BOOKS BY WENDY BYRNE

Hard Targets:
Hard to Kill

Other works:
Mama said…
The Christmas Curse
Fractured

HARD TO KILL

a Hard Targets novel

Wendy Byrne

HARD TO KILL

PROLOGUE

———

"Get the hell out of there. Now." Jenning's voice crackled to life in Sabrina's earpiece.

She ignored his command even while her skin itched, foretelling her sixth sense kicking in. *Yep, she was close.*

"Now, Shaw. His friends are heading your way. You—"

She clicked off the receiver to stop the tirade that no doubt would follow. A few minutes. That was all she needed.

Tiptoeing up the metal staircase in her black combat-style boots, she inched her way to apartment 203. Eddie Ramer might be able to fool the cops but not her. The bottom feeder had been enticing Caitlyn for weeks with his promise of high-paying modeling gigs. And then she'd disappeared.

Coincidence? Yeah, right.

A heavy smell of weed permeated the air, despite the open balconies outside the apartment doors. The metal railing and no-tell-motel appearance of the building didn't shock her. In fact it worked in her favor. The thin walls made her privy to the conversations along the journey to her prize.

201. 202. Finally, 203.

Peeking inside was made impossible by the closed drapes. Instead, she crawled under the window then slid along the wall, stopping outside the apartment door. A cacophony of motorcycle engines in the distance signaled Eddie's friends were getting closer.

Her heart beat heavily while her fingers tingled. Everything inside her longed to grab the gun strapped to her thigh, but she resisted the urge. Only if necessary. She held her breath, keying into the conversation on the other side of the door.

"Let me see what you've got, baby." The voice came from inside.

Sabrina closed her eyes, dispelling the vile thoughts racing around her head. Focus remained the key to her success.

"I thought—" The girl's shaky voice signaled her fear.

"You have a smokin' bod, but I gotta know you can sell the goods. That's the way this works. Only then can I open doors for you."

Enough.

With one strategically placed kick, her boot separated the lock from the flimsy door. Seconds later, she charged inside, tackling Eddie to the ground. He tried to reverse her dominant position, but she was one step ahead of him, bringing the tip of her blade to his throat, a mere flick away from his carotid artery.

She slid off his chest and eased them both to a standing position, never wavering on the location of the blade. "Now Caitlyn and I are going to leave without any trouble from you or your ragtag group of merry men. Got that?"

His brow furrowed while his lips curled into a smirk. "Caitlyn? She's ancient history."

A sinking sensation settled in her gut as Sabrina turned toward the girl. Hovering close to the bed, a young Hispanic girl with striking looks and long, dark hair stood, her blouse partially unbuttoned. Definitely not Caitlyn Collins.

Not good.

That half-second of non-focus on her part was all Eddie needed to grab her forearm, dislodging the knife and sending it flying across the room into the wall. Despite his bulk, the alcohol reeking from his pores slowed his reflexes. She easily ducked the clumsy punch he sent her way. When he grasped her bicep and pulled up, that left him open for her counter strike to the round part of his shoulder, followed by a punch to his liver through the intercostal nerve, robbing him of breath, then a chop to the side of his neck, hitting his vagus nerve with enough force to stun.

Sabrina grabbed the girl and ran.

Dread chilled her bones as she bounded down the steps, yanking the frightened girl along with her. For the first time in her life she'd failed her mission. She'd given the Collins family hope when she'd promised to rescue their daughter. Now she was coming back empty-handed. There had to be another way.

* * *

Eddie's words rang in her ears: *She's ancient history.*
What did that mean besides the obvious? Over the course of the
last day and a half, those words had cycled through Sabrina's
brain constantly as she waded through every possible meaning,
from the mundane to the tragic. Yep, she was grasping at straws,
but right now that was all she had to hold on to.

Right now she couldn't think of anything worse than
stepping up to the Collins' door in Scarsdale and seeing the
evidence of failure reflected in their eyes. They'd trusted her
above everyone else at The Alliance, and she couldn't deliver.

Instead of dwelling on things she couldn't change, she
sucked in a breath and steeled her spine. Seconds later she
pushed the doorbell.

John Collins opened the door to let her in, but Martha
was right behind him. Both their eyes were red-rimmed, while
Martha had a tissue to wipe the perpetual leak of tears clogging
her nose. Evidence of the perilous hold on her emotions was
displayed in the tight clench of her jaw.

"I'm so sorry." Sabrina shook her head. How could she
make the words come out to mitigate the impact? She couldn't.
And that was what hurt the most. "She wasn't with Eddie like we
thought."

Even though this wasn't new information, Martha sucked
in a sob. "Isn't there anything else you can do?"

"I've got to take another look at what she was doing
online." While it was a shot in the dark, it was the only possible
lead she had. They'd already explored friends from school, and
that had resulted in a big fat zero. None of them knew a thing
about what happened to Caitlyn, except to tell her about Eddie.

They looked at each other, and tears began to leak from
the corners of their eyes. *Kill me now.* Failure was tougher than
she could ever have imagined. The taste of it rolled around her
mouth until she felt like the she might gag on it.

"She never gave us any trouble." John shrugged. "Except
for her fascination with Eddie. We were so positive..." His voice
trailed off into the abyss of grief.

"Let me see what I can figure out. Show me her room again." Sabrina trailed them down the hall, praying for a crumb of information, even while knowing the possibility of success was remote.

The pain of being in Caitlyn's room must have been too much for them to bear, as they left her alone seconds later. She chewed on her lip and flexed her fingers as she searched Caitlyn's computer history, finding nothing unremarkable. Then Sabrina dug a little deeper and found the deleted history. The search instantly got more interesting.

Something called Trinity Modeling had been deleted by an eraser program through the website. Interesting.

There was almost always a way to get deleted information, unless the hard drive had been physically damaged—which, thankfully, it hadn't. She needed to find a way of retrieving what had been expunged, but it would no doubt be a painstaking process given the level of sophisticated data cover-up she'd encountered so far.

Untangling the information must have taken hours, but she'd lost track of time so couldn't say for sure. Finally a sliver led to a thread, which led to another, which led to a chat room Caitlyn had apparently been visiting over the last couple of weeks. Sabrina's heart kick started inside her chest as hope bloomed. Gotcha.

"Martha. John. You need to see this."

When they arrived seconds later, she pointed to the screen. "Caitlyn had been corresponding with somebody named Marco about modeling in Europe."

Martha sucked in a breath even as fresh tears began to flow. "She's had this modeling bug for a while now, but I told her no. Why didn't I—"

"You couldn't have known. This Marco guy took advantage of her naiveté and made a lot of promises about putting her in runway shows in Paris with something called Trinity Modeling Agency." She held up her hand to stop their questions so she could finish. "I did a search. There is no such modeling agency."

"How did you find all this stuff?" John asked.

"Even when you delete information from the computer, it's never really deleted." The itch started as her sixth sense kicked in. Without a doubt, she'd hit the mother lode.

Martha grasped her hand and held tight. "You've got to help us."

"Count on it."

All she knew was she couldn't face this family with another failure. She was going to get Caitlyn back or die trying.

CHAPTER ONE

———

Sabrina ran to her laptop when the ping sounded, and pulled up the new message. *Grace, There's a ticket waiting for you at JFK for the two p.m. flight to Paris tomorrow. You'll be walking the runways in no time. Regards, Marco.*

Uncertain whether she should be elated her ruse had worked or terrified, she sat down to finish the rest of her packing. Even though she'd already dyed her hair and had secured fake IDs, she needed to start mentally preparing to become Grace Williams, nineteen-year-old college student.

Glancing in the mirror, she scrutinized every wrinkle and line on her face as she worried about passing for someone ten years younger. Photoshop worked wonders, but in person would they buy her ruse?

Before she had a chance to think about it any longer, the downstairs buzzer sounded. She glanced at the camera mounted outside her Manhattan condo. Crap. Her brothers Jake and Max stood outside holding pizza boxes and wine. After she'd told them of her impromptu trip, she should have known she wouldn't get out of New York without a little complication.

Before she let them in, she closed down her laptop and hid any evidence of her impending mission. As for her newly colored hair, she'd figure something out.

She pushed the release button, opened the door, and waited until they appeared in the hallway. "Nice of you two to bring me dinner."

It was difficult to lie to them. She never had before. They were the only family she had, and she trusted them with her life. But they wouldn't understand her need to rescue Caitlyn without the backing of The Alliance.

They walked inside, taking turns giving her a kiss on the cheek before placing the pizza on the coffee table in front of the couch and walking toward the kitchen. Max opened the cabinet door and pulled out glasses for the wine while Jake grabbed some plates.

"Why the impromptu trip to Paris?" All six foot, four inches of Max plopped down on the couch and helped himself to a slice of pizza. Considering he was still wearing his charcoal gray Brooks Brothers suit and teal silk tie—his fancy Wall Street attire—he must have come from his office.

"With a little more notice I would have vacationed with you." Even though Jake was a year younger than Max, most people thought they were twins with the way they looked so similar in physique and mannerisms. With dark eyes and hair that had a tendency to curl when it got too long, they'd left a string of broken hearts across Manhattan with their charming ways and good looks. The only difference was the way they dressed. Max tended to indulge in tailor-made suits, whereas Jake was all about the grunge look, with tattered jeans and concert T-shirts as his wardrobe du jour most days.

She shrugged as nonchalantly as her guilty heart would allow. "I was in between assignments and figured what the heck."

"And the whole red hair thing, is that part of your adventure?" Jake asked.

"What? Don't you think it makes me look haute couture? Trendy? Younger?" She smiled as both her brothers raised their eyebrows simultaneously.

"Truth?" Max didn't wait for an answer but barreled on. "You know I love you, sis, but the red hair." He made a face. "Not so much."

"Ditto," Jake added.

"Glad you two agree on something." She sat between them on the couch, feeling diminutive by their standards, even though at five foot six, she was above average for a female.

"Where are you staying in Paris?" Jake asked.

She should have known neither of them would be happy with minimal information. "The Shangri-La." With a great location near the Eiffel Tower and amazing amenities, it would be an obvious choice if she were really going for a pleasure trip. She brushed back the surge of guilt. Lying to them felt all kinds of wrong, but she knew if she told them the truth they'd try to talk her out of it. And she was hellbent on doing what she'd promised.

"You going alone?" Max asked.

"Of course."

"You sure you're not hiding some boy toy?" Jake said as he finished off his wine and grabbed another piece of pizza.

"You two will be the first to know if I decide to get myself a boy toy." Despite the worries, fears, and what-ifs running through her brain, she managed a giggle as she grabbed the last slice of pizza before Max or Jake had a chance.

* * *

Sabrina readjusted her position as best she could even while her brain pounded like it wanted to escape the confines of her skull. Every inch of her body screamed for attention as the drugs they'd given her began to wear off.

Numb. Just go numb, dragi, as Petrovich used to say. She hated how easily he invaded her thoughts.

Fear kept her from opening her eyes. But the poor girl needed her. Fast. That superseded any strategy or game plan for the time being.

Memories tumbled around her head, but nothing clear rose to the surface. Waiting for the A Train to JFK Saturday morning was the last slice of recollection she had.

Where was she?

Curiosity overruled fear as she slid open her eyes. Rough cement flooring chilled her bare skin, making her bones ache even more than they already did. The crude structure of the stone walls let her know the basement of the building they'd brought her to was old, clearly predating building codes.

Two small hexagon-shaped windows, covered in dirt and grime, were misaligned along one wall, letting in no light, making it impossible for her to tell if it were night or day. Illumination came from a lone bulb hanging in the center of the room.

After taking in her surroundings, the next thing she noted was the person lying on the other side of the room. Sabrina breathed a sigh of relief when she saw the shallow rise and fall to the women's chest. Like her, the woman was naked with both hands chained together, one arm tethered to the wall by a length of chain.

In her naiveté she'd assumed they wouldn't attempt anything until she'd gotten to Paris. But she was wrong. She'd bet money she'd somehow landed in Europe, but how had they done it? How she'd been overcome and how she'd gotten to this dungeon-like place remained a mystery.

With a little luck, Marco had taken her to the same place he'd brought Caitlyn. Maybe Sabrina was headed in the right direction after all—if she could stay alive long enough to figure it all out.

First she needed to escape the chains. Given the technical sophistication of remote data erasing, she had to believe they kept all their client names and addresses, as well as the names of the girl they bought on a computer. All she'd need to do was hack into it and suck out whatever data she could about where Caitlyn had gone. She twisted at her already chafed wrist and tried to readjust to a comfortable position as she examined the floor for anything that might help her pick the lock. Since she hadn't planned on being stripped naked, the lock picks she'd hidden in the seams of her shirt were of no use to her now. And what she wouldn't give for a few acupuncture needles to help relieve some of the achiness running roughshod through her bones.

The girl on the other side of the room moaned as she shifted her position on the floor. The chain rattled with each move she made.

"Are you okay?"

The girl shuddered then coughed as spasms shook through her body. She whispered something indiscernible before her fragile voice came through on a gasp of air. "I want to go home." Tears flowed freely down her cheeks as sobs racked her small frame.

As much as she wanted to, Sabrina couldn't offer any comfort given the distance between them. Impotence surged through her veins, making her fingers shake, her heart beat faster. *How could she make this right?*

The girl had a patrician nose and a head full of deep auburn hair. Pure terror reflected in her almond-shaped brown eyes.

"I'm going to get you out of this. I promise." Sabrina's voice, even to her own ears, sounded more like some kind of primal growl as disgust twisted her guts into a knot.

"How?" The girl shivered from the cold and more than likely the kind of fear that made the blood in your veins turn icy.

Sabrina's brain still felt scrambled from the drug she'd been given. But when she got her bearings, she'd figure something out. What other choice did she have?

"You let me worry about that," Sabrina replied, keeping her voice light and positive. "What's your name?"

"Liz…Elizabeth." She shuddered out a breath. "My mom and dad call me Lizzie. I hated that name. It sounded like a little kid…but now—"

"I'm Sabrina." Needing to distract the girl, she interrupted. "I'll get you out of this."

She felt a little like Scarlett O'Hara in *Gone with the Wind* uttering words of conviction without a clue how she could accomplish the task. But it didn't matter. Just like Scarlett, who swore to never go hungry again, Sabrina wouldn't give up until this girl was free.

Failure is not an option. The words of Petrovich echoed unchecked inside her head.

"I'm scared." Liz whispered, as if to say the words out loud would make the sensation disappear.

"So am I, honey. So am I." Admitting she was scared rolled off her tongue so easily Sabrina almost thought another person had uttered them. Fear hadn't been a part of her internal makeup for a very long time. By the time Petrovich had taken hold of her psyche, fear of anything but disappointing him had been exterminated.

She shook off thoughts of the past and the melancholy that accompanied it. "Can you sit up?" Lying prone felt powerless. While the change in position wouldn't help their situation, sitting up might offer a much-needed change in perspective and clear the fog invading her brain.

"I feel kind of dizzy," Liz said.

"Let's give it a try. Me first."

Sabrina used her elbow to maneuver to a sitting position. Her muscles screamed in protest but she managed to right herself. As soon as she did, flashes of lights danced before her eyes and the room began to spin. She brought her head between her knees to keep from passing out.

Damn. Whatever they gave her, it was powerful. The effects, combined with lack of food or drink, lingered like a bad hangover with a getting-the-crap-kicked-out-of-you chaser. An almost overwhelming urge pulled at her to give up the fight and slump back to the floor. She fought against the impulse, knowing all too well the line between momentarily caving and capitulating was tenuous.

Caitlyn needed her. Now Liz needed her. She needed to figure out a way.

"Take it slow, Liz."

After a feeble attempt, Liz slid back to the floor. Sabrina didn't want to scare her, but they both needed to shake off this bout of lethargy and concentrate on how to get out of this alive.

"Come on, you can do it. At the count of three. One, two, three." With her encouragement, Liz maneuvered to a semi-upright position and even managed a small smile.

"Do you know where we are?"

Liz shook her head. "Wherever we're at, they don't speak English."

Just as she suspected. Traveling by air would make sense if they wanted to make a quick getaway. But it would also mean Marco, or whoever was the mastermind behind Trinity Modeling, had a private plane at his disposal as well as an airfield that was willing to look the other way when transporting semi-comatose women. How did they manage that?

"Are there other girls here?"

"There was a girl named Caitlyn, but she left yesterday, or maybe the day before. It's hard to judge time down here."

Sabrina gulped back the dose of victory. To know she was headed in the right direction didn't feel nearly as good as it should being that she was naked and chained to a concrete wall without so much as a stray nail in sight to help her pick the lock. "What's your story? How did you get involved in this?"

"I met this guy, Francois, on the internet. He said he was studying in Paris and dabbled in modeling. It sounded so…fun. We had a lot of things in common. My parents were pressuring me to stay in college. I wanted to travel." A trickle of a tear slid down her cheek. "I figured I could do both."

Her story sounded familiar. The name and the ploy used were different, but the results were the same. "It's not your fault, Liz."

A sob traveled through Liz's body. "Francois said he wanted to meet me. I took the train into New York. The next thing I remember is waking up here…I'd give anything to be back home right now."

Before Sabrina could respond, a man threw open the door. "I see our guests are awake." With thick, dark hair and beady eyes, he looked to be around thirty-five or so, and spoke English with a German accent.

Sabrina brought her knees closer to her chest to at least partially hide her nakedness. "You might need to work a bit on your hosting skills, Marco or Francois, or whatever your name is today." She stared back at him and immediately determined what she'd already suspected. He didn't have the swagger of a man who might run this type of operation. And most times the Man-in-Charge didn't like to get his hands dirty. This guy was definitely a middleman. Probably one of many at Trinity Modeling Agency. But if she could stay here long enough to break into his records, she might be able to figure out where they'd taken Caitlyn.

He bit off a cynical laugh. "A sharp tongue won't serve you well where you're headed." He shook his head and smirked. "But I'm guessing you're one that has to learn that the hard way."

"And I'm sure, based on your looks, you have a hard time getting dates. But kidnapping, really?" She needed to think. And apparently she needed to think fast.

"Your smart mouth is going to get you in trouble." Marco stalked close enough that Sabrina thought he might hit her. The deep creases in his forehead told her he was angry, but he had enough restraint to keep from acting on it.

She'd become accustomed to physical pain over the years. And right now a part of her welcomed it like the comfort of an old friend. Wounds healed over time: broken bones mended, scars faded, muscles became strong again.

"It's freezing down here. We need blankets." She wanted to rattle him and figured asserting herself might be one way to do it.

Liz shivered and made a moaning sound, making Sabrina all the more aware of her own words and their impact. Fear radiated like a sound wave off Liz's body, bouncing off the walls of this dungeon-like place.

Another man hissed as he walked inside the room. Sabrina couldn't determine if it was anger or frustration fueling his movements as he dropped blankets over both of them.

"If they catch pneumonia, they won't be worth shit," the man recited in perfect German.

His look intensified as he examined her as if searching for any chink in her façade. Goosebumps rode down her arms as she fought through the inspection thrown her way. At least for right now, the bone-chilling cold sweeping through her body had abated a bit.

"Always worried about the bottom line, Evan. I like that. But they'll be long gone before pneumonia sets in." Marco let loose a creepy chuckle.

Sabrina kept her face impassive. They didn't need to know she understood every word they'd said. Feigning ignorance might help her survive this ordeal.

Evan took a position next to Marco, hands clasped behind his back in military fashion. Unlike Marco, Evan didn't look German. Even though he spoke the language perfectly, there was something off—the slightest pause that might not be obvious to most people, but it gave her a clue. Definitely not his first language. In Europe that wasn't saying much. Most people spoke several languages. She spoke English, French, German, Italian, a mishmash of Serbian, Croatian, and Bosnian, and knew a little Czech as well.

With her plans for escape, she had to weigh her opponents carefully. *Look into their eyes, Saby. Study their body language. Examine their weaknesses so you may be victorious.*

Evan was tall and muscular; probably at least six inches or more taller than Marco. Definitely bodyguard size, and had that intimidation face down to a T. His eyes told the real story. There was something in the way he stared that differed from the maniacal look in Marco's eyes. She liked to think she'd spotted a hint of compassion there, but that might be pure folly on her part.

As a physical threat, he would be a challenge. Much more so than Marco, based on size alone. But with timing, skill, and a whole lot of luck, she could do it if the opportunity presented itself.

Marco would be the easier mark, although she doubted he would ever put himself in a position of vulnerability. He definitely had a bit of a paranoid vibe emanating around him. Maybe drugs. Maybe pressure from those above him on the food chain. She couldn't tell for sure.

"Where are we?" If she knew for certain their location, she'd have a thread to hang on to. Right now that was all she craved so she could plan an escape for Liz, and information gathering for her.

Marco sized her up, as if contemplating whether to give her the information, before he finally spoke. "My home in Austria."

Confirmation of what she'd assumed. That meant connections to people who could be bought or blackmailed. Even though she'd suspected as much, an organization this big could make her and anyone they wanted to disappear pretty quickly. Which only meant she needed to act fast if she hoped to save Caitlyn.

"And me without my passport. Guess you'll have to take me back to the States," Sabrina said.

"Very funny. You're quite a comedian, Grace, aren't you?" He placed his hands on his hips and eyed her.

"And you're just a flunky, aren't you, Marco?"

He moved in close. So close she could see the flaring of his nostrils and smell the coffee on his breath. "I'm somebody who could make your life a living hell should I so choose."

"Into sex trafficking?" She winced, knowing the impact her words would have on Liz. While no doubt the girl knew where this whole thing was headed...*denial is a very powerful tool to the human psyche. Petrovich 101. Don't let yourself get sucked into it.*

"Bing. Bing. Bing. Very clever girl."

"Not all that clever. Waking up naked and shackled was a big clue."

"But after all the trouble you gave my men, you should consider yourself lucky to be alive." He chuckled at his own vile personal joke.

This cat-and-mouse game was starting to get wearisome. Her stomach growled, signaling its thoughts. "Grateful is not quite the word I'd use."

He laughed again, the sound much more menacing this time. "You should be. You damn near killed me with the knife hidden in your clothing."

"I would have been successful if I wasn't strung out on the drugs you gave me." A vague recollection of pulling her knife trailed around her brain like a whisper.

He bit out a laugh. "It's your fault you're here."

"A little twist on the blaming the victim."

"You modern American women, always ready to claim victim when in fact we both know that's not true."

"So we're both clear, I'm nobody's victim. But to make this whole thing fair, you could un-handcuff me. Believe me—that would separate the men from the boys, so to speak."

He laughed again, the cynical sound reverberating within the confines. "I'm no fool."

"That's funny, I was thinking the opposite."

"I haven't been around this long without having the ability to size people up. Maybe I'm a soft touch...maybe you remind me of somebody. After your display in New York, it's your luck I thought I might find a use for you, besides feeding the fish. Given the proper incentive and motivation, and maybe a few choice drugs, I'm sure you'll be more than willing to cooperate with anything asked of you. Besides, some of my clients enjoy their women with a little spunk."

Sabrina gritted her teeth and denied the vile implication. "I'm feeling awfully cooperative right about now." Her fingers flexed while she tried to restore blood flow. Even though she was playing into his hands, she couldn't help herself. She needed to tone down the rhetoric and concentrate on being a sheep. But that had never been part of her makeup. And it seemed that even having been half drugged out of her mind, it hadn't been either.

Marco drew in a breath, "What do you want, Grace?"

"Right now I gotta pee. I'm losing circulation in my arms and legs, and I'm damn uncomfortable." She tsked, rolling her shoulders.

"I'll show you I can be reasonable." He flicked his finger in a command gesture. "Evan, escort these ladies to the bathroom."

"Wait a minute. I'm not being picky, but taking a leak is a solitary kind of moment," Sabrina said. She needed time to plan and another place to search for a weapon, or at least something to get rid of these shackles binding her.

Marco shrugged. "Don't be confused by my friendly demeanor. I always take the necessary precautions."

Without further word, Evan helped both her and Liz to their feet and unlocked the chains tethering them. The blankets he'd covered them with earlier slipped to the floor, and he brought them up around their shoulders once again.

"Where did you put those clothes, Marco? They might as well get dressed while they're in there," Evan said.

Before Marco could respond, the walkie-talkie clipped to his side sputtered to life. The conversation began with a string of English expletives then reverted to Czech. While it was hard to catch every word, Sabrina picked up the gist of what was said.

Something about getting the women ready and making sure they behaved. Neither comment made her happy. Marco didn't seem real happy either. Maybe he didn't trust her, or maybe he didn't like being told what to do.

That Evan guy remained impassive, staring at some spot on the wall as he awaited further orders. His hands laced behind his back, he presented the epitome of tough and in charge. Once again, she calculated her odds with him as an opponent. He would not be an easy mark.

Marco's conversation on the walkie-talkie came to an abrupt halt. Another man appeared at the door seconds later. Dressed in dirty fatigues and boots, his hair a greasy mess, he looked downright nasty. A scar cut through his left cheek to the corner of his lip, stopping in a ragged half-circle right under his eye, almost as if someone had attempted to remove it. Based on the leer he graced upon both her and Liz, Sabrina could understand why.

Pig.

Scar Man handed Evan the clothes, but he kept an intimidating eye on Liz. Sabrina felt powerless.

But as the Scar Guy left, Sabrina found something to admire. Strapped on the guy's back, like a big old present on Christmas morning, was an AK-47. If anybody could figure out how to relieve him of that, it was her.

CHAPTER TWO

———

Sabrina attempted to shake off a bit of the lingering lethargy from the drugs they'd given her as she splashed cold water onto her face. The hint of coolness gave her the kick-start she needed.

With her head bowed over the sink, she glanced around in search of something she might use as a weapon. Resourceful was her middle name, but aside from a whole lot of dust bunnies along the floor, there was nothing even semi-lethal residing in this room. Given a few moments alone and with the door locked and closed, she might be able to twist something off the sink to fashion a makeshift weapon, but not with Evan standing vigil outside the partially open door. She hated to give up so easily, but she had no other choice for the time being.

Evan knocked then came inside to hand them some clothes. Both she and Liz were given identical outfits, including long-sleeve peasant-style white blouses, red skirts, and ballet flats with a black fabric sash to encircle their waists.

"Where are we going?" she whispered to Evan as she began to dress. Would he respond? Did he even understand English?

Even the thin fabric brought warmth to her chilled skin. The shoes kept the damp cold cement floor from shooting straight up her legs and through her body. For the first time in what felt like years, a trickle of warmth stopped the internal trembling.

"Into town. Somebody wants to see you." His English was spot on without even a trace of an accent. He was either educated in the States or he was born there, which brought about the question of why he would get involved in this kind of stuff.

Then again, for the right price, some people would pretty much do anything.

Even though he answered her question, he gave nothing away by his expression. Normally, she could spot a flinch, a chink in the armor a mile away, but this guy showed nada.

"How long until we get to this dog and pony show?" If she had an idea of where they were in Austria, she could start calculating their escape. Then again, she had to assume Marco was being truthful when he divulged the location and wasn't trying to throw her off track.

"A little over an hour." Shifting his weight from one foot to the other, he seemed distracted, refusing to make eye contact with her. Not a good sign. While there were tons of reasons why, she couldn't help but be a little curious what kept his mind so occupied.

Deciding to push the envelope, she moved close to his ear and whispered, "I can get you money. Lots of it, if you help us escape." The smell of soap and spicy aftershave drifted beneath her nose as she pondered which way he'd land.

Based on the neutral look in his eyes, and the firm set to his jaw, she couldn't guess. But it didn't matter, as he didn't get a chance to respond when Marco's voice filtered through the door, reminding them all of his close proximity.

"We need to get going if we hope to get there before sun-up."

While Evan left her hanging as to his decision, it didn't matter. She could accomplish this on her own. All she needed was a tiny break in the wall of impenetrability and she'd jump on that in a hot minute.

As if reading her thoughts, the gaze Evan leveled at her spoke of distrust while he secured plastic cuffs on both her and Liz. No doubt he was gauging her strength, trying to see how much damage she could do if given the opportunity. Having done the same type of calculating appraisal herself on numerous occasions, she knew exactly what was going through his mind.

He said nothing, but instead opened the door and led them to the outer room. Marco seemed a little anxious as he waved his hand in the air to move them along.

"Where are we going?" Sabrina had spent the first twenty-two years of her life in Europe before escaping to New York, and knew it like the back of her hand. Marco had given her an advantage he hadn't counted on. She knew when and where to hide and, more importantly, how to survive.

A disgusting kind of smile inched up the corners of his lips. "We're heading into town to meet some friends."

"I have plenty of those already. But the three of you fellas go on and have a really good time. Liz and I will find something to amuse ourselves."

"Ah, Grace, I'll miss your witty banter. But our time together has come to a close," Marco said.

As if to reinforce the point, Scar Man grabbed the bicep of her right arm, squeezing in a bone-crushing grip. She tried to angle away, but with the cuffs she didn't have a lot of leverage and he left little room to maneuver.

Evan eyed the contact, but didn't say a word. Marco still had that damn smile on his face.

"You have certain attributes that carry quite a price to some people," Marco said.

"Really, that's interesting. Most people I know can't wait to get rid of me." Sabrina bit back the expletives at the tip of her tongue and ignored the pain tunneling through her arm due to Scar Man's brutal grip.

"In a very short period of time, I guarantee you will be more cooperative than you ever imagined."

Dread skipped along her spine as the impact of his words hit home. How quickly she had gone from a kickass, nothing-could-stop-her woman to a fearful, vulnerable one with a few targeted threats. With the drugs, the cold, and the nakedness, their indoctrination techniques rivaled most. The slide into capitulation inched closer as the pressure on her arm reached "unbearable."

Every word she uttered came with a swagger of confidence to counterbalance the pain both inside and out. Maybe there was something in the drug that brought her to a state somewhere between catatonic and submissive. She fought against it with every ounce of resistance she had.

Scar Man pushed her up a narrow set of stairs leading to an open kitchen space. A traditional home in Austria, the house had wooden beams in the kitchen, stone floors, and an enormous fireplace. There was a door leading to the outside on the left-hand side.

Maybe it was being out of the cavern they'd been housed in, but Sabrina felt a resurgence of her old self—the one that had taken a leave of absence from her psyche not ten seconds ago. She'd do her best to cause trouble, like she'd done from the earliest of ages. "You haven't drugged us, so what's going to ensure my cooperation? If we don't behave you'll sell us to the highest bidder?" She narrowed her eyes. "Oh yeah, that's right, you've already done that."

"But I have a secret weapon." As Marco spoke, he brought a gun to Liz's head and cocked the hammer. "I know exactly how to control you."

Liz's eyes went wide in fear. While her body began to shake, her lips moved in silent prayer.

Sabrina should have figured he'd use leverage to keep her subdued. No doubt she'd tipped her hand she wasn't in fear for her life, but someone more vulnerable was a different story. That wouldn't stop her from coming up with a plan to outwit, outmaneuver, outman them despite the odds against her. She'd never failed a mission before and didn't plan on failing this one.

Ingrained instincts had her surveying the room to identify areas of vulnerability, strength, and potential weapons within reach. The set of knifes held in a wooden block next to the stove made her heart go pitter-patter. While she tried to keep her gaze from straying too long, her brain ticked off her moves.

Trepidation lit up her spine, enticing her gaze to the counter once again. Six knives, three men—could she do it? Speed and accuracy were key, and she had both. But timing wise it would be tricky.

Negotiating around the counter toward the stove would take five seconds. With her hands together in cuffs, and Scar Man corralling her bicep, could she grasp and possibly injure one of the men? And, more importantly, could that happen before they got to Liz?

Evan stared at her as if reading her thoughts. He shook his head almost imperceptibly then glanced at Marco, his point made without using words. Then again, maybe he was considering her earlier offer?

"I'll get you some bread before we leave," Evan offered, earning a frown from Marco.

"Why are you giving them food?" Marco screeched in German.

"Because they haven't eaten in days and you don't want them passing out before we even get into the city. I might be a numbers guy, but you brought me here for a reason. I plan to make your operation more efficient and less costly. Let me do my job."

Evan's expression remained indecipherable. He had a good poker face; not a speck of emotion gave anything away. Was it a hint of concern that reflected in his eyes when he handed her the bread? She couldn't tell if it was genuine concern, an agenda, or if he intended to go along with her earlier offer and getting them food was a sign of good faith.

"Some water would be great as well," Sabrina said.

Marco glanced at Evan and shook his head. "What did I tell you? Give them an inch and they ask for a mile."

Evan shrugged but returned a few moments later with bread and bottled water. He handed the offering to both of them with no eye contact whatsoever. Mercifully, Scar Man let up on his death grip enough for her to gobble down the nourishment.

"You wouldn't want your meal ticket to pass out in the middle of negotiations. No doubt that would lower the price considerably," Sabrina said between mouthfuls.

Marco nodded his agreement with a smarmy smile. For once Sabrina didn't want to be agreed with.

"You have a point. While G can be a little…ahem…shall we say, creative in the methods he uses to ensure complacency, he does expect his merchandise to be in good working order at the time of purchase."

"Oh, Marco, you make a girl feel so important—like one of those blue-light specials at Kmart," Sabrina replied, mimicking a Southern accent.

She glanced at Evan. Imagination or not, he had a strange look on his face. While his lips were drawn tight into a thin line, he worked his jaw back and forth a few times as if trying to figure something out. Was he going to rat her out? Or had her big mouth made him suspicious?

She half expected him to blurt out the tale of her bribe. But he didn't. It was too soon to conclude that meant victory.

After finishing off the last of the bread, she felt stronger. Much more herself and able to do what she needed to do. Once she chased it down with a bottle of water, she felt like she could tackle the world.

"I don't want a word from you, Grace. Not one single word." Marco motioned toward Liz. "Or you know what will happen to your friend. You certainly don't want her to pay the price for your big mouth."

He held the gun to Liz's head, and Sabrina closed her eyes and bit her tongue. She knew it was a test. For now, she'd be willing to play along.

Marco smiled, looking pleased by her complacency. He nodded in that I-knew-that-would-work kind of way and handed the gun to Evan, who placed it in a holster under his jacket.

"It's time to leave," Marco said.

"Home?" Liz squeaked out the word like a two-year-old would after a long day away. Emotionally frayed and physically exhausted, Liz appeared to be near the breaking point. While her hands shook, her voice trembled. And she looked to be about ten seconds away from bursting into bone-racking sobs.

Sabrina willed the poor girl a hint of composure by grasping her hands, trying to convey a measure of control with her touch. Liz's eyes remained downcast as she twisted at Sabrina's fingers.

"But I thought you hated your life. You wanted adventure and to see the world. Now you're crying to go home." The mocking tone in Marco's voice rippled in the air. Sabrina didn't have to be psychic to recognize his words hit their intended target, effectively cutting off any further pleading by Liz.

A vivid fantasy of grabbing Marco by the throat and bouncing his head of the cool concrete floor kept Sabrina from acting irrationally. Besides, this was a waiting game. Her time would come sooner or later. And it was all about timing.

* * *

A Mercedes sedan awaited them at the bottom of a series of cobblestone steps. Ironically, the exterior of Marco's house resembled a home from a fairy tale, with its cottagey appearance surrounded by a forest of trees. She could envision Little Red Riding Hood paying a visit any minute now.

As picturesque as the setting might be, any hope for an immediate escape was dismissed when she recognized they were in the middle of nowhere with mountains on all sides. Definitely not an easy way out that she could see so far. Running through the forest hampered by mountains was not a recipe for success.

Given the presence of the moon, and the miniscule amount of light, Sabrina guessed the time was close to three, maybe four in the morning. Once the terrain became more visible she might have a few more clues as to their location.

Based on the abundance of mountains, the house had to be in the southern half of Austria. By US standards the acreage was miniscule, but by getting-out-of-Dodge standards, it was as vast as the Pacific Ocean. They might be close to Italy if in the southwest, Switzerland or Germany if straight west. Getting her bearings was high up on her list of things to figure out.

Evan ushered her into the back seat then came around to the other side, assisting Scar Man then Liz before closing the door. He got behind the driver's seat while Marco occupied the front passenger seat. Scar Man positioned himself between her and Liz, stretching out in the back. No doubt satisfied the two of them were subdued and under control, he made himself comfortable, resting his arms across their shoulders, and slid down until his knees bumped the front seat.

Within a few moments, he began to snore while his chin bobbed intermittently against his chest. Sabrina leaned against him. Not that she had a whole lot of choice considering the confines and his arm pressing against her shoulder. She feigned sleep, resting her head, and tried not to gag on the aroma wafting around him.

The car heater brought the sensation of warmth to her chilled bones, allowing for a reprieve to her overworked psyche. With one less thing causing a brain drain, she could get down to the business of planning an escape.

Scar Man's breathing slowed as he slid into a deep slumber. Capitalizing on the moment, she inched her tethered hands along his side, betting that he'd be sporting a pocketknife somewhere on his person.

Securing some sort of a weapon before they got into town ranked as her number one priority. Being outnumbered she could handle, but without something to help even the odds, any attempt at freeing herself and Liz was a lesson in futility. She kept a vigilant eye on the driver's rearview mirror while her fingers snaked along the pudgy area above Scar Man's pants. Seconds later she touched what felt like a pouch. The resultant sliver of victory felt good despite the circumstances.

Being orphaned at a young age, she and her brothers had learned lessons in survival. Pickpocketing was one of those skills, so the task wasn't difficult, even with her hands still bound. The weapon wasn't nearly as big or as lethal as she would have liked, but given the right angle she could perpetrate some damage. She slipped the knife into the pocket of her skirt while Scar Man continued to snore. Now she had to strategize how to take full advantage of her prize.

They drove for an hour, maybe more. She tried to get a feel for the direction based on the countryside, since the sun hadn't yet started to rise in the sky. But darkness seemed to be her enemy.

Evan and Marco remained eerily quiet in the front seat. Scar Man continued to sleep while Liz whimpered against the outside door. In a perfect world, she would offer the girl promises and reassurances of success, but that seemed impossible, especially since her main objective was escape and survival.

Signs of the emerging town began with intermittent homes along the roadway. Within a few moments, two-story buildings came into view, along with groupings of larger structures and streets. Sabrina kept her head bowed, her position relaxed. All while every muscle in her body was charged with a heightened state of alert.

She'd been trained by one of the best. Fooling Marco's merry men shouldn't be difficult as long as she kept her wits about her.

After heeding directions from Marco, Evan parked along a deserted street on the outskirts of town in front of what looked like an abandoned house. He shut off the car, then got out and opened the back doors and helped both her and Liz maneuver out.

She'd have to figure out her exact location later. But right now, she played her part—submissive and powerless—as she shuffled to a standing position outside the car with Scar Man in between her and Liz.

"I'll wait here, with this one," Scar Man said, motioning toward Liz. "You take the other one to the meet with G. They'll be two of you and one of her in case she gets out of line."

"That won't be necessary. She understands the gravity of any mistake," Marco responded, but Sabrina could tell by the tone in his voice that he was digesting the information, second-guessing his decision.

"I don't trust her," Scar Man said while pointing to Sabrina.

"You worry too much, Arte." Marco blew out a breath and eyed her. "She looks agreeable to me. Especially when we're holding her new friend for collateral." Marco ran his hand down the front of Sabrina's blouse, groping her breast. Suppressing the urge to utilize her weapon was a test of her patience. "See, nothing to be afraid of." He let loose a little chuckle.

Scar Man, a.k.a. Arte, shook his head. "If you ask me, we should have taken care of her back in the States."

"That's why you're not in charge." Marco encircled her bicep with his hand. "But you're right. Why show G everything we have from the get-go? Maybe we can up the price a little if we keep him guessing."

"They're both redheads, as he requested, but the young one is a little scrawny; probably looked a lot better in the photos we sent him." Scar Man spat onto the ground, the spittle landing inches from Sabrina's toes. "You already know how I feel about that one."

Right back atcha, bud.

Scar Man was doing the hard sell, wanting to keep Liz around, which made Sabrina anxious. She could handle anything he might try without too much effort, especially with the weapon she'd commandeered, but Liz would be like a lamb brought to the slaughter. Pleading her case or reacting to their discussion in any way would let them know she understood German, so she kept her face impassive and bided her time.

"You're not used to American women." Marco shrugged. "But I have to agree. I prefer peace and quiet to that mouth of hers." He grasped tighter on to Sabrina's bicep. "G has no idea what he's getting." Marco let out a girl-like giggle.

Patience.

Scar Man chuckled. "If you ask me, G deserves her."

While she hated the idea of Liz stuck alone with Scar Man, that meant her own odds were lower. She could get away from Marco and Evan, and head back toward Liz.

Evan spoke for the first time. "Where are we supposed to meet this guy?"

"A man will be selling fresh flowers at a market a couple of blocks from here. We'll take turns bringing the women there so that G can see what he's paying for. He'll be watching from one of the rooms above." Marco stopped, as if formulating a plan. "Once I have confirmation the money has been transferred to the account, we go ahead with the exchange. Since G isn't the most trustworthy guy, I'd rather walk in and leave the car here. That way we keep our options open."

Evan nodded, but his eyes remained on Sabrina. While her head was down, as she pretended she hadn't understood every word they said, she could see his gaze between her lashes. She didn't know quite how to interpret his look, but suspected he, like Scar Man, didn't trust her. Or maybe he was contemplating her offer. Or maybe he'd seen her relieve Scar Man of his knife and was about to go all Rambo on her.

Instead of any of those things, he unclipped the plastic ties binding her hands while Scar Man went back inside the car, dragging Liz with him into the back seat. "Remember, I have your friend. You wouldn't want anything bad to happen to her," Scar Man called through the window.

As if she'd forget. The terrified look on Liz's face would haunt Sabrina until she returned.

They had walked about a block from the car when a police officer pulled alongside them on his motorbike. Even though not a big fan of police officers, Sabrina was tempted to plead her case and tell him all she knew about what was about to go down. But something about Marco's relaxed posture gave her pause.

"What are you doing in town so early, Mr. Peterson?" the officer said in German, while the motorbike kept a steady hum between his legs.

Marco's hand remained secure across the breadth of her bicep, but she sensed no spike to his pulse. No nervous hitch to his breathing. He was confident he had control of the situation.

Sabrina got the impression Marco was well known in this town. And judging by the officer's deference, well respected.

That eliminated her first option. Running to the nearest police station wouldn't further her cause. It would only make Liz more vulnerable.

"Business," Marco responded without hesitation, a broad smile upon his face.

"Bankers must keep odd hours, like police officers."

"If you want to stay ahead, you've got to do what you've got to do." Marco chuckled as he drew Sabrina closer to his side.

Could the whole town be part of this? Probably not. So were they stupid, naïve, or saw what Marco wanted them to see? Sabrina bet on the last.

Which meant Marco was good at covering his tracks. This whole organization was no doubt cloaked in respectability from the top down. The strategist in her couldn't help but wonder how it was structured. Did different operatives work different areas of the continent?

In order for this organization to be so successful, they had to fly under the radar and be the last people anyone might suspect. And he was only a cog in a giant wheel of this operation. She couldn't imagine the level of respectability the man in charge might hide behind if Marco was any indication.

She had to wonder about G as well. Was this whole network a group of well-connected, respected individuals that no one would suspect of wrongdoing, let alone dealing in the flesh trade?

From the start, she'd naively assumed the men involved would be representatives of the seedy underbelly. Disgusting-looking people doing disgusting things. She could pick them out in a crowd by the way they looked, the people they hung with.

But, like most things, that hadn't been the case. They looked like normal, everyday folks, but underneath they dealt in scum. They lived in chateaux and chalets, probably a castle or two, but had a dark side nobody knew about.

Which only meant they would be even harder to find. No doubt there was a protective wall and a sterling reputation a mile wide around the man at the top. When a person had a lot to lose, they did everything they could to ensure their dirty little dealings stayed underground.

"I'll let you and your date be on your way. Don't work too hard." Without another word, the officer revved up his motorbike and sped off.

Sabrina fought against the wave of hopelessness. She'd faced worse odds than this on many occasions. Most missions she'd worked alone, but this felt almost insurmountable, knowing the obstacles in her way. Still, it wasn't time to throw in the towel. Besides, she didn't have a lot of options where this mess was concerned. It was go big or go home, and she wasn't going anywhere until she accomplished her goal.

Marco pulled at her arm. "Come on, let's get moving. We're already running late." She trudged after him, letting the shuffle to her walk and blankness to her expression give him the false impression nothing occupied her mind. She played the part and led him to believe she was scared and powerless and willing to do whatever he wanted, because she had no other option but to be subdued.

The streets were deserted given the early morning hour. A hint of fog hung along the mountains, keeping the town temperate. Even so, Sabrina shivered as the breeze ripped through the thin cotton of her peasant blouse.

Evan eyed her as she walked with Marco. Something in the furrow in his brow made her contemplate the idea there was more to his glance than a status check. But allowing her mind to concentrate on that potential wrinkle would not be a prudent use of her time. Searching for possible avenues of escape remained her number one priority.

She took in the scene, anxious to spot avenues that might allow for an escape. Every doorway, around every corner became a possibility, although it would have been much easier if they'd kept she and Liz together. Then again, the plan to separate them had been ideal from their perspective. If the situation was reversed and she was in the power position, she would have done the same thing.

Never underestimate your opponent, Saby.

Even though Anya had killed him over a year ago, reminders of Petrovich were a constant. He'd been both a blessing and a curse rolled into one. And, being back in the area where he'd been so much a part of her life, the bubbling up of memories was a given.

She shook off thoughts of the past and focused on the present. She was in the open and had a weapon. To add to the good news, she'd spotted a sign indicating Switzerland was five kilometers away—a little over three miles. This was definitely doable.

A sign over an old three-story building read "The Langford Inn," confirming the location in the southwest corner of Austria in the city of Langford. Once they had their break, she could lead Liz toward freedom. Switzerland would be the safest bet for now, since it might be far enough away to be out of Marco's immediate reach.

They walked in silence down one street, then the next, weaving their way to their destination. Sabrina memorized each turn in the road in order to retrace her steps, but shuffled along as if her brain remained in that twilight state of complacency and defeat.

She inhaled, steeling her body and mind for what she had to do. Waiting for the moment when she could make her move.

"Is that the corner?" Evan pointed down the block. When Marco nodded, he continued, "I'll stay with her and you can wait for the flower guy to open up."

She raised her head high enough to track the location for the meeting. While no traffic was in sight, she could imagine no more than a car at a time could pass down the narrow street. This could enhance her success during the escape she'd planned.

Marco flipped his wrist, glancing at his watch. "Why don't you check it out? See if you see any of G's guys coming from the other way? Besides, I prefer to keep Grace in my sights. G's been known to pull a fast one occasionally and he won't be expecting you. I'll stay here with Grace."

Some opportunities are made. *Some fall right in your lap*. She wouldn't have felt this confident if she were left with Evan. Playing the bodyguard role, he had a gun tucked into his holster. But Marco she could handle with or without a weapon.

Sabrina counted to ten as she watched Evan's retreat through the tips of her lashes. Patience was indeed a virtue, especially when it lowered the odds and gave her the more vulnerable of the two targets.

Catching him off guard was easy. Preoccupied and confident, Marco wasn't expecting a word from her, let alone the attack. She felt the relaxation of his hand on her bicep and knew there was no time like the present.

Sabrina knocked the wind out of him with an elbow just below his ribcage, followed by a fist between his legs. When he bent over in pain, she brought up her knee, smashing his forehead against the bony part of her leg.

She pulled out the knife and flicked it open, aiming for his throat, but nicking his shoulder instead when he shifted at the last minute. Moving quicker than she'd anticipated, he kicked at her hand before she had a chance to set the knife tight within her grasp for the second assault. The knife flew into the air and skittered along the walkway.

When she tried to escape, he encircled her neck with his arms, pressing the bend of his elbows into the front of her throat. Her breath stalled from the pressure and Krav Maga mode kicked into gear.

She raked her nails across his face then grasped his hands, pulling them down and away from her neck. Turning, she slipped her head through the opening underneath his armpit. She counterattacked with an elbow strike to the back of his head. As he went down toward the ground, she made one last kick to his midsection before she left, stopping once to smash his cell phone with her heel. The last thing she needed was either him or Evan warning Scar Man.

She grabbed the knife and started running. Even when Marco cursed and screeched her name, following that up with a round of threats, she resisted the urge to look back.

Retracing her steps through the maze of streets was more of a challenge. But after ten intense minutes of running, she spotted the Mercedes.

Knowing Scar Man had an AK-47 and she had a simple pocketknife didn't give her a rush of confidence. But that meant she needed to utilize the element of surprise.

Sabrina took off the black cloth belt around her waist and pulled it tight to test its strength. Satisfied it would do the job, she slunk low and eased her way toward the car.

She had to act quickly. As soon as Evan found Marco, they'd both head back and she'd have lost her window of opportunity. More than likely they'd assume she'd try to save Liz.

Unlike those heartless bastards, she gave a damn. Leaving Liz to fend for herself wasn't even a remote possibility. They knew that.

She spotted the car, but blackout windows kept her from seeing inside. Sabrina could only assume both Scar Man and Liz were in the same position as when she left.

Which meant he was in the back on the passenger side, and Liz was in the middle. Sabrina crouch-walked her way to the back of the car.

"Noooooooo." The strangled plea came from inside the car.

Sabrina's heart bounced against her ribcage as she struggled to regulate her breathing. She yanked open the door.

Letting loose a scream so primal, Sabrina didn't even recognize it as her own, she drove the knife into Scar Man's back. Blood spurted, spraying her white blouse. His torso contorted while he sought to remove the weapon, leaving him open to her next move.

Sabrina wrapped the sash about his neck and yanked. She held on until she heard the snap. Then, with the ease of removing a piece of garbage, she grabbed him by his shirt and pushed his lifeless body onto the street.

Only then did she stop and glance at Liz, who looked as white as a ghost. "We need to get out of here." She urged Liz out of the back seat. Wiping at the tears running down her cheeks, Sabrina glanced into Liz's eyes as she coaxed her into the front passenger side. "Are you okay?"

Liz nodded. At least she could answer questions even if she appeared to be in shock.

Sabrina got behind the driver's seat. She'd been hot-wiring cars for nearly twenty years, but newer models were more of a challenge. Still, she had the engine humming within a minute or so.

"Hey, you two, where the hell do you think you're going?" Marco's voice felt more menacing than normal as it drifted in the pre-dawn morning.

Liz immediately started to moan and shake and looked like she might collapse under the strain of the last ten minutes. The haunting sense of fear crept up Sabrina's spine and took hold. But fear was not her enemy. She needed to channel it to get what she needed. Before Marco could get any closer, she peeled away from the curb and headed toward the Swiss border with an impotent Marco running behind her, shaking his fist.

CHAPTER THREE

———

Within five minutes they were at the border. Within another two they were in front of a police station. Although she hated to send the poor traumatized girl in there alone, she had to be practical. "You need to go in there by yourself, Liz. I'm covered in blood. They'll ask too many questions." Walking in there, looking like she did, would cause huge problems even if she could justify what she'd done to Scar Man. It would take days to sort it out. Even worse, it would put the whole organization on hyper-alert status and it would be even harder to track down Caitlyn. That was a complication she didn't need right now.

"I can't." Liz was shaking so hard her teeth were chattering.

Sabrina took the girl's hand and held it to the side of her face. "Yes, you can. This is the easy part."

She didn't want to push Liz out of the car, but knew time was limited. No doubt Marco's car had a satellite locator, which meant he could remotely have the car shut off without too much trouble. She wanted to be far away from Liz when that happened in case Marco's reach extended beyond the border.

"I feel…so weak…" Her voice trailed off and Liz shook her head. "I can't go in there by myself. Let's keep driving." A trickle of a tear slid down her cheek as she grabbed Sabrina's forearm in a death grip. No doubt if Liz had Super Glue, she'd coat herself in it and adhere to Sabrina's side until she was in her parents' arms once again.

"This is the safest way for right now." She could see fear in the way Liz's gaze kept darting about, as if she were expecting

Marco to pounce any second now. Sabrina could definitely relate to that fear. "You're a strong girl. I know you can do this."

"I need you." The pleading tone seemed to echo through her trembling bones and into her defeated body language.

"No you don't. I wouldn't send you off if I didn't think you could manage." She squeezed Liz's arm but wasn't positive the message of reassurance was received, based on the way the girl continued to tremble uncontrollably.

"I can't leave you here alone." Her voice squeaked.

"I'll be fine." When Sabrina saw the doubt surface on Liz's face, she continued, "You saw what I did to Scar Man. This way we can both escape." She wasn't going to give up so easily and had every intention of getting back within striking distance of Marco. He was the key to obtaining Caitlyn's whereabouts. "Tell the police you're an American and you're lost. Nothing more about Marco or what happened. Ask them to take you to the American Embassy immediately. Then call this number: 555-785-7878. It's an organization called The Alliance. My real name is Sabrina Shaw and I work for them. They'll make sure you get back home and will contact your parents and make sure you're safe in the meantime."

"But—"

Sabrina shook her head, knowing right now this was the only solution they had. She needed to accomplish what she came here to do, and leaving Europe wasn't going to get the job done.

"Remember to say nothing about Marco." She held Liz's hand. "Promise me."

Rather than respond, Liz nodded then opened the car door. Marching toward the police station, she kept her back straight, her head held high, sparing one last glance toward Sabrina with a hint of a smile gracing her face.

After she watched Liz safely enter the station, Sabrina started the car and decided the only course of action would be to return to Marco's. The secrets he kept would lead her to Caitlyn. But she needed firepower. She'd learned the hard way she couldn't go in there as a victim and be successful.

As she pulled away from the curb, she checked her mirrors and slammed on the brakes. Her chest lurched when she spotted a car going slowly down the block. Paranoia reared its ugly head as she watched a car go by. Was that Evan or Marco? She held her breath as the car inched past.

But the car didn't stop. In fact, the old man driving didn't even look her way.

She blew out a breath and smiled as she pulled away from the curb. The last few days must have played havoc with her confidence. She needed to get a grip and think about what to do next.

First order of the day was a different car. Finding another car to steal would give her a fighting chance at remaining hidden. She had little choice but to head toward Italy and her friend Antonio. Coming down on the wrong side of the law most of the time, he was the only person she knew who could pull together enough firepower for her to accomplish the task of taking down Marco.

It wouldn't take long to get to his home. All she would have to do is head south through Austria and hope to find a car along the way before Marco had this one turned off via satellite.

She'd gotten a couple of miles away before the Shaw itch started at the base of her skull and fluttered down her spine, foretelling trouble. As she continued down the country road, a growing sense of trepidation fluttered inside her belly. Her first indication her instinct was right came when a cop appeared in her rearview mirror. She glanced down at the blood splattered across her blouse and tried to think of a logical explanation.

When the cop was joined by another, she knew she wasn't going to make it to Antonio's, nor be given an opportunity to tell her side of the story. When the Mercedes began to slow despite increased pressure on the gas pedal, she knew how this would end. She tried to calm her racing heart, but that didn't seem possible when Marco appeared in the middle of the street in front of her as the car sputtered to a stop.

The locks on the doors popped open without her assistance. One of the cops opened the driver's-side door and yanked her out, tossing her to the ground before she could even think about breaking her fall. As she lay on the ground trying to get herself to a standing position, she waited for the clink of the cuffs on her wrist. Being arrested for murder wasn't part of her plan.

Instead, when she peered up from the ground, she spotted Marco patting the officer on the back. "I'll take it from here."

She should have guessed Marco wouldn't allow her to be arrested. If she were in custody, his dirty little secrets might come to light. Was he powerful enough to have them ignore a potential murder charge?

"Are you sure you don't want to press charges?" one of the officers asked as he eyed the blood on her white blouse.

"Naw." Marco shook his head and wiped at the cut on his face. "I'll drop her off at the gypsy camp she ran away from. That's what I get for being a soft touch. She took advantage of my generous nature."

Sabrina kept her face impassive as they continued their conversation in German. He hadn't told them about Scar Man. Even an outstanding citizen couldn't get away with having the police ignore a murder.

No doubt he planned on bringing her back to his place. But if she broke away once, she could do it again. It would be more difficult this time, as she'd revealed her hand, but nothing was ever impossible.

The police were barely out of sight when he smacked her across the face. His ring scraped across her cheek as he glared at her. "Where's Liz?"

She looked at him, allowing a hint of a smile to turn up the corners of her lips. "Safe and sound, where you can't touch her." She had bet on the fact Marco's reach didn't extend beyond the local authorities. Based on his fury, and the fact he didn't know where Liz was, she had to believe she was right.

"What the hell does that mean?" Without waiting for her answer, he backhanded her.

Once again, he'd underestimated her. She balled her hand into a fist and connected with his nose, sending blood spraying before she took off running.

Even though pretty much out in the open, running along the road gave her half a chance to snag a ride from a passerby. She could only hope the next car she spotted was neither Evan nor the police.

The turn in the road brought her smack dab into the middle of a small village. While there weren't many people, it might offer her a place or two to hide. She managed a quick look behind her and spotted Marco not very far back. This wasn't going to be good.

Plastered against the brick building, she hid among the shadows for as long as she could in order to catch her breath and think of a way out. Plan B: If she were going to be captured, she would use it to her advantage. This time she'd come prepared.

Sabrina's heart pounded in her chest, the erratic beat caused by Marco's presence nearby. The itch crawled up her back. She flexed her fingers in anticipation.

Sweat congealed beneath her armpits then trickled down the side of her chest. That flight-or-fight sensation went into overdrive, triggering adrenaline-soaked nerve endings.

Footsteps. The little twerp must know she was close.

"Here, Gracie, Gracie. Haven't you figured out yet you can't escape?"

His voice crept up her back, causing a shiver to flush through. Schooled in the philosophy of never giving in or giving up, she found the concept of waiting for the inevitable to be excruciating.

Still pressed against the wall, she cowered behind a trashcan, waiting for him to pass by, hoping at least to get in a good shot or two before being subdued. Knowing she had no other option, she waited. The element of surprise was all she had.

First she heard the almost imperceptible slide of his three-hundred-dollar shoes along the street. Since Evan wore jeans and a pair of tennis shoes, Sabrina knew it was Marco. Unless she was mistaken, only one person approached.

Crouching low, she peeked around the corner and spotted the gray fabric of Marco's suit pants. She grabbed his ankle and tugged, bringing him to the ground.

Before he had a chance to react, she stomped as hard as she could on the center of his chest, once again targeting his intercostal nerve. The idea of killing him was a tantalizing thought, but she might still need him to get information about Caitlyn if necessary. While Marco struggled to catch his breath, she ran like the devil was chasing her. Turning onto the open street, Sabrina searched for a miracle.

Sliding to a stop at an intersection, she glanced first in one direction then the other. Crap. Evan stood not twenty feet away to the right. Immediately, she went left. But she could have sworn she didn't hear pounding feet behind her.

Shocked. Stunned. Curious. Temporary bout of insanity? Or was he giving her a head start just for shits and giggles? Dare she think he was offering a get-out-of-jail-free card?

She couldn't say anything for sure. Pushing down both the fear and the questions, she continued to put as much space as she could between her and the enemy.

Her momentum came to an abrupt halt when someone yanked her hair from behind. Instinct had her bringing her hand back to relieve the pressure. Before she had a chance to do anything to counter the attack, she felt the prick in her arm, and everything else was a blur.

* * *

"Where did you disappear to?" Marco screeched at Evan.

"I secured a car to see if I could find them." Evan wasn't lying about getting a car, but had lied about his whereabouts. He'd figured they'd head toward the border, and figured he'd missed them when he checked with the police in Switzerland and found they were in the process of bringing Liz to the American Embassy. He couldn't help but wonder why Grace hadn't gone with. Why would she risk getting caught? The curious part was the phone number Liz kept repeating to the officers. The police hadn't done a follow-up on it, but he intended to as soon as possible.

"Where is Liz? And what did you do with Arte's body?"

Evan shrugged. "Don't know where Liz is. But I dumped Arte in the woods for the time being."

Marco shook his head and pointed to a drugged-out Grace lying on the pavement. "Damn fool woman. Why did she come back? Did she think she'd be able to take me down somehow?" He bit off a chuckle. "Carry her to the car you secured and I'll take her home. Have my car cleaned up, then bring it home." He patted Evan on the back after he laid her on the back seat. "Loose ends, Evan. Whoever she is, she can be dangerous in the wrong hands. She broke Arte's neck. How did she know how to do that?"

"Maybe she's not who she claims to be." Evan figured that was the understatement of the century. The woman had skills. From where was the only question circling his brain.

"I'll get her to tell me the truth." He got in the driver's-side door. "Throw Arte's body into the trunk. We don't want some hiker stumbling over his body in the woods."

Twenty minutes later Kane was on his way back to Marco's. He swore, shaking off his Evan persona in a heartbeat. Undercover work sucked, but never more so than today. He had ingratiated himself into the organization over the last six months as he tried to unravel the inner workings of a very complex financial operation in order to follow the money to the top. When Marco asked him to come to his house to see what he did on an everyday basis, he'd been stoked thinking he'd be able to tap into the computer network and get the name and address of the man in charge. But he'd been there a week without even coming close to Marco's stash of transaction details.

As for ingratiating himself into the sex trade, he thought he'd been prepared. But he'd been wrong.

When he was trailing the money, he could do that objectively, but seeing the women they'd exploited up close and personal and watching them get auctioned off was a whole other thing. That's where he and Nellis, his boss and the SSA, supervisor special agent in charge of this operation, were going to have to figure something out. He couldn't sit around powerless while young women were being brought in as sex slaves and treated as commodities.

Conceptually he understood that going after little fishes like Marco wasn't his goal. They all wanted the big guy. The man they called Trinity. And stopping transactions at Marco's level would only cause the snake to grow another head, so to speak. There'd be somebody else to pick up the slack if Marco was eliminated from the picture.

He thought he could do it. He thought if he intellectualized the whole assignment he could get past the memories buried deep inside his chest. He thought he could ignore the urge to rip Marco's heart out through his chest wall, but that hadn't happened either.

Stuck in town tying up loose ends while leaving Grace vulnerable, drugged, and in Marco's hands hadn't been part of the deal. Without a choice, he stayed to finish what had been asked of him while at the same time trying to figure a way out.

Which brought him back to exactly where he was— speeding in excess of ninety miles an hour toward Marco's chalet, hoping he wasn't too late. Frustration rocked through him as he punched in the numbers on his cell.

He didn't even let Nellis respond. Instead, as soon as the ringing stopped, he blurted, "I'm not doing this anymore."

Pissed didn't even begin to describe how Kane felt about this disastrous assignment. He wanted Trinity as much as the next guy, but didn't have the stomach for working through the normal channels, especially if it meant he'd have to sacrifice more young women.

"We need Trinity's identity." Nellis spoke in an even tone, in direct contrast to Kane's current temperament. While it forced him into focus, it only increased his anger two-fold. "The only way to get that is if you stay undercover as Evan. Marco trusts you. We know he's a stepping stone to the man."

"You don't get it. Marco's pissed and a woman is in the middle of his crosshairs right now. She might very well be dead." The thought made him sick to his stomach. Kane couldn't remember another time when he'd felt this helpless.

"That would be unfortunate."

Kane's body shook as adrenaline and rage rocked through. "Unfortunate? That's all you can say about a woman who was dragged halfway around the world to be sold to the highest bidder." Even though he knew there was more to her story, he wasn't about to tell Nellis that, instead choosing to play the guilt card.

"We all know sometimes there are casualties out of our control. This type of thing is very unpredictable. You have to remember the big picture."

Kane ground his teeth together so tight, his jaw ached. "Screw the big picture. It's my call and I'm bringing her away from the danger, and I'll nail Trinity to the wall as well." He blew out a breath. "That is, if she isn't dead."

Nellis didn't seem to hear Kane's last comment, or chose to ignore it. "Like it or not, you can't make up your own rules for these things."

"The hell I can't." With that, he pressed the end button and threw the phone onto the passenger seat.

If Grace had been a little more patient, he'd had a plan. He wasn't going to let her or Liz get sucked any further into the clutches of Trinity or his organization. But then she took matters into her own hands and went crazy ninja on him. That had been unexpected. Sure, he'd known she had some wits about her. He'd known she could stand up to pressure, but where had all that come from?

Certainly she wasn't who she presented herself to be. Young, naïve college students looking to break into modeling didn't have the lethal skill set Grace possessed. Kane allowed a smile to ease up the corner of his mouth.

She'd made quick work of Arte. Breaking somebody's neck was an expertise that most people—especially women—didn't possess. So that meant she was skilled. What was that number the police told him Liz kept reciting?

555-785-7878

He texted IT and asked them to run the number for him. Seconds later came the response. *The Alliance. An organization offering services in hostage retrieval and security.*

He couldn't help but think Arte deserved her brand of street justice more than anybody he knew. Which was saying a lot when, due to the nature of his job, he brushed elbows with a lot of dirt bags.

Prime example—Marco, as well as the elusive Trinity. Marco had a few bruises and bumps as a result of his altercation with Grace. Another feel-good for Kane.

But she couldn't do it alone. Especially not now, when Marco was on the proverbial warpath and she was right in the middle of a shitstorm of trouble.

What was she thinking? The rate she was going, she'd get herself killed and he'd be unable to stop it.

After leaving Special Forces, Kane had worked for the FBI for ten years. In all that time, he'd thought he'd seen every inhumane treatment imaginable. He'd become numb. Immune to it all. Then he'd become one of Marco's merry men. And learned how naïve he'd been. Marco knew more about torture and brainwashing than Kane could have imagined.

Grace.

Kane sucked in a deep breath as he pushed the car over a hundred in his race toward Marco's estate. At some point, in everyone's life, a man had to have his *I'm mad as hell and not going to take this anymore* moment. This was his.

Kane screeched to a halt on the driveway, threw open the door, and raced inside. Knowing what Marco was truly capable of, fear rattled his brain, de-focusing his objectivity once again.

Kane rushed inside the house and past the guards into Marco's office. As he entered, Grace's head snapped back and she tumbled against the desk. The slap Marco gave her with left a giant red welt across her cheek. With her hands tethered with plastic ties, she had no way to protect herself.

Kane clenched his hands while he fought down the urge to tackle Marco to the ground. Going off half-cocked wouldn't help Grace. More than likely, it would only get them both killed.

As repugnant as the thought was, he needed to start thinking like Marco if he had any hope of saving her from disaster. Money. That was the man's Achilles' heel.

Her head dropped to her chest like a rag doll that had lost its stuffing. The sick feeling in Kane's gut spread throughout his body as she used the top of the desk to steady herself.

Just as he worried she was going to pass out, he saw her grasp a loose paperclip and hide it in the palm of her hand. He had to wonder what she planned on doing with it.

"You cost me, bitch," Marco screamed.

He hit her again. This time a trickle of blood oozed between her lips. Hauling her from the desk, Marco forced up her chin. He held it there until her eyes opened.

"Now maybe you'll learn not to cross me."

"Don't count on it," she said moments before head-butting Marco. She didn't have a lot of leverage given the angle, the lingering effects of the drugs, and her constraints, but the impact forced Marco back on his heels. Kane hard a hard time suppressing a smile.

"You bitch," Marco screeched as he rubbed his forehead.

When he drew back his fist, Kane grabbed Marco's arm. "I wouldn't do that, Marco." She couldn't take much more based on the way her eyes were glazed and unfocused. Kane couldn't fathom how she'd garnered the strength to strike back at all.

Marco glowered, his rage now directed toward Kane. "Give me a good reason why I shouldn't beat this slut senseless."

Kane dialed down the testosterone arcing between them. "Number one—this isn't the time or the place." Kane glanced around, playing into Marco's paranoia. Let him believe there might be some members of the household who might dare tell others Marco had lost it. "And more importantly, she's no good to you covered in bruises with possibly a broken nose or cheek— or worse yet, dead. If you promise a high-quality product, you need to deliver it. Since I imagine that virgin sacrifice thing is out of the question with Grace, you need to give them the beautiful redhead they requested. And right now she's not looking so beautiful."

When Marco paused for a few more precious seconds, Kane continued, "G didn't see the fiasco, so he doesn't know. I called to say the women became ill suddenly. It's all smoothed over. He's still anxious to go ahead as long as she looks as good as she did in those pictures you took. I set up the meeting for next Saturday." A little white lie for the time being would give him some more time to think through his options.

Kane maneuvered his body so that he inched between Marco and Grace. "You've got at least a couple of days' worth of healing to make her presentable as it is."

Now that she'd piqued Marco's ire on several occasions, the woman probably wouldn't survive more than a day or two. Which was how he came up with the strategy of theoretically continuing on with the deal as planned. It gave Kane a couple of days to come up with something that wouldn't get the two of them killed.

Appealing to Marco's greed might circumvent anything worse. Concentrating on Marco's need to accumulate money, no matter what the cost or sacrifice to others, was the path of least resistance for the time being.

Marco paused, his shaky hand poised in the air as rage and adrenaline poured out of him like a dike springing a leak. In his current state, Kane couldn't say for sure what he'd do next.

"I know what this is about. You want her for yourself."

Kane chuckled despite the circumstances. He guessed perverts thought everyone wanted the same thing. "Are you crazy? She's way too much trouble. I like my females willing and subservient without the use of drugs. We both know that's not Grace." He hesitated for a few seconds. "You know I'm all about the bottom line, and she's bringing in a good price. Besides, the big guy won't be too happy if you damage the goods before he gets his cut. You've already lost one. I'd be willing to bet you wouldn't want to answer to Trinity if you lost both."

As expected, Marco shifted his attention from Grace onto Kane. "Screw Trinity. I can do whatever I want." Sounding more like a whiny six-year-old than a grown man, Marco slowly lowered his arm despite his words.

"But he's got the connections. He makes it all happen for you, doesn't he?" Kane knew he was pushing it, but he needed to get the attention off Grace until it was a fair fight. If Marco continued to take his frustrations out on her in the condition she was in, she'd be dead within the hour.

"I could kill you right here and now for that." Marco straightened his posture, trying to look all badass.

But Kane knew the real truth. More than anything, Marco was terrified of enduring Trinity's wrath. While he didn't know the man's identity—and he wasn't all that sure Marco did either—he did know Marco would do anything to avoid crossing him. Rumor had it that acts of unspeakable violence happened to those who dared cross Trinity.

Despite an instinct to go in for the kill, Kane gave Marco back a little of his dignity. "If you're going to kill me, make it for the right reasons. Don't make it because I'm telling you what you don't want to hear."

Kane kept his posture relaxed, non-threatening. With four guards milling about, he'd be a dead man in less than a second if Marco so chose. Kane had no illusions that he was indispensable.

"I'll clean her up. Let her come off the drugs. Before you know it, she'll be good as new and off your hands. And you'll be several thousand dollars ahead of the game in a few short days."

Kane didn't wait for a response, but gathered Grace, putting a tight grip around her biceps. Her eyes slid open a fraction and she gave him a half-smile.

Kane shuffled past Marco with an arm about her shoulders. Before they made it to the door, Marco stepped in front of them, blocking their path.

He stuck out his hand, bumping against Grace's right shoulder. "No woman ever hits me," he hissed inches from her face.

"You're wrong about that." She sucked in a breath, "I just did. In fact, more than once today."

This woman had a death wish. Why else would she continue to push Marco's buttons at each and every turn?

"Must be the drugs," Kane offered as a feeble excuse as he ushered her down the hall and out of Marco's reach.

He brought her downstairs to the room adjacent to where she'd been held earlier. Not much different than the other one in terms of dampness, but at least there was a cot. As soon as her butt hit the thin mattress, she slumped to a prone position. He slid her legs under the thin cover and eased the hair from her eyes.

"Liz?" Her voice was barely above a whisper, as if the effort cost her more than she could endure. Cracked and bleeding, her lips were so swollen that the inside was exposed and stretched dry and taunt over her teeth.

"She's safe. The Swiss police brought her to the American Embassy." He whispered into her ear rather than take the chance Marco was listening. Offering that little bit of good news was easy. It was staring into those eyes filled with pain that was the hard part.

She looked like crap. Her wavy red hair was a mass of tangles, with clumps of dirt and drying blood adding to the disarray. The white blouse she wore earlier was in tatters and spattered with blood. Kane couldn't tell if it was hers, Arte's, or maybe even Marco's.

Her right bicep had deep bruises circling it, and her forearm sported a large red welt. There were scrapes and scratches over almost all of her exposed skin.

A bruise marred her right cheek as the beginnings of a black eye formed on her left. A deep red scratch from Marco's ring cut through her right eyebrow. She had drying blood below her nose and fresh blood oozing from her bottom lip.

All of which would be good. It would give him a couple of days to figure out how to get her out.

Kane went into the bathroom, rinsed out a towel, and set about the task of cleaning her up. Determined to figure out a plan and get her out of this death trap.

"Where did you come from?" He whispered the question into the air, thinking she was too out of it to respond.

Seconds later he was surprised when her eyes slid open. She smiled while her voice croaked from strain. "Haven't you learned about the birds and bees yet?" Her eyes slid closed seconds later.

He stifled a chuckle. But first things first.

As bad as she looked, he snapped off a picture and sent it to the FBI. Sooner or later they'd match it up with facial-recognition software and he'd get the lowdown on her story and how she got hooked up with The Alliance.

CHAPTER FOUR

———

Sabrina readjusted her position on the cot while pain radiated from the top of her head to the tips of her toes. Everything ached, but especially her head. With every beat of her heart, her pulse baboomed inside her skull. The drugs Marco had used this time on her were a powerful concoction that had instantaneous results and a kickass lingering effect of dizziness every time she moved.

She licked at her parched lips and cracked open one eye, hoping for solitude. Instead, she saw him. The guy they called Evan.

His long legs stretched out in front of him, his hands behind his head while he tipped the chair against the wall. His eyelids were closed, masking those deep brown, calculating eyes—the ones that seemed to take everything in and then file that information inside his brain in a folder labeled "for future use."

Memories of him ministering to her needs floated about her head. Cold towels placed upon her face, tepid water cleansing her hair, his soft hands massaging away the clumps of dirt and blood as he whispered assurances that Liz had made it out safe and sound.

Was it a dream?

Vaguely she recalled his interference with Marco yesterday, or maybe the day before. She wasn't all that certain how long she'd been out of it.

Don't expect and you won't be disappointed. But she still had to wonder why.

In her experience, nobody did anything without an angle, so what was his? Was he a soft touch? Did he intend to take her up on her offer? Or did he have an agenda of his own?

She couldn't remember how long it had been since she'd eaten. Her stomach had stopped growling several days ago.

Shifting first to her elbow, then to an upright position, she closed her eyes and waited a few moments until the room stopped spinning. When she opened them again, he stood in front of her, his hand inches away.

She had to admit, the guy was good. He moved like a cat.

"You need to use the bathroom?" he asked.

She nodded, although the effort cost her. "Alone," she managed to croak.

Something resembling a chuckle escaped his lips before he helped her to her feet. In a different room than the last time she'd been in this dungeon of a basement, the rudimentary bathroom was identical. Dirt covered the floor and cobwebs littered the corner. There was a mirror over a sink stained with rust. After attending to necessities, she examined her reflection.

Sabrina touched her cheekbone and poked at the large red welt covering the right side of her face. When she did so, she once again experienced Marco's slap.

Don't get mad. Get even. Petrovich's mantra tumbled through her brain.

But find Caitlyn first.

Shaky, she held on to the sink for support while she searched the waistband of her skirt for the paperclip she'd managed to grab from Marco's desk. She allowed a satisfied smile to cross her face before burying the clip once again. After inserting her hand into the hole in the door where the doorknob should be, she hobbled toward the cot.

"You hungry?" Evan asked.

"Starved." There was something in the way he looked at her that was different from the others, even if she couldn't quite quantify the difference.

"I've got coffee, and some bread." He shrugged, offering up no further explanation.

"I'll take it." She needed nourishment if she expected to last. As it was, the nauseous roll in her stomach signaled she was a hair's breadth away from passing out again. "But you take a sip first to make sure."

A smile eased up the corner of his lips before he brought the edges of the cup to his lip and took a sip. He winced.

"Strong. A shot of caffeine mainlined right to the bloodstream," he responded, a grin spreading across his face.

He handed her a tin plate filled with chunks of bread and an apple, which she promptly wolfed down. Although she kept her eyes averted, she sensed his watchful presence.

"What happens next?" she asked.

He shrugged. "Marco's in charge. You'll have to ask him."

"Really?" She let that one word hang in the air for a few minutes to see how he might respond.

"What do you mean?" His eyebrows rose, conveying a façade of innocence.

"Somebody else is pulling Marco's strings." She was poking around to see if he'd bite.

"I don't know what you're talking about."

"We'll forget that for now." She bit out a cynical laugh. "Answer me one question then: why?"

"Hmmm?" While he said that one word as a question, his eyes seemed more cautious than normal.

"Don't play dumb. Why didn't you go after me when you had the chance? Were you going to let me go?"

"I don't know what you're talking about." His face remained impassive.

"You were a block away from me and stood there. What's your angle?"

He shook his head. "Whoever you saw, it wasn't me." The only sign he was the least bit uncomfortable was his refusal to look her in the eye before he clamped the handcuffs onto her wrists.

"So that's how you're going to play it?" She drew in a deep breath while her mind raced with possibilities. Maybe Marco had a camera hidden in the room. She searched the corners of the room. "You were there right before Marco grabbed me. For some reason, you didn't make a move. I want to know why."

"I didn't come around until after Marco subdued you."

"Whatever." Doubt rattled around inside as she questioned her memories. With the drugs she'd been given, anything was possible. "You did stop Marco from killing me."

She needed that bit of reassurance she hadn't lost her mind. Sabrina needed to know she was right about at least one thing, and it wasn't her imagination or some drug-induced hallucination.

He nodded in affirmation. "We need you healthy. It's all about business."

"Bull." She let her denial hang in the air even while he eyed her without saying a word. This guy had such a great poker face he could make millions playing cards in Vegas.

"I'll let Marco know you've come around." Rubbing his thumb across his bottom lip, he left, closing then locking the door behind him.

Despite what he might say, Evan had interfered on her behalf with Marco the other day. Now she needed to know why.

* * *

"What was that about?" An enraged Marco confronted Kane as soon as he got upstairs.

Given the depths of Marco's paranoia, Kane knew most rooms were wired for sound. Instead of denying the accusation, which would only increase Marco's insistence, he avoided his question for the time being. "She's awake."

"What did she mean by you let her get away?" He grasped Kane by the shirt and tugged.

With Marco's normal paranoia, what went down in Langford, and his suspiciousness about Kane's behavior, Kane's days here were numbered. He'd willingly oblige and get out of Dodge once he figured how to get Grace out at the same time.

"The girl's been on heavy-duty drugs for a couple of days. You know that stuff makes people hallucinate." Kane threw out a pat answer but knew it wouldn't suffice.

"But you went missing for a long time." Still flush from anger, Marco folded his arms across his chest.

"I got a car to go looking for them. Nothing sinister involved."

"Maybe you thought about letting her go so you could keep her for yourself."

Kane shook his head. "I told you before—I want nothing to do with this woman. If you don't trust me, you should let me go, because I'm not going to be scrutinized for every step I make." He let his voice go louder with each word he spoke and hoped Marco didn't call him on his bluff. At least not until he could figure out a way to get Grace out of there without jeopardizing his investigation.

It might be time for him to investigate those underground tunnels beneath the house he'd heard about a couple of days ago. Rumor had it they were installed prior to WWII and used as a means of escape on many occasions. He knew there was an entrance behind the bookcase in Marco's office.

Marco eyed him with a suspicious glare. "I changed my mind and called the local police and told them Grace had gone crazy on our ride home. That she'd killed Arte and escaped before I could deliver her back to the gypsy camp." He smirked. "I figured I should cover my bases in case she gets away from us with or without help. I even put up a substantial reward for her capture. Brilliant, if I do say so myself. No doubt every person within a hundred miles is scouring the countryside trying to find her. One thing you'll learn about me, Evan, is to never cross me. I have a lot of power on my own without Trinity."

Kane figured the situation had just gone from bad to worse.

* * *

As her brain started to focus, the bumps and bruises were still a constant reminder of how close she'd come to getting killed by Marco. Sabrina pushed back the aches and retrieved the paperclip from her waistband. Even though she couldn't see a thing due to the darkness, she'd learned to pick a lock blindfolded, so it shouldn't be too difficult. Right now, sneaking upstairs and getting a look at Marco's computer was her goal. Nobody kept paper files anymore, so if she wanted to find out whom he'd sold Caitlyn to, it had to be stored electronically.

While she didn't know much about the layout of the house, it couldn't be all that difficult to find his office. After ten minutes of working on the lock, she'd made some progress but it was taking longer than usual.

Patience, along with skill, was crucial in getting the tiny tumblers to cooperate, even if the tip of the clip was too large for her purposes. The first satisfying clink made her pulse speed up. The urgency factor tripled within her chest. Time was of the essence.

Once she got free, securing a weapon was her number one priority. The kitchen had the display of knives that would come in handy, but a couple of guys with guns would mow her down in record time. Knives were silent killers, which made them more lethal if the opportunity presented itself. She'd choose a knife over a holstered gun any day of the week.

Given the awkward constraints, her arm felt numb, while her fingers focused on the process. As another tumbler clinked into place, she heard footsteps coming down the stairs. It was the middle of the night; couldn't their never-ending policing tactics wait?

She sucked in a breath to settle her nerves and thought about ways to utilize this impromptu visit to her advantage. Maybe if the guard got close enough she could wrap the chain around his neck and secure the key. She slumped to the mattress, pretended she was asleep, and hoped the opportunity would present itself. This might very well be the break she was looking for.

His knees creaked when he bent closer to the bed. The wash of fresh soap assaulted her nose as he got closer.

Evan. He was the only one of the guards who showered on a regular basis.

Shame. She kind of liked him. Well, as much as she could considering the circumstances. She drew in a calming breath and fisted her hands in preparation.

One. Two. Three.

She struck, hoping luck would be on her side and she'd be able to get the length of chain around his neck. Instead he brought her hands up over her head and whispered in her ear, "Don't say a word. Listening device."

With one hand tethering her two, he reached beneath the mattress and gave a yank. Then stood and crushed the receiver with the heel of his boot. While he was distracted, she clenched her hands and took a swing in his direction.

He stopped her hand and held tight. "I'm here to help you, not hurt you." Without another word, he handed her a pair of camouflage pants and matching long-sleeve T-shirt. "It was the smallest size I could find."

Despite the lack of light, with his face so close, she spotted fear in Evan's eyes, combined with a sense of urgency reflected in his furtive movements. Her scalp prickled. Something had happened or was about to happen. And it wasn't good.

Sabrina pulled at the handcuff while he worked the lock with his key. If he'd noticed any of her tampering, he didn't mention it.

"Who are you?" If things were going south, why would his first stop be her?

"I'm working undercover for the FBI. My real name is Kane Travis."

"What?" Even as she asked, the question pieces of the puzzle started to fall into place.

"I overheard Marco. You're getting picked up first thing in the morning. He's selling you to a guy who makes Attila the Hun look like Mother Teresa." He swore softly. "I had hoped to have more time, but he found out I lied to him about G and thinks I went AWOL. He's got guys out there looking for me as we speak. But I need to get you out of here."

She gulped, the fear crawling up her throat threatening to choke her. "I have to get into Marco's computer first."

He perched his butt on the floor and stared at her. "Why?"

She swallowed hard. "I need information. I can't leave without it. I need to know where the girls go."

Kane shook his head. "Marco is too paranoid to keep that kind of sensitive information on his computer. He keeps all of his client transactions on a thumb drive he has attached to his wrist."

"I'll cut his arm off if I have to. I need that information." Trusting people hadn't been part of her nature for a very long time. She wasn't about to start now. She didn't much care if he was part of the alphabet soup of US government agencies.

"I know you'd put up a fight. But it's not possible. At least not now. Especially with his back against the wall."

"What happens to the girls who leave?" She knew the answer to the question but needed some time to process the recent turn of events.

"I'm still trying to figure that out. But I've got to assume the worst."

A shiver wormed along her spine as she pictured Caitlyn alone and powerless and at the whim of some sick bastard. "Why should I trust you? This could be a trap."

He sighed. "Put those clothes on. Anything is better than what you're wearing for what we're going to need to do. I also have a pair of boots for you."

He turned his back while she dressed. She appreciated the gesture, despite the fact he'd seen everything she had on more than one occasion. In fact, he'd been more intimate with her than most lovers she'd had.

Sabrina shook her head, not liking the direction this was headed. Everything he said made sense, but she didn't want to go anywhere without figuring out where Caitlyn had been sent. "If it's all the same to you, I'll make this escape on my own."

He grasped her wrist. "Your chances of getting out are less than zero." He stopped her protest with a finger to her lips. "I know you work for The Alliance and you have mad skills, but this isn't my first rodeo, and believe me when I say now is not the time. Our best bet is the underground tunnels."

Underground tunnels sounded suspiciously like a get-out-of-jail-free card. Even though it went against her grain to go along with someone else's plan. Having him lead her to freedom sounded like a mighty good proposition for the time being. Besides, after getting some firepower, it would be a great way for her to return and retrieve the information she needed.

But still something didn't ring true. "Why would you risk your life to escape with me? If Marco's going to dog my every move when I get out of here, he'll do the same with you. So what gives?"

He blew out a breath. "I set it up so he believes I stole one of the cars. All the roads out of here will be swarming with Marco's men. That's why we're going through the tunnels. He doesn't think I know about them." He reached to his back and pulled out two guns. He held out his hands, each containing one. "Are you okay with a Glock?"

"I can hold my own."

"I bet you can."

He ushered her out the door and past the body of Petre. Evan dragged him inside before he shut the door firmly in place.

She grabbed the Glock and followed. He led the way, maneuvering through the dark hallways with his gun drawn. When they passed through the kitchen she had a nearly irresistible urge to snag a knife out of the block, but resisted.

"Who's pulling Marco's strings?" she asked. "I know he's not bright enough to orchestrate this on his own."

"The guy I mentioned earlier. They call him Trinity. But I'm no closer to finding out who he is than I was six months ago."

She was uncertain whether to believe him or not, but in the end, it didn't matter. He was her ticket out of here. And right now, "out of here" was one step closer to finding Caitlyn.

After twisting through a series of darkened hallways, they went up some steps and into the main area of the house. While dark, she could tell by his calculated movements that he anticipated trouble around every corner.

He used a pin trigger to unlock a door. Leading with his gun, he eased inside, pulling her behind him. She looked around at the bookcases and immediately began to rifle through the drawers of the desk.

"What are you doing?"

"There might be something in here."

"I already checked. Even the file cabinets have nothing but office supplies—reams of paper, pens, paperclips."

She blew out a breath. "You sure?"

"Yep. We've got to get going. Rounds will be back this way in less than ten minutes."

Reluctantly, she stood behind him while he moved a picture, uncovering a series of buttons.

"This is when it gets a little tricky," he whispered. He clipped a device to the keypad, and after a series of beeps, he punched in the code displayed. The bookcase shifted open, revealing a passageway. "Try not to use your gun inside the tunnel. If you miss, the bullet will ricochet."

She grabbed at his shirt, pulling him close. "Don't assume I'll miss."

"If you do, it might very well bounce back and hit you in the ass. Or worse, in mine."

"I'll keep that in mind."

It took her pupils at least twenty seconds to adjust to the dark inside the tunnel. The walls and ceilings were within touching distance, making it feel even more claustrophobic. He reached inside his back pocket and pulled out a folded-up piece of paper and a small flashlight.

"A map?" She shook her head and laughed. "You really don't know your way out."

"Nope. But I did know where to find the map." He pointed to a spot on the map. "Some of these lead to dead ends, some circle around underneath the mountain. One, maybe two, will get us out of here."

"Are there guards down here?"

"More than I care to think about. But the good news is, most of them are out looking for me right now." He grasped at her arm. "I estimate maybe twenty or so might be milling about down here." His glanced shifted, taking in the scene before them. "We need to be careful."

"I'm all about being careful." And losing this so-called partner as soon as possible.

For the most part they both stayed close to the slime-covered walls as they inched their way through the maze. Sabrina didn't want to think about all the critters and rodents residing peacefully in this dark home. Give her a trained assassin and fear didn't even come into the picture. Put her in a room full of creepy crawling things and she was a hot mess. Instead, she focused on getting out of there as quickly as possible.

Kane had the penlight to illuminate the way. He was in charge, since he had the map. For now, she'd be more than happy to play things his way.

He stopped suddenly, shut off the light, and turned, holding a finger to his lips. Seconds later she heard footsteps approaching. Based on the number of voices, she'd guess two, maybe three people.

She followed his lead, and pressed herself against the walls. When he yanked out his gun, she did the same. She rested the handle against her thigh.

The men laughed and spoke mostly in German about Marco's predicament with Trinity, confirming what Kane had said earlier. Then they talked about her inferring she must be a witch since she was able to kill Arte with her bare hands. Under different circumstances, she might have found her villain status laughable, but not now.

Then they said something that let her know their shaky window of safety was about to come to an abrupt close. One of the men was off to relieve Petre. Since Petre was currently lying on the floor of her former prison cell, it wouldn't be long before they discovered her missing.

She felt a heightened sense of urgency in Kane as they wound through the hallways. Once the men were far enough away, she put the gun back in the waistband of her pants.

"They'll figure out you're missing any second now," Kane whispered.

"We don't have much time."

Seconds later, an alarm began to pulse. The piercing sound seemed to bounce off the claustrophobic space, making her ears ring. Feet stampeded against the crude stone floor, but it was impossible to decipher what direction they were coming from. The hair on her arms stood at attention, as she and Kane raced through dark hallways that suddenly became even more ominous without the benefit of his penlight and with thundering steps as a backdrop.

Beep. Beep. Beep.

The shrill tone reminded her of a death march as it reverberated down her spine. The blood thumped in her veins while they continued to run their way, hopefully, to freedom.

She charged into Kane's back when he jerked to a stop. Then he turned and signaled for her to wait. Seconds later she heard the crash of a body hitting the floor.

Kane returned and grasped her hand, yanking her along while footfalls echoed through the hallways. Between the ever-present blare of the siren and the tunnels shooting in every direction, tracking movement seemed impossible. They'd have to depend on luck, which seemed to be in short supply lately.

But she had to give kudos to Kane for the takedown moments ago. No unnecessary noise. Maybe he was a fed with some skills after all. If she had to pair up with somebody temporarily, he'd be as good as any. At least he could carry his own weight.

Kane swore seconds before his fingers disengaged from hers. The darkness was so pervasive she couldn't see, but heard a scuffle a few feet away. Her heart rate tripled as she fought the frustration of not being able to help.

She trailed the curve of the wall with her fingertips, and finally spotted Kane. He was in a mess of trouble, trading punches with two guys but still managing to somehow hold his own. Deciding to even the odds, she snuck behind one guy, landing a kidney kick, bringing him to his knees. From there, a chokehold put him out of the picture.

Kane was giving it to the other guy, but had yet to finish him off. As she was about to help out, the barrel of a gun poked into her temple.

Instinct had her grabbing his forearms, misdirecting the angle of the gun in case he was stupid enough to shoot. While she had him bent over, she delivered a series of quick kicks to his groin, driving him back until she could deliver a chop to his vagus nerve to subdue him. When he collapsed onto the floor, she relieved him of both his gun and dagger.

Now Sabrina felt in control. Glancing to her left, she saw Kane finishing off the guy while the blare from the alarm continued to slice through the air.

Footsteps seemed to be coming from all directions when Kane grasped her hand and yanked. They slipped together down yet another corridor. He hadn't looked at the map so she could only hope he knew where he was going.

While she had faith in her abilities, trouble seemed to be escalating. Pretty soon, if things continued on this disastrous course, she'd be dead and Caitlyn would be left floundering on her own.

Kane felt along the wall then rubbed his fingers together. "This way," he whispered, then added, "I think."

Nothing like a bout of confidence to settle her nerves. But she wasn't about to quibble, especially since she didn't have a better idea. "I hope there's some logic behind your decision."

"The dampness isn't quite as pronounced. We've been on an incline for the last few minutes. I think that means we're heading out of the mountain. Besides, I'm fresh out of intelligent answers."

She chuckled despite the circumstances. "Gotta like a man who admits he doesn't know where he's going."

The strike came out of nowhere, catching her across the cheek with a blow that nearly took her head off. Her already sore jaw vibrated. Her teeth ached. When she recovered from her position on the floor, Kane was standing with a gun pointed at his head.

"I have your boyfriend, so you might as well surrender." The guard spoke with cockiness.

"He means nothing to me," she replied, keeping any show of emotion out of her voice. Which, for her, was relatively easy. Most men considered her a stone-cold bitch, void of emotion, even on a good day. Forced into a life/death situation, such as now, there wouldn't be so much as a telltale quiver. Petrovich had made sure of that.

While the guard was trying to figure out if she was telling the truth, she launched the dagger. Dead on accurate—as always.

The man didn't even know what hit him when the point severed his jugular vein. He stood motionless before collapsing onto the floor.

Kane brought his hand up to rub his cheeks, as if trying to decipher the last few moments. Despite the darkness of the tunnel, Sabrina saw his eyes dart back and forth between her and the guy lying on the ground. Shrugging, he grabbed the guy's gun and pulled out the knife, wiping the excess blood on the man's shirt before handing it back to Sabrina.

"I don't even want to know where you learned to do that. Because you know what, it doesn't matter. You saved my ass. That's all that matters."

"Sure did."

"I half expected you to abandon me on the spot."

"Don't kid yourself. That was my Plan B."

"I figured as much."

Despite the tenor of their conversation, he once again grasped her hand and headed toward the end. They were so close—a soft breeze filtered inside. Freedom was palpable.

Sabrina allowed a sense of victory to overshadow her penchant for caution. For a second. Until a shiver along her spine alerted her seconds before the attack.

The larger of the two men went after Kane, the smaller after her. He lunged with a knife. To counteract the attack, she burst toward him with the weight of her body, deadening the arm holding the knife while striking his windpipe with a closed fist, collapsing his trachea.

Out of nowhere another man came at her, bringing her to the ground, forcing his thumbs around the front of her throat. Breathing became a struggle within seconds as stars burst inside her skull.

Pop.

Just when she'd thought she'd drawn her last breath, he tumbled on top of her. Pushing him aside, she looked up to see Kane standing with a gun.

"Now we're even," he muttered.

"I had things under control." Sabrina's head ached and nearly every bone in her body throbbed. But she'd come out of it alive, proving anything was possible.

While she couldn't see a mirror, she figured she looked about the same or maybe a little worse than Kane. He had a deep bruise forming along the right side of his face and blood seeping out of a cut above his eye. He was holding his arm in a manner that made her believe he might have injured it. On top of all that, he was walking with a limp.

"I have two questions. Do I look as bad as you? And what happened to your leg?"

"I've seen you look better. And it's an ankle sprain. It will heal in a few days."

He smiled. For the very first time, Sabrina noted the dimples on both sides of his mouth. Cute. Not that she noticed such things.

Besides, she wasn't certain this FBI agent had the same goals she did. Bringing Caitlyn home—that was all Sabrina needed to think about. Not official investigations, undercover agents, or what happened to Trinity once Caitlyn was safe and sound. And certainly not cute dimples.

The trees obscuring the sun gave way to an open clearing as they moved farther and farther away from the entrance of the tunnel. A slight breeze stirred the air around them. Miles of lush green hills were all she could see, except for the country road winding its way through.

Was it divine intervention that brought that dilapidated pick-up truck into her vision? She couldn't say for sure, but right now it seemed a good an exit strategy for what she had to do.

She eyed the truck as it made its way around the curve. Favoring that leg the way he was, she could outrun him. As long as she stayed out of his reach, she'd have no trouble making her escape.

"I know you're part of The Alliance, but where did you learn to do that stuff?" Kane asked, the words coming out in staccato breaths as he swayed toward her on his troubled ankle.

It was a question she wasn't willing to answer. For anyone, let alone some FBI agent with an official agenda.

"Here and there."

"That's not an answer," he said, stepping closer.

She raised her chin, ignoring the masculine scent enveloping her. Testosterone, adrenaline, and spicy aftershave. For a woman with less willpower, it would be a heady combination. "No. It's not."

He stared at her for a long moment before he must have realized that was all he was going to get from her. He glanced to the road. "Don't go off on your own. We're better off combining forces on this. Working for the FBI does have some perks."

She huffed out a breath. "No thanks. I'm not interested in the FBI's perks."

He shifted his weight off his sore leg, leaning heavily on the other, signaling defeat. "But you're in more danger than you think..."

His voice trailed off as Sabrina sprinted away and hopped into the back of the open pick-up truck. Leaving him out of sight and out of mind.

CHAPTER FIVE

———

Kane's leg gimped out when he tried to chase after her. What did she think she'd accomplish on her own? He'd been chasing Trinity for weeks now, and this agent from The Alliance thought she was going to just waltz in and…what? She'd asked where the girls went. Was she tracking one of the girls? Tracking Trinity? Whatever she was doing, it had ruined the slow, steady progress Kane had been making the last few weeks, gaining Marco's trust and following the chain of command up the ranks toward his ultimate goal: Trinity.

Kane ran a hand through his hair. Like Grace, he knew there were girls who were in trouble right now. But if he didn't get to Trinity, if he wasn't patient enough to follow the money to the top, as soon as one girl got away, another would take her place.

And he couldn't let this woman jeopardize that no matter whom she worked for.

He watched the green blip travel across his cell phone screen, reporting her steady progress. Like it or not, he'd hook back up with her soon. But for right now, he had no option but to sit down and call for help.

"Who is she?" Kane asked Ron, his friend at the Bureau. He didn't dare contact Nellis. No doubt the guy was still pissed.

"Her name is Sabrina Shaw. And yes, she works for The Alliance. She's been with them for seven years. Typically does eight to ten missions a year at the average of fifty grand a mission. Emigrated from Serbia when she was twenty-two. Speaks German, French, Italian, Serbian, and some Czech. Lives in Manhattan. Her brother Jake works for The Alliance as well. Her other brother Max is a trader on Wall Street."

Kane whistled. "That's some major dough. Doesn't need to play by the bureaucratic rules, and makes about four times as much as me. I need to find me a new job. Is she military trained?"

"Not as far as I can tell. Not sure where she got the street cred to hook up with The Alliance. They don't take just anybody."

"Why is The Alliance involved? What's she doing here?"

"You know that stuff is confidential, but it so happens that I have connections. And rumor has it she's doing a freebie for Mr. and Mrs. Collins to find their daughter Caitlyn, who they believe was abducted. The local police blew off their claim, citing the girl as a runaway."

"Damn." Kane drew his hands through his hair again. "She's no runaway. They shipped that girl out the day I got there. I wasn't in on the deal so I have no clue where she was sent. You got anything else?"

"Car should be at your location in about ten minutes. Can you hold out that long?"

"Is there another option I don't know about?" Kane chuckled for the first time in what felt like years.

"Guess not. What's your current plans?"

"First? Find Ms. Shaw. If I had to guess, she's going after the thumb drive and Marco's client list. I need to be there when she gets it."

"Lofty goal considering you don't know where she's headed."

"I suspected she'd bolt, so I put a tracking device in the clothes I gave her. Sooner or later the fact that there's a substantial price on her head is going to catch up with her."

* * *

Sabrina stretched her legs and tried to make herself presentable. Her messy hair partially covered her face, which was good, since she probably still sported bruises on her cheek and forehead. Since she didn't have a brush, she finger-combed through her waves the best she could.

Sleeping in the hay of the farmer's barn had been a necessity yesterday—maybe as a result of the drugs she'd been given, or maybe it was just pure exhaustion that had forced her body into hibernation. In the end, she had no choice but to bunk with the cows and horses.

It was a risky proposition stopping so close to Marco's place, but with her head aching and her body trembling, she'd known she had no choice. Now, feeling refreshed, and alone, she was ready to figure out how to find Caitlyn.

The clothesline hanging next to the barn had been a godsend. While most of the clothes were too large for her, she did manage to snag a sleeveless undershirt to wear under the long-sleeve camo shirt Kane had given to her. Of course, her first choice would have been a nice size 34B bra, but she made use with what was available.

She splashed water from a nearby stream on her face and arms, cleaning up as much as possible. Immediately, she felt more refreshed and rejuvenated than she had in several days.

She used acupressure points between her thumb and forefinger and in the indent just below her kneecap to relieve some of the aches and pains at various parts of her body, and tried to formulate a plan. At this point, she was out of leads and out of everything else. But, at least in some ways, she was closer to finding Caitlyn. She knew where the girl had been kept. Now she needed to retrace the footsteps to find out where she'd been sent.

Everything hinged on getting back into Marco's house and getting information from him about Caitlyn's whereabouts. As for the elusive Trinity, that was Kane's problem, not hers.

Hitching a ride would be easy. Besides, she didn't think she had the strength to walk the fifteen miles to the nearest town.

Knowing Marco controlled the area around Langford, she opted for the opposite direction. Underestimating the far reach of his powers would be a mistake. But she had to take a chance. And she had to get moving. Antonio would be her best bet, but she needed to get to a phone.

The gun was secured in the waistband of her pants, covered by the shirt that hit her mid-hip. The dagger remained in one of the pockets as her primary measure of security.

Never underestimate your opponent, Saby. Petrovich's sage advice rung in her ears. Never trusting or believing anybody except her family had been the part of her core that kept her alive.

So why did she find herself second-guessing cutting Kane loose? Sure, he might have been a little trouble, and she did prefer to work alone. But he was with the Bureau. That had to open some doors, free up the information highway, so to speak, especially since recovering Caitlyn wasn't part of her duties working for The Alliance. Confessing to her brothers what she'd been up to and asking them for help was a possibility, but there was little they could do from the States.

She'd always been a take-charge, by-the-seat-of-her-pants kind of gal. This experience was no different. She still had her wits, wasn't without her own network of connections throughout Europe, and had an ache in her gut that couldn't or wouldn't be willed away. The toughest part was being in this area brought up memories of Petrovich. He'd been her savior and her nightmare rolled into one.

* * *

When Sabrina hit the streets of town, people were milling about, stopping for coffee or lunch at local cafes. The weather was brisk and the clothes she had on were doing little to prevent the cool breeze that had set in.

But she needed money. Without a credit card, or a passport, or a phone, there was only one way to acquire it. She needed a mark.

For survival, she and her brothers relied on pickpocketing as a means to an end when they'd lost their parents. By the time she was eight, she had out-mastered her brothers. They said it was her innocent appearance rather than skill that allowed her to be so efficient. But she suspected they were jealous. After they had been taken in by Petrovich, her skill level had only increased. Even though she swore she'd never fall back on pickpocketing, the old adage about never saying never came to mind. Right now it was a means to an end.

Tourists were always the mark of choice. They normally carried more money and were also more distracted, spending time enjoying the nuances of the culture rather than worrying about their wallets.

She scanned the crowd looking for prey: *Nope, too old. Nope, too young. Nope, too poor*—the guy looked as if he hadn't had a good meal in weeks.

Finally, she spotted an excellent mark. She couldn't tell if he was a tourist or not, which probably meant he wasn't, but he fit the other criteria she was looking for.

Distracted by the ramblings of a teenager who seemed bent on making her very existence a drain on anyone within earshot, the guy might very well be perfect. His daughter—or at least Sabrina hoped she was his daughter rather than a very young girlfriend—had blue hair and more visible piercings than she'd seen in quite a while, even by Greenwich Village standards. The girl whined and pointed into a storefront window with all the theatrics of a six-year-old wanting the newest shiny new toy. Dad nodded and feigned interest as he tried to encourage the girl to move on.

Sabrina moved next to the couple, gazing at the display. It took her less than a second to understand the reason behind the terrified look in the dad's eyes.

The window display held an array of clothes bordering on obscene. Sprinkles of bright satin colors of fuchsia and purple were mixed with black satin and lace attached to dresses that had an erotically Gothic twist. Deep, plunging necklines and thigh-high slits bordered on the perverse in a combination that could only be described as the No-Daughter-of-Mine-Will-Ever-Wear-That Display.

She almost felt a little bad at the idea of lifting his wallet. The guy had more than enough on his plate with a rebellious teen, but right now she didn't have a choice but to follow through with her plan. Nerves skittered along the surface as she flexed her fingers to relieve the building tension.

Listening to their one-sided conversation, conducted in French, Sabrina tsked and uttered a "Mon Dieu" in support of dad even while she slipped her fingers inside his pocket to relieve him of his wallet.

She moved away discreetly. After turning the corner, she flipped open the wallet, snatched the money she would need, and tossed the Italian leather to the cobblestone sidewalk, where hopefully it would be found and returned.

She stuffed the euros inside her pocket. While it wasn't much, it was enough for until she could hook up with Antonio, who could score her a fake passport and loan her some money.

Even though it was a little indulgent, she bought a pair of tennis shoes to replace the too-big-for-her boots Kane had confiscated. As if her stomach knew she had some money, it began to rumble. She purchased some food at a local pub and gobbled it down. As she paid the man behind the bar, she contemplated her next step—finding a car to hotwire.

Eyeing the phone in the corner, she walked over and dialed Antonio. He lived close, with a residence in Northern Italy, and he had enough money and firepower to set her up for what she needed to do.

Damn it. No answer.

Didn't people carry their cell phones with them all the time? She left a message, but without a number at which to reach her, she'd have to keep trying.

As she hung up the phone, she became more aware of the quiet surrounding her. It took her a few seconds to realize the hum of conversation had dissipated, with only occasional whispers breaking through the silence.

When she glanced around, all eyes were riveted on her. They held some kind of paper in her their hands and were pointing to it, then looking at her. Uh oh. This was going to get ugly.

"That's her, isn't it?" one of them shouted from the back as they all started to converge.

She eased outside with as much finesse as she could muster, given that half the local population seemed to be nipping at her heels. Armed with nothing but their bodies and a will to subdue her, she had a fighting chance.

Certainly she could outrun a bunch of middle-aged men going soft in the middle. She hit the street desperate for an escape.

But it was hard to think when a mob of angry Austrians was in hot pursuit. Luckily she spotted a pick-up truck idling outside a store with the owner nowhere in sight. Backed into a corner, she couldn't get picky. It was a crime of opportunity.

With only a vague sense of where she needed to go except as far away from the crowd as possible, she let out the clutch and pressed the gas pedal to the floor. The old truck swerved on the uneven pavement until she was able to regain control.

A shot of adrenaline gave her the boost she needed until she glanced at the gas gauge. An eighth of a tank? She banged on the dashboard. "Are you frickin' kidding me?"

She blew out a breath and reined in her fear. *Calm down. This is doable.* Even with that miniscule amount of gas, she should be able to get far enough away to work on a Plan B.

Feeling much more calm, she glanced into the rearview mirror. Instead of reassurance, her pulse rate shot through the roof when she spotted a pick-up filled to the brim with men carrying rifles. The locals must have called in reinforcements with guns. But why?

She glanced at the passenger seat and spotted a piece of paper. A picture of her with the caption that read *Wanted for Murder, Reward Offered*. With a sinking sensation in her gut, she glanced at the gas gauge as it slid closer to the E.

Could this whole thing get any worse?

CHAPTER SIX

———

Sabrina swore as the truck rolled to a stop in the grass. She threw open the door and sprinted to a dilapidated farmhouse about a hundred yards away and hoped she could get there before bullets started to fly.

Her lungs pounded against her chest while she struggled to catch her breath. A bullet ricocheted off the wood behind her, splintering the edge into tiny fragments. She peeked through one of the many holes in the wooden structure and spotted a guy creeping toward her.

These were innocents caught up in the thirst for making a quick buck. They were pawns in Marco's game. She didn't want to hurt them. Instead she aimed for a tree branch overhead to scare the guy back while she tried to figure a way out. As she'd expected, he crawled back to the cover of trees. She had no doubt the group was strategizing about how to take her down.

"Hey," one of them yelled. Then he said in broken English, "We don't hurt you."

A sound over her shoulder grabbed her attention.

She turned, her gun pointed behind her. "Need some help, Ms. Shaw?" Kane whispered as he scooted under a hole in the boards along the back, carrying an Uzi.

Even while she wasn't thrilled at his appearance, and the fact he'd somehow figured out her name, his timing was impeccable. "I'm doing fine on my own. But you can leave that Uzi and the ammunition and we'll call it even."

"I wasn't aware I owed you anything," he whispered, a slow, easy smile on his face as he sidled up next to her and shot off a round into the trees. He looked cool, calm, and rational. But then again, he did carry with him enough ammo to destroy an army. She'd be cocky too if she were carrying that kind of firepower.

"Not telling me about the price on my head was an oversight, I presume?"

"I tried to warn you, but you were too busy abandoning a wounded man."

Sabrina clucked and rolled her eyes. "I work alone."

"You've made that clear on multiple occasions so that even a dumb-as-a-rock FBI agent could understand."

She eyed her target and shot a foot over his head to drive them back. "I've gotta commend you on your firepower. Impressive."

He raised his eyebrows. "There are some perks working for a bureaucracy." He glanced through a hole in the wood. "As far as I can tell, there's about ten or fifteen of them."

"Not bad odds if they're as unskilled as they appear." Sabrina shrugged, easing off a round into the trees. "But they've come close a couple of times." She pointed toward the wall behind her, which had a few embedded rounds.

He examined the wood, fingering the splinters and fragments. "Kindergartners with guns, if you ask me. That's the problem with these Wanted Dead or Alive scenarios. You get every two-bit loser anxious to score easy cash. I imagine earning a couple thousand euros by doing a little target practice sounds easy."

"Okay, you're the big bad FBI guy, how do we get out of this?"

"We don't want to hurt anybody. Let's spray the trees with bullets so we can slip away into my waiting car."

"A car full of gas?" When he nodded, she smiled as relief shimmied through. "I better cover for you. You'll need extra time with that bum leg?"

"I'll do okay."

"You're hobbling around like my ninety-year-old grandma. Well, if I had a ninety-year-old grandma."

His brow furrowed as a hint of a smile turned up his lips. "I could still beat you in a race."

"I wouldn't be too sure about that. You didn't do so well last time."

"That's because I let you get away."

She rolled her eyes. "Yeah, right." She encouraged him to come closer by curling her fingers. "Let me see. Is it sprained?"

"Twisted it during that last takedown in the tunnel. If you had stuck around, you would have known that."

"Pull up your pants." She rubbed her fingers together. "I'd be much better with my needles, but they're gone. Along with my cell phone, my money, and my luggage."

"Needles? What the hell are you talking about?" He glanced through a hole and let off a couple of rounds before he backed away.

"I know acupuncture. At least enough to ease some of the discomfort. I prefer using my needles, but in a pinch, I can ease it with acupressure as well." She shook her head and smiled. Despite everything going on outside, with him shooting off a round or two every thirty seconds or so, this whole thing felt like a slice of normalcy. "Now stop being such a baby."

She held the pressure points and counted. Little by little she felt the relaxation of the muscles underlying the injury. His injury wasn't bad, but it was enough to slow them both down.

"Feels a little better."

"Hate to say I told you so, but this gal has skills." She glanced outside. "There's no time like the present to do a little disappearing act."

Letting loose a barrage of bullets, they covered the area, keeping it up for several rounds. Taking short breaks in between kept the men outside off balance, never quite knowing when the shooting would start up again.

"You didn't think you'd get far in that pick-up, did you?"

"I was in a jam. I opted for what was handy."

He wiggled his eyebrows up and down. "Good thing I have connections. The car is on the other side of that set of trees. Next break, we make our move."

With one last explosive round, they set off into the trees behind them with her in the lead, grasping his hand to pull him along. A few moments later, she spotted the old Volvo ready and waiting.

Despite a sincere desire to the contrary, she'd hooked herself up with a partner.

* * *

Sabrina settled against the front seat, feeling a sense of relief wash over. Although she knew this respite was short-lived, it gave her the opportunity to catch her breath.

"How did you find me?" Now that the dust settled, she was curious. It wasn't coincidence.

"I listened for the bullets, and followed the sound to trouble."

She gave him her best "oh pleeeez" look.

"I got into town right after you and heard you'd stolen a pick-up."

She shook her head and urged him on with her fingers. "That doesn't explain how you found me. I'm a good ten miles out of town."

"I put a tracking device in the clothes I gave you." He had the good grace to look sheepish. "I figured there was a strong chance you'd book it if we got out of there alive, and being proactive is what I do best."

What was wrong with her? As many tracking devices as she'd put on others over the years, she didn't even consider the possibility Kane had done the same thing to her. Shame on her. Petrovich had taught her better. Patting down her pants, she squirmed around in the seat to touch at every possible hiding place: the seams, the pockets, the waistband. When she found nothing, she stripped off her shirt and finally found the receiver—smaller and thinner than one of her acupuncture needles, neatly tucked into the band of her shirt. She ripped at the seam and wiggled it out of its hiding spot before flicking it out the window.

A smile etched up the corners of his lips. "Don't give me the evil eye. I told you about it, didn't I?"

"I would have figured it out sooner or later." As soon as he said "FBI" and let her get away so easily she should have known he had an ace in the hole.

He snorted. "It wouldn't have taken you too much longer, which is why I confessed."

She put back on the shirt and brought up her legs so that she sat cross-legged on the front seat. "Tell me, are you the good brother or the bad brother?" she asked, changing the subject away from her own blunder.

"I don't have a brother. Only a sister," Kane remarked while a hint of confusion marred his face. He shifted into third and stared at her across the front seat. Their respective Uzis were placed between them for easy access.

"Cain and Abel, as in the Bible. I'm sure you were named after the evil one."

He shook his head, but a small smile played at he corner of his lips. "I saved your butt, didn't I? That wasn't so evil."

"Contrary to your belief, I was doing fine. My butt didn't need saving."

"If you call almost out of bullets, surrounded by fifty guys wanting to kill you, and being miles from anywhere without transportation doing fine, then yeah. You were." He nodded, glancing over in her direction. "I'll leave you to your delusions."

She sighed and fought the urge to smile. The last thing she wanted was for him to believe his charm was working. "For the record, I believe you said it was only fifteen guys, and I still had my knife." She tapped at the holder strapped to her thigh. "Evil twin," she added.

"I hate to disappoint you, but Kane is a family name. Spelled K-A-N-E as opposed to the biblical version, you know, C-A-I-N."

"Well, I'm not much on Bible reading."

"That makes two of us."

For a second or two she contemplated what he meant by that. Not interested in delving too deep, she opted for a more impersonal question.

"You must have made nice with your bosses to score this ammo."

"Not so much, but I still have some friends."

She tapped her kneecap with her finger. "Which reminds me, why isn't there a price on *your* head? After all the run-ins we had with guards in the tunnels, they've got to know you're helping me."

He shrugged. "Many of the guys we ran into don't know me. Besides, the car I stole from Marco I drove into the lake. If they found it, they might assume I'm dead. They're a lazy lot so probably didn't bother to look for a body."

"Too bad you couldn't come up with an equally brilliant plan for my untimely demise." She paused. "Speaking of which, since I've got to get back inside to get that thumb drive, you can leave me with a few weapons once we're in the clear and I'll sneak back in." She brought the Uzi into the palm of her hand. "As for now, I'm prepared."

"This isn't Gunfight at the OK Corral." He raised his eyebrows. "Did you watch too many westerns when you were a kid? Is that the problem?"

"Very funny."

"I was about to say I've rigged the back seat so it pulls down. I suggest you hide in the trunk." He stopped to grace her with a dimpled smile before he continued, "And yes, you should bring your new toy as well as a couple of rounds of ammo. I don't think you'll need either because I'm going to be a"—he placed a baseball cap backwards on his head—"student on holiday." He spoke the words in French.

"I'm impressed. Let me crawl into my cave. Give me a signal if you want me to come out guns blazing." Sabrina drew in a breath as she yanked up the seat, cloaking her in darkness. Not wanting to appear too chicken, she neglected to tell him how pervasive her claustrophobia could be at times. All those times she'd be hiding in a cave while her brothers went out to gather what food they could had been a lingering memory she'd prefer to forget. She drew in a few calming breaths and centered herself.

"Believe me, you'll be the first to know," he hollered.

* * *

As much as he wanted to project confidence, Kane didn't have a whole lot of faith. He knew he'd never be able to talk her out of going back to Marco's place to retrieve the records, but convincing her to take a more planned approach would be the difficult part. But for right now, at least he'd be there when she confronted Marco. If he did have financial information about Trinity's clients on it, it would be one step closer to Trinity and making sure no more Caitlyns ever went missing at his hand.

Once she'd closed the back seat, he relaxed a little. That was until he spotted the roadblock up ahead.

Despite the rigidity of his military posture, he slumped his shoulders and tried to appear unassuming before he lowered the window. "Are you guys looking for somebody?" He spoke the words in French rather than German.

"We're looking for a woman," one of the men said.

"You and me both." Kane laughed. "It's been a while since I've seen some action."

"Then take my advice and don't get married. You'll never get laid again." One of the men spoke as the others snickered and swapped insults back and forth in German.

The man in charge quieted them all with a raised hand. "The woman we're looking for is armed and dangerous and already killed a man. She wounded another when a group tried to take her by force."

"What does the woman look like?"

"Red hair, small but strong. We heard she killed the guy with her bare hands."

"She sounds like a total badass. What should I do if I see her?"

"Don't approach. Call the police," the officer in charge said. "There's another road block a little further down the road."

"And don't pick up any strange women," one of the men called.

"No problem. Thanks for the warning. I'll be on the lookout."

He wasn't surprised when he heard the creak of the back seat coming down. "Stay down for a few more minutes. They're still watching the car."

"How much longer?" She opened up the seat, but stayed prone. "Did I mention I'm a wee bit claustrophobic?"

He raised his eyebrow and smiled but didn't dare comment. "You need to stay right where you are for a while."

"Can I leave the seat down at least?"

He turned to see her hovering near the opening, as if she needed to suck in fresh air. It was the first time he'd seen even a speck of vulnerability, and he couldn't help but wonder about her demons. "I'll let you know when we're close to the next checkpoint." He barely finished saying the words when he saw a group of men in a line across the road. "Close it up. Now. I think it's some of Marco's guys," he barked as the sense of trouble raced down his arms, contracting his muscles.

Six men lined up, breaking into groups of three on either side of the road. There was nothing lax about their posture, or in the way they held their weapons. The difference between them and the last group was night and day.

Kane stopped the car and told the same story, except the tenor turned hostile almost immediately. "How long have you been in Austria?" One of the men leaned into the car window, glancing around the interior as he asked the question. "Let me see your passport."

"I'm on holiday and going to visit my girlfriend in Germany." Kane handed over his French passport.

"Where did you say you were going?"

"I'm headed to Munich." Kane figured he'd better look for an escape route. Unless he missed his guess, this was going to go bad quick, and he needed to be prepared.

"Why are you traveling through Austria if you're from France?" The man asked as he put a hand on Kane's shoulder and squeezed.

"I grew up in Avignon, but I was visiting some friends in Austria." Out of all the languages he spoke, French was his strongest. Most people thought he was a native.

"How did you meet your girlfriend?"

The guy was coming on strong, trying to make a point, while the others had lost interest. Which worked in his favor for the time being.

"At university." He said the first thing that came to mind, but he could tell the guy wasn't buying it.

God only knew what Sabrina was doing inside the trunk. If he had to guess, she was a hair's breadth away from bursting out, guns blazing.

Between her trigger finger and this guy's persistence, this had all the makings of DEFCON 1 waiting to happen. It was only a matter of time before he had six guns pointed in his direction.

"I know you from somewhere..." The guy's voice trailed off.

"Yeah, I get that a lot. I guess I have one of those faces." Kane shrugged and held his breath. Being undercover for several years, this kind of thing happened. Most times it was inconsequential. Waiting it out was the only possible way to play this for now. He hoped Sabrina was equally as patient.

"Inspect the vehicle," the guy commanded in German as he raised his gun and pointed it at Kane's temple.

Immediately, the others snapped to attention and moved toward the car. One of the guys started to pull on the handles of the locked door. Next thing he knew, Sabrina kicked out the panel and fired a quick barrage, catching the guy mid-chest. Wiggling her body through the opening, she scooted onto the seat. She threw the guy's body out the door and closed it while Kane sped away.

Kane glanced into the rearview mirror and spotted three men hopping into a car. Considering the hilly terrain and their military-style Jeep, Kane figured the odds were in the bad guys' favor.

"Hurry." She pounded her fist on the back of the front seat as a bullet shattered the side mirror.

Kane drove, inching the speedometer toward ninety, taking the curves and the bumps at the same speed. She held on to the passenger side headrest as if her life depended on it.

"How close are they?" A rumble of fear skittered along Kane's spine. He never worried much when he was alone, but working with somebody else he always felt responsible for them as well.

A spray of bullets riddled the back of the car.

"There's your answer," she called back.

"Any ideas?" He gripped the wheel with both hands as the tug of the rough terrain fought for control.

"Other than drive faster? No. I'm leaving it all in your capable hands."

She eased out another round. They returned her fire, destroying the back window.

"You okay?" he called. They were getting closer. More accurate.

"Yeah. But I think I should take over the driving. I do this sort of thing all the time."

"When there's a break in the action, I'll give you a crack at it if you think you can do better." He reached into the compartment between the seats. "In the meantime, do you know how to use a grenade? Oh, hell, what am I thinking? Of course you do." He handed them to her. "I only have two, so use them wisely."

"Going old school, huh." She tapped on the sunroof. "Open this up." Seconds later, she let them fly. "I suggest you move it, Kane."

The car lurched as the explosion rocked behind them. The grenade landed a few feet ahead of the car chasing them, but it seemed to have stopped them in their tracks.

She seemed unfazed. In fact, it seemed almost like she was in her element. Once again, he couldn't help but wonder where she'd been trained prior to coming to Alliance. Maybe the Israeli Army?

"Nice shot." For the first time in a while, he was able to take a deep breath. "There's an intersection coming up. We'll ditch this car, then head the other way on foot."

"Except for the almost-getting-killed thing, that was kind of fun. I now have a new favorite toy." She crawled from the back seat to the front to sit beside him. He didn't know how or why, but it felt oddly reassuring to have her there.

"Grenades are a little messy. Causes a lot of attention, so it's not the way to go unless you're desperate."

She turned, bringing her left leg onto the seat. He couldn't believe how relaxed she looked. And people thought he had nerves of steel. He had nothing on this woman.

"What happened back there?"

"One of the guys recognized me and pointed a gun to my head right before the shit hit the fan."

"I didn't jump the gun, did I?" she asked.

"I couldn't believe you waited that long."

"I'm still getting used to the gun, so I didn't want to miss."

"Yeah, well, a few seconds later and my brains would have been spilled on the front seat."

"That had to be a little scary."

"Not for me. I'm the big bad FBI guy." He laughed. "Truthfully, I was scared shitless. If I weren't, I'd be an idiot."

Weird. Never had he been so comfortable with anybody that he knowingly admitted fear, especially when she was displaying none. From an early age he'd always been able to project being the epitome of calm and confident despite the chaos going on at home or on the job. Maybe she was able to do the same. Something about Sabrina was making him more aware of that prickle of self-doubt lurking underneath his surface.

"Hooking up with me has brought about a whole set of problems you hadn't figured on." She chewed her lip, signaling to him she was hedging about something.

"Undoubtedly. But then again, you have that sparkling personality that more than makes up for it."

If he had to guess, she was trying to weasel out of this pseudo-partnership they'd developed. But that wasn't going to happen. He knew what she was after, and even if it wasn't for exactly the same reasons, he wanted it too. No way was he going to let her get to Marco before he got what he needed from the man.

Sabrina tapped her finger against her thigh. He could see the wheels turning inside her head. "I have some connections in Italy. We're not very far from the border. If you bring me there, I can go off on my own."

He reached across the front seat, securing her hand in his. "Like it or not, you could use my help. It doesn't hurt I've figured out a way to take down Marco without him seeing it coming. We're going to sneak right into his backyard and find out all his secrets."

So he exaggerated a bit. He wanted to get at the information as much as she did. While he might need it for a different purpose, that didn't mean they couldn't work together on this.

"You've piqued my interest. How are we getting to Marco? As I remember from that lovely experience, he has a ton of guards." A smile pulled up the edges of her mouth. "I'm good, but I'm not sure about you."

A rumble of laughter erupted from his chest. "You're good, all right. But we're both even better when most all of Marco's guys are eating up the countryside trying to find a certain redhead that's royally pissed him off. There's also that little thing with G that's got his underwear in a twist and him in hot water with the big man. And now that he knows you're still in the area, the countryside is going to be crawling with dirt bags. And on top of that, no doubt Marco's still pissed about you helping Liz get away."

Despite the light tenor of their conversation, it was difficult not to fixate on the elephant in the room—all the poor women who'd already been sucked into the system. Memories of a childhood filled with worry about his mother's safety seemed to pulse at the base of his skull. Maybe Nellis was right. This assignment struck too close to home.

"Which reminds me, who is G? Do you know any of the other buyers?"

Thankful for the reprieve from his memories, he said, "Haven't a clue. Everything is in code. All I know is most have more money than I could ever dream about, and most are regular customers of Marco's."

"How do you know all this?"

"I planted some devices that allow me to be privy to tactical information. Somebody will probably find them sooner or later, since they regularly sweep for bugs, but for the time being, everything that goes down there is being sent straight to the FBI."

"Speaking of which, what is your plan for breaking in?"

This was the part that hadn't gelled in his head. While it was risky, there weren't any other options. He didn't know why, but there was no doubt in his mind Sabrina was going to attempt this, on her own. She wasn't letting go. And neither was he. Together there was a slim chance they'd be successful.

"Marco's got lots of vehicles, but not a motorcycle. With most of his guys scouring the countryside, he won't be expecting us. We seize the element of surprise and take the dirt path that winds through the forest. There's no way a car could fit through there."

She threw her head back and laughed. "You've got to be kidding me. You call that a plan?"

"Come on, haven't you seen *The Great Escape?* Steve McQueen riding that motorcycle?"

What had Nellis called him? ADD with an adrenaline junkie chaser? He was beginning to believe maybe he was right.

"If I remember correctly, he was captured by the Germans in the movie."

"Minor detail. We'll be in and out before you know it." They needed luck and massive amounts of firepower. Just in case.

"What about the tunnels?"

"They've been sealed off after your breakout."

"They figured out you were the one to help me escape?"

"Marco doesn't want to admit he trusted somebody who betrayed him. It's a much better tale to say the woman he lured happens to be one with superpowers who can kill with her bare hands. It makes all the guys think they're going to be the stud who takes you down once and for all."

"Guys are so sophomoric sometimes." She giggled. The sound seemed so contrary to what he'd seen of her so far, he stared to make sure he'd really heard it. And, yep, she had a big old smile on her face and even a hint of a twinkle in her eye.

Seconds later, she morphed quickly to the tough-as-nails persona once again. "Hmmm. While it seems a little bit crazy to ride in on motorcycles like some version of Hells Angels, I do have unfinished business with Marco. I need to know who he sold Caitlyn to. And, if I'm lucky, maybe make him sorry he was ever born."

"Oh no you don't." He grabbed her arm between the seats. "I need him to give me information about Trinity. He's the best lead I have so far." He was in enough trouble going off script. Now he needed to justify to the powers that be that he made the right decision.

"Just so you're clear, nothing is going to stop me from getting the information I need about Caitlyn Collins."

CHAPTER SEVEN

———

Kane glared at Sabrina in that intimidating way that cops did. Maybe he thought that would make her back down.

"Why? Getting Caitlyn wasn't sanctioned by The Alliance."

She shook her head. *The fed information highway strikes again.* "I'm trying to help the Collins family because it's the right thing to do. Just because The Alliance decided the mission was too risky to undertake doesn't mean I could say no."

Petrovich had his own little arsenal of young killers, starting with the KOS and later recruiting orphaned youth to his own personal army. He played God, deciding who he thought was worthy of living and dying, and sent the minions he trained to do his dirty work. Trinity's organization was doing the same thing, making a handsome profit preying upon innocent young women for sexual exploitation, had pushed more hot buttons than she cared to think about. But that was not her problem. She only had one objective. Caitlyn Collins.

"You've got some skills, so don't take this the wrong way, but if I hadn't gotten you out of there, you'd be another one of the statistics. Those guys would have been able to capture you and bring you to Marco."

"I've gotten out of much more difficult spots." Like when Max had nearly died. A twisting sensation in her gut wound her nerves a little tighter. Thinking and dwelling about Caitlyn's predicament, intertwined with her own up-close-and-personal experience, made the situation more urgent than ever. "The local police filed Caitlyn as a runaway. After a couple of hours on her computer I found the conversation with Marco he thought he'd remotely deleted, with the mention of Trinity Modeling as the lure. At that point, I couldn't say no, especially after seeing her parents cling to that one sliver of hope I was offering. They wanted their girl back, and I promised them I would do that for them."

"And once you make a promise, there's no turning back."

"Exactly. I'm going to find that bastard and string him up by his balls." The conviction steeled her nerves and brought a sense of calmness throughout her system.

"Where were you trained? You've got the Uzi down, and with your Krav Maga skills I'm guessing Israeli Army. Am I right?"

She felt the uptick in her pulse at his far-from-innocent questions. He didn't know about her past with Petrovich, and she'd just as soon keep it that way. "Let's say I've managed to acquire some skills in my life."

"A woman of mystery?" He shook his head even though she knew he wanted to probe further. "While I appreciate your need for vengeance, do not kill Marco. He may have information I need."

She brought her foot up onto the seat, relaxing back against the door. "Can I torture him just a little?"

He laughed and she glanced his way. Darn it, those dimples sprang to life and she felt this tiny flutter in the pit of her stomach. Girly thoughts were not her normal modus operandi. She enjoyed sex as much as the next person, but it was the emotional piece she didn't take kindly to.

"As long as he can tell me what I need, I'm okay with that."

"Now that we have a plan—such as it were"—she glanced at him and rolled her eyes—"and firepower, we need to get to Marco. How soon can you get the dirt bike?"

Despite the lack of sleep, a surge of adrenaline at the mere mention of progress made her ready to go full steam ahead.

"It's not quite so easy."

"Why did I have a feeling you were going to say that?"

"It's about timing. You're going to need a disguise."

She nodded her agreement. "My natural hair color is dark brown anyway. I dyed it to make myself look closer to twenty than thirty."

He glanced at her and smiled. "I'll get some hair dye at the next store we see. And a pair of scissors."

She held up her hand. "I'm far from a prima donna, and know guys don't care much about their hair, except when it's falling out, but a pair of scissors outside of a licensed professional is kind of scary for a female." She fingered through her shoulder-length locks.

"Big bad Sabrina Shaw afraid of a measly pair of scissors?" He winked. "No need to worry, I'm a wizard with a pair of scissors."

Sabrina rolled her eyes again. "And I'm sure when my hairdresser gets a look at your handiwork she'll probably faint on the spot."

He held his right hand across his chest. "Because I'm a guy you think I can't cut hair?"

The amusement in his tone didn't surprise her. It was the reaction running deep into her bones that made her body sit up and take notice. Somehow, and for some reason, this guy was different. And the only reason she had for that didn't sit well with her.

Not at all.

* * *

With night closing in, most of the shops were closing or getting ready to by the time they walked into town. While Sabrina waited outside with an Uzi tucked in the duffle bag and his baseball hat covering her hair, he went inside the grocery store to get some water, food, hair dye, shampoo, and scissors.

He came out a few minutes later. "Let's find a spot where we can take care of this before we look for a place to eat."

They walked into the wooded area where he applied the hair dye and then rinsed it out with the water he purchased.

He snapped the scissors. "Allow Monsieur Kane to give you a fabulous cut."

She couldn't help but laugh, even though the sight before her was ominous. Trusting this man with her life was one thing, but her hair? "This does not seem to be a good idea."

"You're chicken."

"For good reason. You don't look as if you'd be good at this. In fact, you pretty much look all thumbs."

"Once again you insult me." He spoke with an exaggerated French accent and motioned with his hand. "I'll do such a great job you'll want me to cut your hair all the time. I guarantee it."

Without a mirror, she couldn't do this herself. "Oh, this is going to be ugly." She brought her head down and acquiesced.

Bringing a comb through her hair, he brought the scissors near the nape of her neck and snipped. She cringed. But that was only the beginning. It was an excruciating twenty minutes before he finished.

Hair touched the base of her neck, tickling her nape. Bringing her fingers through the waves and curls, she couldn't help but mourn the loss.

"Beautiful," he remarked.

"You have to say that. Otherwise I might take a knife to you," she grumbled.

"Don't think I wasn't feeling the pressure."

"Wait until I see a mirror, then I'll decide." She huffed out a breath, and drew her fingers through her hair once again. "Let's go back into town. We have to get the motorcycle. Which reminds me, how exactly are we going to do that?"

"A friend of mine from the Bureau is trying to hook us up, but nothing's guaranteed."

"I need to borrow your phone to text my brothers and let them know what I've been doing. No doubt they've tried to contact me and are worried sick."

"Max and Jake?"

"Been doing a little research?"

"Pays to know who I'm partnering up with." He graced her with a smile.

"Don't get too cocky. I'm always a hair's breadth away from ditching you." When he handed her the phone, she texted, *I'm fine. But this is an FBI guy's phone so don't text back. I'll fill you in on what's been going soon. Saby.*

Her stomach rumbled. Lunch this afternoon was a long time ago. Fresh clothes and a warm bath were a distant memory.

"I searched the internet for hostels, but we'd have to walk about ten miles, so we might be stuck in town and hope for the best."

"It goes without saying I have no money, so anything more than free is too rich for my blood."

"I've a couple hundred euros so that should cover us for dinner and maybe a night at a small inn if we're lucky." He grabbed her hand. "There's a place down the road. I thought we'd head there for a little food."

"Now you're talking. I'm starving. I could go for a beer and some stew." As tempting as it might be, remembering the consequences last time she picked somebody's pocket shifted her to a scared-straight mentality.

She had no desire to repeat the fiasco from earlier in the day. Besides, she didn't have the energy.

They walked inside the small, dark tavern. Only a few people sat at wooden tables, some choosing to sit along the bar. To her relief, none of them paid any attention. She headed straight for the bathroom to check out her hair while he secured them a spot.

A few moments later, she met him at the bar and peered into the mirror along the back, confirming what she'd already seen in the bathroom. It was her, yet it wasn't. Her fingers twisted in the hair at her nape, while her breath hitched in her throat.

"What do you think?"

"Weird. I've never had short hair before. It's going to take some getting used to." Fleeting memories of her mother's long, dark hair shot through her mind. Most times she kept those thoughts at bay, but her mother's effervescent smile flashed before her even while a kind of controlled fear tunneled through. What had happened the night her parents died? Snippets of memories seemed to float around her brain, but they never coalesced into anything she could make sense of.

"More importantly, it will take people a lot longer to match you up with your picture."

His response interrupted the trajectory of her thoughts. Getting caught up in something that might never produce any answers wasn't on her agenda right now.

When their stew and ale arrived, they both dug in. Too famished to stop for even a second, they were finished before he spoke again. "What's your story? I know you were born in Serbia, but how you got to the US is sort of a mystery."

"And here I thought the FBI knew everything." She avoided his question with a sip of ale. The brew slid down her throat, quenching a thirst she hadn't felt in a long time. Being in Europe did strange things to her; memories—both good and bad—tugged with every step she took. "All I'm interested in right now is how fast we can get back to Marco's place and find out where he sent Caitlyn."

"They're expecting us to run the opposite way, but we're heading straight for him. Is tomorrow soon enough?" When she nodded, he continued, "First we need a good night's sleep and to secure the motorcycle."

"Right about now I could lie down in the middle of the floor and fall fast asleep, I'm afraid."

"You're still coming off those drugs that Marco gave you." He shook his head and she couldn't help but wonder what he was thinking.

"Does he have a chemist in residence or something?"

"Not him personally, but Trinity does and sends Marco concoctions to produce different effects, from an aphrodisiac to excruciatingly painful to euphoric. The whole thing is beyond sick."

If they continued to discuss the inner workings of the organization, she'd never get to sleep tonight. Instead, she chugged the last of her ale and changed gears in their conversation. "Any idea where we can bunk for the night?"

"I checked with the bartender while you were in the bathroom, and they have a room above the bar. Sound okay to you?" He stood and helped her out of the chair.

She nodded as exhaustion pressed down on her shoulders, permeating every muscle of her body. The bartender escorted them through the kitchen and up the back steps to a room at the end of the hall. After Kane gave him money, he unlocked the door and walked away without another word.

The modest room had a small bed, a table with a lamp, and a bathroom outside the door. She'd stayed in worse places in her life. But, being in such close proximity to somebody, she hadn't decided whether trust was an issue.

Still, in some ways, she felt that she knew Kane better than most other men, aside from her brothers. Which was odd, since she'd known him for only a couple of days.

"Small bed, huh?" He glanced at her and grimaced. "I'd let you take the bed and I'd sleep on the floor, but I don't think there's enough room."

She plopped onto the bed and slipped off her shoes. "As long as you keep your hands to yourself, I'll be fine."

"Never let it be said that I don't know how to show a lady a great time." He placed her bag and his on the floor and took off his shoes.

He squirmed into position next to her. The makeshift cover was barely enough for one person, let alone two, but they somehow made do.

Being in close proximity was doing something very strange to her libido. Her body tingled as he slid against her.

"Get a good night's rest, Rambo. We've got a big day ahead of us," he whispered into her neck, before he planted a soft kiss at her nape.

How did he do that? An unexpected shiver skittered along her spine, tingling her nerve endings, waking up areas she was sure had gone into dormancy long ago.

She wanted to elbow him and tell him to back off. Something to avoid that sensation tiptoeing up her spine. But she didn't. Because for once, the touch of another human being felt comforting rather than claustrophobic.

Despite being bone weary beyond what should be humanly possible at this very moment, the last thing on her mind was sleep.

CHAPTER EIGHT

————

Kane stirred from a light sleep when he heard the words *Teufel Hexe*. He'd heard the words *devil witch* used to refer to Sabrina more often than he could remember over his final few days at Marco's home. Hearing them again brought him wide awake. They'd been found.

Going downstairs would make them sitting ducks. The dormer window above the bed was their only option. He placed his lips close to her ear. Even if the bartender didn't put two and two together, he couldn't take the chance.

"I think we might have been found."

She propelled out of bed as if shot from a cannon, yanking at a non-existent knife at her side. He held out his arms to calm her even as he wondered about the demons that caused her hyper-vigilance.

"Somebody's downstairs. I heard them say 'devil witch' in German."

She brushed off his attempt at calming her fears. Without a word, she put on her shoes, grabbed her backpack, and pointed toward the window with her thumb.

No doubt she'd fit through easily. As for him, he wasn't so sure.

He gathered his stuff while she pulled out her gun in preparation. He brushed back any thoughts of her demons for now.

"You go first. You might have to pull me through." He opened the window as wide as possible.

She shimmied through as the sound of footsteps inched up the stairs. For a minute he thought she'd cut and run when he lost her in the shadows of the night, but she reappeared with her back against the dormer to give her leverage. She stretched her arms in front of her, grabbed his hands, and yanked. He shifted his shoulders to get through the frame.

"You're heavier than you look," she whispered as she struggled to get his chest through the small opening.

With one last heave she got him through, only to have him land on top of her in the process. "Sorry. Did I hurt you?" He scrambled up and helped her to a standing position.

"I'll survive." She winced as shouts reverberated through the air. "Any ideas?" They held hands and raced over the steep rooftop.

"We're safe for a few minutes because none of Marco's men will fit through that window. They'll expect us to make a jump for it and will be waiting for us on the ground. How are you at climbing trees?" He stopped and glanced at a low-hanging branch.

"Are you kidding? I'm practically half monkey." To demonstrate her skill, she jumped up and wrapped her hands around a sturdy branch. It didn't take her long to shimmy toward the trunk before reaching across to grab the next branch.

He couldn't help but admire her agility as he followed behind her. Still he had to wonder what kind of experiences she'd had to prepare her for the life she now led.

* * *

After spending most of the night and half the morning in a tree branch next to Kane waiting for Marco's men to leave the area, Sabrina was more than ecstatic to scramble to the ground. As he had predicted, there was a motorcycle waiting for them, hidden within the trees a couple of miles up the road.

She still didn't feel all that secure riding on the back of that dirt bike, especially after the last couple of days. Kane knew how to handle the machine, but there wasn't all that much protection on the back of a bike. Despite the Uzi housed in the backpack strapped to her and the additional firepower in the pouches lining the sides of the bike, she didn't feel safe.

Not to mention the flak jacket Kane wore filled with explosives. He forced her to wear one as well, sans the explosive firepower. It was heavy, weighing her down, but did offer additional protection.

They came prepared for a war. Which was good. That was precisely what she was expecting.

Kane turned off the bike and they dismounted. He pushed it aside and covered it with some fallen branches. Satisfied it was well hidden, he removed the two Uzis from the side pouches, handing her one and keeping one for himself.

Then waited until past midnight to make their move.

"You ready?" he asked.

"Uh huh," she mumbled in return. "Do you think he's kidnapped any more girls in the two days we've been gone?"

"I'm sure he's on probation with Trinity. There's not a doubt in my mind he won't get any more...shipments—for lack of a better word—in the near future, until he clears up the mess we made for him. My best guess is one guy on the outside patrolling. Maybe a half-dozen inside." He drew in a breath. ""Let's take care of business," he whispered, grasping her hand and rushing off through the woods.

Finally, the house came into view. Inexplicably, her heart rat-a-tat-tatted inside her chest, and her fingers began to tremble. She'd never felt so anxious before about a job. And this was a job. Even though it felt personal. The bottom line was that everything from now on brought her one step closer to finding Caitlyn.

They crept along the perimeter, Kane leading the way. He stopped. She listened, trying to figure out what he'd heard that she hadn't.

Snap.

Someone was close by.

Her pulse pounded inside her veins, making her head throb.

Baboom. Baboom. Baboom.

Trepidation spider-walked up her back as an eerie silence enveloped her. Her breath caught in her throat. Picking up on Kane's unmoving stance, she didn't dare flinch.

One minute she was pressed against his back, the next she wasn't. If not for the telltale sound of a breaking neck, she wouldn't have known what happened. "Be right back," Kane whispered.

Seconds later, she heard the rustle of leaves as he dragged the body to the cover of trees. As she waited for him to return, someone slipped in behind her.

"I've been waiting for this," the man growled against her neck as he put her in a chokehold.

Breathe.

Marco's men had always seemed cocky about their abilities. He'd never see it coming. She'd practiced the move thousands of times and successfully pulled it off more times than she'd cared to think about. She turned her head ever so slightly, lowered her center of gravity, grasped his arms, and threw him over her back and onto the ground. Before he had a chance to recover, she stomped on his throat, crushing his windpipe.

Despite the swiftness of the takedown, adrenaline wove through her extremities, giving her the shakes. She hated killing people. It wasn't who she was, regardless of what others might say about her past misdeeds. Still, she couldn't seem to take her gaze away from the man's lifeless body.

"Killing people sucks." Kane touched her elbow. He turned her face so that she looked into his eyes. "But it was either him or you. I'll hide him in the trees. Be back in a second."

She sucked in her lip in order to get herself together before he returned. After everything that had happened over the last forty-eight hours, now was not the time to fall apart. Instead of giving in to the emotion rolling around inside her head, she bit off the first words that came to mind. Projecting the ball of anger that simmered inside her was a good distraction when he came back. "You said one guy."

He shrugged but didn't break eye contact. "Okay, I miscalculated, so shoot me." A hint of a smile played at the edges of his lips.

Somehow, after knowing her a handful of days, he knew what to say to get her off her spiral of coulda, shoulda, wouldas. "Tempting offer, but I need every bullet I have."

He chuckled as they moved silently toward the house, stopping outside the door. She struggled to keep her breath even.

"I don't hear anything, but I'm sure there are a few guys milling about. We'll go in slow and see what we find."

Neither said a word as they ventured inside. At nearly one in the morning, the lights were out, and the entire place was shrouded in darkness. Moving quietly, they slipped through the living room.

An eerie silence surrounded them as the itch crawled up her spine. Something was off. Kane must have sensed it as well, as he stopped. He pushed her into a closet when noises filtered from the back of the house, and followed in behind her.

A cacophony of curses sounded before one of the men shushed the others. A guy mentioned something about Marco needing his beauty sleep, which brought raucous laughter, followed by more shushing.

Kane stood in front of her in the claustrophobic closet, but she still readied her weapon. Any moment now she expected them to realize two of their own were lying dead in the grove of trees. She counted out the different voices to determine how many men they'd be up against. Factoring in one reticent voice, she figured six. With them together, she didn't like their odds. Best to keep hidden until they could pick them off one by one. She let that ominous thought slide to the back of her mind and waited.

Cupboards started banging as if they were looking for food. This continued for several minutes, followed by another series of curses. While she and Kane dared not take in a deep breath, the men debated who was the better poker player.

Then, almost as quickly as it started, it stopped. One of them mentioned going outside for a smoke. At least a couple of the men left, but a few voices still came from the opposite side of the house.

Sabrina let out a shaky breath and squeezed Kane's hand. His lips were pressed against her ear when he whispered, "The odds just went down. Let's move."

He eased open the closet door. She cautiously followed behind. It was not difficult to find the men, as their conversation drifted through the air.

Kane peeked around the corner then put up two fingers. She nodded even while unwelcome fear traversed her spine.

He led with his gun and instructed them in German to move into the other room. She wasn't sure if it was fear or a kind of lethargy due to excess liquor consumption, but the men were submissive rather than resistant when they were tied up, gagged, and shoved into a back room.

"A couple more outside," he whispered as they walked back toward the door. "With a little luck they'll be as plastered as these guys."

As if on cue, the men barreled inside, bringing their raucousness along with them. Kane hit the first guy with the butt of his gun, knocking him to the floor. The third guy went after Kane, while the second guy came toward her swinging. His knuckles caught the end of her jaw before he put her in a chokehold. She made a fist and struck between his legs, then came up with her elbow to catch him in the throat. A targeted strike to his vagus nerve and he was toast. They secured the men, putting them in a separate room from the others while they went in search of Marco.

Kane grabbed her arm and pulled her so she faced him. He stared into her eyes for a good ten seconds before she shook her head and brushed him away. The last thing she needed right now was for him to spot the fear lodged in her chest. Somehow she needed to shake the feeling of vulnerability that had enveloped her since she'd woken naked and chained to Marco's wall.

Instead of giving in to the sensation, she charged up the stairs even while the hairs on her arms pricked in anticipation. She tried to shake off the uncharacteristic bout of fear as Kane pointed to the room at the end of the hall and nodded.

Kane snatched her in close. "You okay?" he whispered.

"Always," she whispered back.

But the quiet bothered her. It was as if they were waiting around for the proverbial shoe to fall. Adrenaline poured like a faucet through her bloodstream and hyper-vigilance followed. She'd been in tight spots many times before, but this felt different.

This. Was. It.

Kane turned the knob and eased open the door. Guns drawn, they slipped inside, each taking a side of the room. She glanced at the bed and shook her head.

Empty.

How could that be? Was Marco even home?

Before either one of them could formulate what to do next, somebody barreled inside and went after Kane with the butt of a rifle. He stumbled backwards, knocking her over as he fell to the ground.

She struggled to extricate herself from beneath him. Even in the dark, she spotted the lump forming on his forehead. She didn't have time to check his fate, as the man grabbed her around the waist, lifting her off the floor before she had a chance to retrieve her gun. The breath squeezed out of her lungs as he increased the pressure. She tried to break his grasp by yanking at his forearms, but his grip was fierce.

Instead, her fingers inched down her thigh until she reached the handle tucked inside the pocket of her cargo fatigues. The sensation of the steel against her fingertips gave a boost of adrenaline she hadn't thought possible.

Striking wildly, she brought the blade up high, hoping to catch his throat but missing the mark. Preoccupied with the blood pouring out of his cheek, he opened himself up for the dagger she drove deep into his chest. The impact of his body hitting the floor reverberated along her spine.

Her fingers trembled at her side, and it seemed to take an inordinate amount of effort to keep her nerves attached and inside her skin. She hated killing people. It reminded her of the blackness inside her.

She squashed the thought and forced herself to think. Marco had to be close. Bile backed up into her throat as vulnerability made a resurgence. She heard a lock click down the hall and ran in that direction. No one would run and hide except for Marco.

"Where's Caitlyn Collins?" she shouted before breaking the lock with a kick.

The room was small and dark with a large wooden desk, a small couch, and two cathedral-style windows along the back. Marco spotted her and immediately ran toward the windows.

She launched herself onto his back as he attempted to escape. Immediately, she regretted not retrieving her knife. And shooting Marco was too good for him. Besides, she kinda sorta promised Kane.

"I'm going to kill you." He tried to flick her off his back, but she wouldn't budge. Marco's words were punctuated by short, choppy breaths as he struggled to remove her hands from around his neck.

"Not likely." She yanked tighter. But the angle was wrong for sufficient leverage.

He propelled backward into the wall, sending a shockwave of pain along her spine. Still, she hung on. As oxygen deprivation started to cloud his thinking, he tumbled about the room, determined to break her hold. Then he went toward the window and drove her back through the glass. Shards embedded themselves right through the flak jacket, accompanied by pain.

Numb. Just go numb, Dragi.

Blood trickled down her back and onto her arms as her strength began to wane. But she used a last surge of energy to tighten her chokehold.

Finally, Marco's knees began to buckle. She jumped off right before he face-planted onto the floor.

She ran into the other room to check on Kane, but he was still out. She checked his vitals, and once she found his pulse, a sense of relief shimmied through. When she reached for his gun, someone grasped her ankle, pulling her to the floor.

While she kicked and twisted to shake free of his grip, he slid her back to the other room. She fumbled for purchase, certain since he had the upper hand, he would easily toss her out the window. His dominance was clear. Her weakness evident. Panic took hold as her fingernails splintered while she tried to dig into the floorboards, all while the glass drove ditches into her skin.

Her body continued to helplessly slither toward him. Nothing could prevent her slide toward the inevitable.

He'd kill her. No doubt about that. And he wouldn't be quick about it. Based on the laugh he emitted, which rumbled like a death march from his chest, he was enjoying her struggle. He sensed her fear and was getting off on it.

He chanted, in a tone so macabre it dredged up every horror film she'd ever seen, "Come on, Sabrina. Winning isn't an option. You should know that by now."

He used her name. Somehow he'd figured out who she was. And if he knew, then Trinity did as well. Funny how that thought stuck in her head. But it somehow gave her an idea.

Figure it out. No one will ever save you.

She forced her muscles to go limp. Her hand slid along the floor lifeless rather than grasping and clawing.

But as she feigned defeat, her fingers touched something beneath the desk. A syringe. She thought of the many times he'd poked her with the same instrument and filled her with poison. It would only be fitting if he was the victim this time. Maneuvering it within her grasp, she let him continue to pull her along the floor as if a willing victim.

He stopped when she was next to him. As he straddled her body, his fingers surrounded her throat, which gave her an ideal target. With an oomph that rocked her whole body, she stuck him at the vulnerable point in his neck, plunging the needle deep within his flesh and emptying the contents. She didn't have a clue what was in it, or what it might do to him, but there weren't a lot of other choices.

He grasped at it with trembling hands, yanking to pull it out, but it was too late. The poison was already mainlining through his system. He struggled for breath, but she felt nothing but a sense of vindication.

"Where's Caitlyn Collins?" Her fingers trembled. Before he passed out, she needed to know.

He coughed and grabbed at his throat, a combination of blood and spittle spurting from his mouth. She'd seen it more times than she could count, and knew death was in his eyes. So close it was only moments away. What had been inside that needle, she couldn't even guess.

"Who's Trinity?" she growled. He couldn't die without telling her something.

A weak smile pulled up the edges of his blue lips. "I'll never tell."

"Where's Caitlyn?" she screamed, pulling on the front of his shirt. "Do not die on me, you heartless bastard."

But it was too late. His head tilted to the side, the color drained from his face along with the life out of his body. She didn't feel a sense of victory.

She ripped the wristband from his arm without much trouble. Too numb and too tired to feel much of anything. Her breath squeezed from her lungs while blood dripped along the floor as she scooted away. She stayed that way until the shakes subsided enough that she felt she could stand and check on Kane.

"Kane." She stroked his cheek and pushed down the fear and paranoia rising to the surface. She realized the uphill battle she faced to find Caitlyn. For the first time in a long while, she questioned her ability to see this through to the end.

As desperation seeped in, she shook his shoulders. "Kane."

He moaned before his body shifted. "What the hell?" he muttered.

"Marco's dead." While ninety percent of her body wanted to collapse, that luxury no longer existed in her world.

Still unsteady, he somehow managed to get to his feet, and reached down to bring her along with him. "Shit." He picked at the shards of glass littering her back, causing the pain to finally reach her senses. "What happened to you?"

She tried to keep her "ouches" to a minimum. But it hurt. Bad.

"Close encounter with a window, courtesy of Marco."

Quiet pervaded as he yanked pieces of glass from her back. The prickle of awareness snaked down her spine, a prelude to trouble. Her body shook as adrenaline, shock, and terror penetrated through and sounds from below seeped into her awareness. The men were starting to gain momentum in their quest to be free.

"Do that later. Grab his laptop and let's get out of here."

He touched her hand, signaling his agreement. The men must have heard the scuffle and recognized what was happening. It sounded as if they were moments from breaking free.

A sense of urgency fueled her movements as they sprinted down the hall toward the front door. While they ran into the woods, shouts came from behind right before shots peppered the trees around them. All she could think of was *not now*. Not when she'd come this close.

Every bone in her body cried for attention. Her back felt on fire. She was convinced her muscles were as well. It didn't matter. They kept running until they reached the small grouping of trees with the brush covering the bike.

Kane started up the bike, and she hopped on the back. Gunshots continued but sounded farther and farther away. When they were out of reach, she expelled a shaky breath.

They rode while the silence and relief invaded her inch by inch. With each mile away from that chalet the sense of reprieve settled inside her bones, even while pain dulled her mind.

Kane stopped the bike by the edge of a lake. By now the sun was beginning to break into the morning sky and warmth invaded her chilled skin. The clear blue water lent a calmness to the setting despite her rapid pulse.

Sabrina eased off the bike, the adrenaline shakes making her limbs twitchy. Finally, she felt the stirrings of vindication. They had survived. Marco was dead. While he hadn't divulged his secrets, she had his computer along with the thumb drive he so closely guarded. While it wasn't victory yet, it was a step in the right direction.

"I cannot believe we made it out alive." The cuts along her back hurt, but with adrenaline pumping through her veins, she could embrace the euphoria of success.

Finding Caitlyn was within her reach. She could feel it with every bone of her body. Despite the odds, she'd bring that girl back home.

Kane's smile began to form slowly, as if he wasn't quite sure if he should indulge in that bit of comfort for now. First, the line appeared in his cheeks, then the indentation got deeper and deeper until it was a full-on, dimple-wielding grin. A grin that could no doubt melt a woman's heart. Not hers, but the ease of it made a warmth spread from her head to her toes.

"I can't believe we actually pulled that off." He winked and moved closer.

She jumped, bumping his chest. "Ouch. I guess girls weren't meant to do those. Either that or your chest is too hard."

"Or yours is too soft."

"Be careful, you're sounding like Goldilocks."

He ran his fingers through her hair, letting his thumbs rest at the spot on her neck right behind her ear. With gentle pressure he rubbed up and down beneath her jaw as he looked into her eyes. A kind of nervous energy blossomed inside her chest.

Anticipation.

And then he kissed her. Sensations she didn't recognize bombarded her, making her knees weak and her heart pound in her chest.

This was crazy. Stupid. Ridiculous. But man oh man, it felt incredible. This wasn't the Sabrina Shaw she knew. That woman didn't believe in any connection beyond the level of lust. But this felt different. A tingle vibrated at the base of her spine and permeated through her body until every square inch of her pulsed and radiated with a need so consuming she wasn't all that sure it would ever be satisfied.

Which was ludicrous.

She'd never heard of anything so lame. But why was it that what her rational mind knew was true, her body wouldn't believe.

When he broke the kiss, it wasn't because she gave him any indication she wanted him to. A fact that embarrassed the crap out of her.

Rather than say anything, he pulled her in tight about the waist and rested his forehead onto hers. They stood there, for the longest time. In that position.

And somehow, with everything they'd gone through, it felt so very right.

CHAPTER NINE

———

"I need to look at your back," he mumbled, his head next to hers, his hands affixed to her waist.

Sabrina sighed. The furthest thing from her mind right now was letting go. This respite of serenity felt a lifetime in the making. Some strange and foreign part of her wanted to suspend this moment indefinitely. Another inkling that the Sabrina Shaw she'd become accustomed to was bound for a change.

"You could be sliced up pretty bad. We won't know unless I check." He slid away from her to illustrate his point. "Thank God you had on that flak jacket; your back would have been cut to shreds."

She inched away as he helped remove her protective vest. He pulled out small shards still embedded in the fabric of her long-sleeve fatigues. Then he lifted the shirt as well as the T-shirt beneath it over her head.

Immediately she crossed her arms over her chest, not that it mattered. First of all, he'd seen her naked. Second of all, his attention was focused on examining her back. And thirdly, it didn't much bother her if Kane saw her naked. Which was not a good sign either.

"If that bastard wasn't dead, I'd go back and slice him to pieces for this," Kane muttered.

Even with the light touch, pain radiated down her spine. Yep, the adrenaline had definitely left the building. "Ouch." She bit her lips to keep from crying out more than she already was.

"Matter of fact, I might go back and blow up his damn body for good measure."

"There's that machismo thing rearing its ugly head. You know I can take care of myself."

With an innocent shrug, he muttered, "Can't help it."

He shook out her shirt, letting any pieces he'd missed fall into the grass. Then he walked toward the water, immersing the fabric and rinsing it out. Satisfied, he cleared it of any debris, wrung it out, then shook it again.

"I'm going to wash off some of the blood and try to clean up the cuts. You need some ointment to make sure you don't get an infection. The windows in that house are old and haven't seen a good cleaning in a while."

With a gentle touch, he tended to her cuts. The sting of the water on the open wounds caused her to flinch, but he continued apologizing each time she let out an *ouch*.

Keeping her hands across her chest, she turned when he stopped. Oblivious to her nudity, he removed his flak jacket then his own shirt. This whole preoccupation with Kane was starting to irritate her. But the female side to her couldn't help but notice the tightly bound shoulders and arms, defined with muscle. Her eyes strayed a little too long for her own piece of mind on the combination of all three. Finally, she turned once again toward the water.

"Put this on while yours dries," he said.

If he noted her uncharacteristic fixation on his bodily attributes, his expression didn't give her a clue. Good. She'd never want him to know she was human after all.

"Let's turn on Marco's computer and see if we get anything."

He yanked it out of his backpack. The screen flickered to life, displaying a naked woman as a screensaver. "I would have expected that from Marco." Kane shrugged and fiddled with it to gain access.

"Put in the memory device from Marco's wrist and see where that gets us." She stuck it into the port, only to get a bunch of gibberish rolling across the screen. "I knew this wasn't going to be easy. The good stuff has to be hidden with a password." She shook her head and tried to tamp down the frustration.

"The battery's running low, and I've already arranged a cottage for us over the border into Italy. We'll charge it up and work on it there. I'll have Ron have some antibiotic cream dropped off along with the food and clothes." He opened the map. "If we follow this trail we shouldn't meet any border guards."

* * *

The only thing that hurt worse than Kane's head was his chest every time he thought of how close they'd come to getting killed. And she'd killed the only lead he had in Marco. Between the computer and the flash drive, he had to hope there was a whole lot of data they could recover that might salvage the operation.

His discomfort of riding on the bike was tempered by the fact he kept remembering the gouges on her back. Her milky white skin was cut as if she'd gotten fifty lashes. Every time he even touched her, she about jumped out of her skin. And the wash of anger settled low inside him. He'd failed in his mission of securing Marco to get him to talk. Getting to Trinity would be even harder now.

A couple of hours later, Kane pulled in front of the cottage. "We're here." After she eased off the back, he flipped down the kickstand and got off. He found the key in the plant hanging along the porch and unlocked the door.

"Plug in the computer." As usual, Sabrina didn't want to waste any time. Then again, he didn't expect her to.

"Outside or in?"

"Outside." She held out her hands and he complied.

"I'm going to take a quick shower—then I'll bring out the food."

"Hurry up. I'm starving."

After his shower, Kane grabbed the tray of food from the small refrigerator. Gotta give it to Ron—he thought of everything. He peeked inside an envelope left on the nightstand, and spotted enough money to tide them over for a while, along with a duplicate passport for Sabrina.

The cottage was small, but comfortable. A large bed stood in the center against the wall, adorned with a white lace coverlet and an abundance of pillows. Floor-to-ceiling windows let in the cool, dry evening air, and candles decorated the fireplace. The table outside on the terrace gave a breathtaking view of the mountains. For right now, it offered a sense of security.

"Here's some cold pasta and vegetables, some fresh fruit, and a bottle of wine." He popped open the cork. "Gotta love these Italians. They know how to eat."

Hunched over the computer, she stuck a fork into the large bowl and twirled the spaghetti around before she slurped it inside her mouth. She smiled and clicked away on the keyboard.

"How is it?" Kane handed her a glass of wine.

"Incredible." She twirled another forkful of pasta and roasted vegetables, holding it up to Kane's mouth for a sample. "Taste for yourself."

"Man, this stuff is good." He reached for another forkful, but she batted down his hand.

"Get your own fork."

There was something intimate in the gesture. Maybe more comfortable than intimate. He couldn't say for sure how or why it happened.

"Find a way to get around the password yet?"

"Still working on it." She shook her head and took a sip of wine. "I can't get this screen to stop spewing gibberish."

"Ron also dropped off a change of clothes for both of us—including new underwear. How's about that for the good old FBI handling everything."

"Hmm, sounds as if he thought of it all. But I don't imagine he picked me up a bra."

"Taken care of. As well as a duplicate passport for you." He shrugged. "I guessed at the bra size —34C?"

"In my dreams." She giggled. "Hey, a little Kleenex here and there and I'll be good to—wait—got in." Her jaw clenched tight as she tapped on the screen, but then she swore. "What is this? It appears to be a list of account receivables and payables. While the receivables are in the five digits, and the bottom line is substantial, it doesn't give me what I want."

"Patience. Maybe there's a hidden file somewhere."

She twisted to look at him. "This doesn't make sense. Why would he guard this thing so much if there was nothing on it? What am I not getting?"

"Let me have a look." He tried every trick he knew to get at something beyond the statistical info to secure names or even account numbers. Trinity. The name drummed in his head until he couldn't think straight. "What do these codes mean?"

"It can't be complicated. Marco wasn't the sharpest tool in the shed." She scooted back in her seat and took a long sip of the wine. "What am I missing?"

She still was in loner mode of thinking, feeling, knowing that everything she did, she did alone. He had to wonder about her and her brothers, and why the FBI didn't have more information about their entry into the US. There was a whole lot she wasn't telling. And rampant speculation on his part was serving no purpose.

"I can send the files we found to FBI headquarters and see if they can unlock it or figure out the code."

She shrugged. "Now that we've got the big dogs on the case, I'm going to take a long, hot bath. I need to wash the stink of Marco off me."

It probably was a little bit of wishful thinking when he thought she might invite him to join her. "Be careful about your back. Ron dropped off some ointment along with the clothes. I could put some on the cuts when you get out."

"I'll be fine." She gave him a cheeky smile. "Believe me, I've been through a lot worse."

Kane continued to work on the computer, anxious as she was to figure out what all the data meant. At first glance, it looked as if a series of random numbers and letters, but it had to mean something. But what?

She must have been in the bath for at least a half an hour when she reappeared wrapped in a fluffy white robe, looking more relaxed than she'd looked since he'd met her. Even the dark circles beneath her eyes seemed to have dissipated a bit.

"Figure out anything?" She peered over his shoulder.

"I've tried all the obvious ways to uncover the names behind the numbers but I'm still coming up with zero."

"Maybe the FBI will come up with something."

"Always a possibility." He closed the computer. "Why don't you lie down, and I'll take care of your back." Without waiting for a response, he opened the tube of ointment and pulled down the bed covers.

She loosened the belt on her robe, slipped out of the sleeves, and lay on the bed, her arms wiggling around until they found a comfortable spot buried beneath the pillow. "Time to work your magic."

Kane tugged at the collar of the robe until her back was exposed. "That glass really cut you up." He tried not to apply too much pressure as he put the salve on her back. Every time she winced, he couldn't help but think about payback. Marco was dead, but Trinity was the reason behind all of this.

"I hope I don't require stitches. Based on your handiwork with my hair, I'd hate to see you with a needle and thread putting together pieces of my skin."

"I've stitched up wounds before. They're not the prettiest, but in the middle of nowhere you do what you have to do."

She plumped the pillow beneath her head. "Is there anything you can't do, Mr. Hotshot FBI Man?"

He grimaced. "Can't dance worth shit."

She burst out laughing. "Well, that and you have a really soft head. A little tap and you're down for the count."

"Are you kidding? I think he used a brick to hit me." He rubbed her shoulders just because he could. "Now that we have all my spectacular achievements out in the open, I'd like to know a little more about your superhuman powers, Rambo."

"Apparently I'm hard to kill."

"I've been meaning to ask, did you work in one of those traveling carnivals or something? Because I gotta tell you, your knife skills are amazing. Maybe you could give me a few pointers. "

She chuckled. "No traveling carnivals in my past. And no to the free lesson."

"I'd pay you for it." He stopped a minute, letting his hand expertly work at the muscles in her back. "Somehow."

"First of all, I don't teach my superpowers to just anyone. You might not be worthy of the gift. I'd have to ensure you'd use it for good, not evil."

He quirked up one eyebrow and looked at her. "Hmmm. That's asking a lot. It does depend on the definition of good and evil. Although it might seem all black and white, it may not be."

To illustrate the fact he was in this to win, he rubbed his thumbs along the base of her neck then zeroed in on her shoulders. When he sensed an ease in the tension within her shoulders, he felt as if he were making progress.

"Oooooooh, that feels so good."

"I'm a master." He pressed beneath her collarbone. "A few minutes of this and you'll be my slave forever."

Swiveling her head, she glanced at him. "You know me well enough to recognize that would never happen."

He shrugged. "Thought I could plant the seed. Maybe get you under my spell so you could spill all your secrets. You haven't told me much about yourself."

"Not much to tell."

He bit off a laugh. "Yeah, right. I know I asked you this before, but why did you leave me in the middle of nowhere? And did I mention I was injured?"

"I work alone." Her smile looked forced. "Besides, you were cramping my style."

"Hey, I work alone too but I'd never leave a man behind."

"US military. I should have guessed."

"What's that supposed to mean?"

"Nothing." She shrugged. "You have that way about you."

"So do you. But I suspect you weren't in the military."

"That's right. You're privy to all sorts of personal information about me and everybody else you want."

"Not really." He shook his head. "Besides, your file is buried so deep somewhere I'm not even sure the president could touch it."

The tension in her shoulder seemed to dissipate. "So you say." Her expression turned stubborn, as if whatever secrets she had, she intended to keep buried.

"It's true. What's your story? Where were you trained?"

She chewed her lip as her eyes narrowed. "Why should I be the one spilling secrets? How about you?"

"Ah, you're one of those. You show me yours and I'll show you mine." He smiled and hoped she'd let down her guard at least a little.

"In that case, you need to strip naked, because you've seen everything I have." She smiled, and that tension eased a fraction more, as evidenced by the slow, easy smile tweaking the ends of her lips.

He shook his head. Where this was headed was written in neon colors. Instead, he played along—at least for the time being. "Babe, you do not want to see that. I have scars."

"In case you weren't paying too much attention, I do too." She turned on her side and pulled up the edge of her robe to reveal a long, smooth leg. "I got six stitches in my calf, broke my arm a couple of times and they had to put in a pin the second go round, the usual appendix scar, and a nick right above my heart—the list goes on and on."

"So this is a competition now." He stood and ripped his shirt over his head. "Caught a bullet with my chest. Found out I wasn't Superman after all."

The wound had puckered and diminished over the years. She fingered the scar, then trailed her fingers up his chest. "Is that all you've got?"

"I have more, but they're inside." He brought her fingers to cover his heart. "Just like yours…" He trailed off as she sat up in bed, wiggled out of the robe, grabbed his shoulders, pulled him against her, and kissed him. A full-on kiss involving tongues. Not one of those little pecks she'd laid on him before.

A straight-up diversionary tactic for sure.

* * *

Sabrina felt the rapid beat of his heart as his naked body slid off hers. He nuzzled the spot on her neck that he'd already discovered drove her crazy before he drew her body against his. As far as trying-to-avoid-the-inevitable conversation, the sex was an excellent diversion.

"I like your way of avoiding the subject." He rubbed his hand up and down her arm, as if he'd noticed the sudden uptick in her pulse.

Sabrina turned to face him. She wasn't ready for this. Not yet. Maybe not ever. Instead, she kissed behind his ear and down his neck, hoping maybe he'd settle for round two. "Don't tell me you're one of those psych majors into analyzing everyone and everything."

"Matter of fact I was, but even if I wasn't, a blind man could see what you're doing here."

She harrumphed her disapproval. Why couldn't he be like any other red-blooded American man and get laid, go for round two, and then move on. But noooooo, he had to get all new-age sensitive on her. "I don't like to talk about myself."

She wanted to say something clever and funny, but at the moment the only thing more frazzled than her body was her brain.

Push. Pull. Push. Pull.

The universal truth: disaster was around the corner. But she had no ability to stop it. Knowing and wanting were at opposite ends of the sanity spectrum.

She knew every inch of his body now, if not by feel, by sight, and erotic thoughts zinged through her bloodstream. It had been a long time since she'd given in to pure lust. But compromising what they had to do weighed heavy on her mind.

Intimacy between them would screw up this mission only if she allowed it to. She could keep herself detached like she always did. Besides, if things got a little too close, she could always shake him loose.

Push. Pull. Push. Pull.

And maybe, just maybe, she could gain a little perspective. Because right now she didn't want to think about caution. She didn't want to contemplate going slow. She wanted to be with him—skin on skin. To feel the touch of his hands on her, which was one more un-Sabrina-like thought to add to her growing list. But being with him had made her feel alive for the first time in a long while.

Damn, she needed something to clear this muddled mind of hers.

"I told you before I had scars inside as well. My dad beat my mom for as long as I can remember."

She drew in a breath. After their casual conversation, his revelation had been unexpected. "I'm sorry."

He shrugged. "I'm over it. That was a long time ago."

"You have a sister, right?"

"Yeah, she's in med school. We've both dealt with what happened in similar ways. While she threw herself into her studies, I threw myself into risk-taking as a profession. I never met an impossible mission I didn't volunteer for: deep into enemy territory with a three percent chance of getting out of there alive and I'm your man. It was as if I wanted to go back in time and save my mom from what had been brewing for as far back as I remember."

"I…don't…know…what to say."

"Nothing to say. My dad's an asshole and there's nothing I can do about that." He drew in a breath. "My mom never tried to run away from the bastard. In fact, when he found a new woman, she begged him to stay. I signed up for the Army ROTC my senior year of high school, and they put me through college. I had a knack for languages and figured, what the hell? Became an Army ranger, got shot up, and went to work for the FBI. Haven't talked to my dad in more than fifteen years and don't intend to. My little sister escaped most of the crazy. My mom sits by the window and hopes for the day my POS dad will come back. It's sick and twisted, but that was my screwed-up barometer of family life. I thought I could separate my personal experiences from my undercover job when I went to work for Marco, but found out pretty quickly that was impossible."

"I…" She thought about responding, but couldn't get the words to form through the clog of emotion inside her throat. He'd shared something of himself. Could she do the same? Getting comfortable is never good. Even as she pushed away the memory, the words bubbled on the edges of her lips. "My parents died when I was seven. My brothers and I lived on the streets, foraging for food, begging for places to stay, and then hiding out in caves, barns, anything that kept a roof over our heads."

He wrapped his arms around her. "How did it happen?"

She shook her head, even while sensation shuddered within her. "I was young. I don't really remember. I can feel the fear." She rubbed her hands down her arms. "Then they were gone. My brothers and I have never talked about it. At first, Max convinced me the whole thing was an adventure." She shook her head. "We developed some survival skills along the way."

"Yeah, I could see that. I spotted you pickpocketing Arte's knife in the rearview mirror when we drove into town." He took her hand in his and kissed her knuckles. "But there's more, isn't there?"

She drew in a deep breath. No one outside her brothers knew the truth. "Have you ever heard of Goren Petrovich?" Saying his name out loud took every ounce of fortitude she possessed. For years she'd worked so hard at obliterating his name from her vocabulary, but she'd failed to erase the memories of what he'd made her become.

"I don't think so. Who is he?"

"My brothers and I had an especially bad night. We had crawled into a cave. I remember being cold and hungry, shivering and crying, asking for my mama. I think I had a fever. It's all kind of fuzzy now. Max went out to get us some food but returned with Petrovich. That's when the real adventure began."

"What do you mean?" Although he said the words as a question, she could see by the set of his jaw and the pity in his eyes he already knew the answer wasn't pretty.

"He trained us. To…well, that's where I learned to take down a man like Marco." Rather than feeling weighted down by telling her secret, she felt better for some inexplicable reason. It was almost as if that blackness inside of her had become a dark, dingy gray instead. "Petrovich took on contracts for hire, and he trained us to do his dirty work. To carry out the…hits."

"But you were just a kid."

Sabrina shrugged. Trying to shrug off the emotion his words of sympathy stirred. "He told us they were bad men. Maybe some were, I don't know."

"It's not your fault."

"I know that," she snapped back, more intensely than she'd intended. She paused, took a deep breath. "I guess it's why I'm taking this case to heart. I know what it feels like to be used like that."

"Ah shit…did he…" He winced. "You know…"

She held up her hand, even though she couldn't help but be touched by the absolute fear she spotted in his eyes. "No, it was never sexual. On one hand he offered us a roof over our head, food, and an education. It was what he expected in return that gives me nightmares. Of course, he always somehow convinced us we were ridding the world of evil, but I'm not so sure about that."

She turned so that her back was to him and relished in the comfort for once in her life. Somehow he intuitively got her. And that frightened the hell out of her.

CHAPTER TEN

———

Kane was sound asleep when Sabrina made her decision. After last night, she needed to make a clean break. He was getting inside her head, acting as if he knew what she was thinking, how she was feeling, and she didn't want that to happen.

Besides, going alone was what she did best. Having a partner had never been part of her makeup, and hooking up with him had been a mistake. Now that she had a direction and a way to go, she wasn't going to allow him to hold her back, even for a second. She needed to find Caitlyn ASAP and not get mixed up in his official investigation into Trinity. Not her problem.

Antonio wouldn't ask questions. He knew the score, and was an expert at ferreting out codes. Screw the FBI. She had her friend to help her, and he wouldn't feel he needed to tag along for the ride as well. He wouldn't make demands or have any expectations.

After grabbing the memory stick and laptop, it was bittersweet when she snuck out of the room after stuffing the few things she had in the bag, and headed for Antonio's. Kane naively thought he could trust her, but trust was something she'd never been able to commit to in her life, and she wasn't about to start now. As her brothers used to say, "Trusting is for sissies," and she wasn't about to become one of the tragedies of her own stupidity.

She scribbled a note because she felt the sting of obligation after everything he'd done for her. Guilt crept up her back as she pushed the motorcycle—and his only means of transportation—to a spot where she could start it without waking him.

Within moments she was on the road, handling the situation the only way she knew. Alone.

* * *

Kane felt the sun on his face as it filtered through the window and couldn't help but smile. And it had nothing to do with the sex—okay, maybe a little. He patted the bed next to him, searching for Sabrina. When he came up empty, he opened his eyes and jumped to his feet. Even though he searched both inside and out, he knew she'd left.

Reality took about five seconds to slap him upside the face. He spotted the note where the laptop had been.

Sorry, I have to do this my way.

After biting off a litany of curses, he called Ron. "She bailed but still needs firepower. I'm pretty sure she's headed to a friend named Antonio. I have a feeling he might be somehow connected to Goren Petrovich. I don't care who you have to bribe, find out who he is and where he lives. ASAP." He jumped up and looked out the window. "And get me transportation."

* * *

The front door swung open, and Antonio swept Sabrina into his arms. Taller than Sabrina by several inches and solidly built, Antonio had been one of the many orphans who'd been under Petrovich's tutelage while she'd been there. For the most part, she and her brothers stuck together, but at times Antonio would invade their threesome.

"Sabrina, your hair. I hardly recognize you." The man fingered through her short locks with a sense of familiarity she wasn't quite comfortable with. "I like it. You look Italian." He laughed, swinging her around in a circle. "You should have called. I would have prepared a feast."

She laughed even while thoughts pinged around her brain. Guilt. Caitlyn. Instead she focused on a means to an end. "I tried once, but you didn't answer, so I thought I'd surprise you."

"You're not here for a social visit. What can I do for you?"

She plunked the computer and memory device on the table. "Crack the code. I need to find out where he sent these girls."

Antonio's eyes narrowed. "Who's he? And what girls?"

"A man they call Trinity is in charge. Have you heard anything about him?"

Maybe it was her imagination, or her current state of paranoia, but there seemed to be an almost imperceptible hesitation before he shook his head. "I don't think so. What is this man involved in?"

A second passed while she tried to decipher what that look in his eye was all about. She gulped back the wariness and spoke. "Human trafficking. I need some clues."

"Let's see what we can find. But before I do that, let me get you something to eat." He wiggled his eyebrows up and down. "You're looking a little scrawny."

She'd been to his home a couple of times in the past, but he'd made some amazing improvements in the intervening years. "I guess the wine-selling business is going well for you."

"I can't complain."

He placed his arm on her waist and led her to the kitchen, where a humongous La Cornue stove was the focal point of the farmhouse. She didn't know much about kitchens but knew the stove alone cost over thirty grand.

Even though it was late in the day, open French doors allowed in the breeze as the night began to fall. The grounds outside his home were beautiful, and she couldn't help but be lulled into a temporary sense of relief.

He pulled out a bottle of wine and poured her a glass, encouraging her to take a drink with a wave of his hand. "You drink. I make some pasta." He pulled out a chair at the massive island topped with marble.

She knew better than to resist an Italian plying her with food. Instead, she opened the laptop, bringing up the only file she'd been able to find. "This is all I've got."

He clucked as he turned on the stove and began to heat the water. "And here I thought you were the computer whiz."

"I bow to your superior skills."

"It's about time you admitted it." He chuckled and sat next to her as he began to tap on the keys. "Let me see what I can find."

She peered over his shoulder, anxious for any morsel of information. Thoughts of Kane plagued her even though she tried to put them aside. Still, she couldn't help but wonder about him and if he'd made any progress finding information about Trinity.

While she'd come here to escape the discomfort, Antonio wasn't bringing her the sense of relief she'd thought he would. Somehow they didn't feel like old friends anymore.

* * *

Kane had finally managed to doze off when his phone rang. "What do you have?"

"Antonio Bianchi."

His pulse pounded. "Are you sure? She's been gone for nearly twelve hours. I've been crawling out of my skin."

"Yep, positive. We were able to find a photo of them together from a while ago." Ron drew in a breath. "He's rumored to have gone rogue in the intervening years. While he has a legitimate wine business as a front, there's a lot of speculation about where he gets his money, and none of it good."

Kane's fingers started to tremble as his heart raced. "In other words, she walked right into a trap."

"We don't know that for sure, but Antonio has a reputation for being a mercenary of sorts. It doesn't seem out of the realm of possibility that he might be involved somehow in what's going on with Trinity's organization."

A litany of curses threatened to explode from his mouth before he settled on one. "Shit."

"Your truck should be arriving any minute. It might be old, but it will blend in better for where you're headed. Are you going to need any backup?"

"No." Kane spat the word out as he paced the room. "Besides, Nellis would never approve that expense, especially since she's not our target."

"True, but by the time he figured it all out, it will be a done deal."

"I'm good." For that instant Kane couldn't help but think about the fact that he and Sabrina were so much alike. The difference being he knew when to ask for help.

"And the other news is we have a potential break in the information you sent us. We found a couple of hidden files with photos of the girls who've been taken. As soon as it's all compiled, I'll email it to you."

* * *

Sabrina wasn't sure if it was lethargy from the wine or the past several days had finally caught up her with her, but when Antonio walked her up the steps to the second level, she felt as if she could slide to the floor and sleep for a hundred years. He held tight to her waist as they slipped down the hall. She concentrated on putting one foot in front of the other, and he stopped beside a door and opened it.

"I have some business to take care of in the morning, but maybe after that I can get back to the computer and see if I find anything."

"If you can't find anything, then…" She shrugged. She couldn't think about another failure. "Thanks for all your help, Antonio."

He pulled her in close and nuzzled her neck. A twinge of discomfort tunneled inside her.

"Maybe we could spend the night together. Just like old times. We could make love till morning."

"I…I don't think so. What we had together was kids' stuff, over a long time ago."

He withdrew and touched his fingertips to her chin while he examined her face. "What's happened to you? Is there someone in your life?"

What?

"No, no, it's not like that." She blew out a breath as she worked through their conversations, trying to ferret out how he'd come to that conclusion. She'd never mentioned Kane or anything about his involvement. "It's complicated, Antonio." She put a chaste kiss on his cheek. How could she make him understand this thing with Kane when she didn't really understand it herself?

"Ah, my dear Sabrina, love is always complicated, *n'est pas?*"

Without another word, he left. Not giving her a second to protest, even if she could formulate the words inside her head.

* * *

Sabrina's head pounded as she lay in bed, unable to fall back asleep. A dull ache kept her from going from awake to alert.

Depression felt like a veil covering her as she fought through where or what to do next. Footsteps sounded in the hall, but she closed her eyes and feigned sleep when the door slowly opened. She couldn't be sure how long Antonio stood examining her slumber, but it had to be a good twenty seconds. Any moment she expected him to call her ruse and insist she join him for breakfast, but he didn't. Instead, he quietly closed the door. She listened as his soft steps retreated down the stairs.

Seconds later, she heard him talking. "No, I told you before I wouldn't." His voice was quieter than usual as he spoke. Since she only heard one voice, she assumed he was on the phone. "Yes, I have her but she doesn't know anything."

He was quiet for so long, Sabrina thought he might have finished. "I get it. Okay." She heard a long exhale before he continued. "I'll leave in a little while and then you're free… The payment… She won't stay out of it…"

She shook her head as the words fused together in her head. Had he put something in her wine last night? She threw her legs over the side of the bed, but instead of charging down the stairs to confront him with the possibility, she slid back against the mattress.

Maybe it was all one big screwed-up dream.

* * *

Given the remote location, pulling into the dirt driveway would give advance notice of his arrival. Instead, Kane hid the old truck about a half-mile away and ran through the field toward the house in the early morning hours. With the back portion of the land covered in trees, he had a fighting chance of not being seen. Despite concentrated effort on his part, he couldn't keep fear from creeping up his back.

The dossier sent to him on Antonio couldn't have been clearer. The guy would sell out his own flesh and blood for financial gain. With Sabrina, the writing was on the wall. He could only hope he wasn't too late.

He crept along the side of the building, his breath faltering with each step. Knowing what Antonio was capable of didn't make him feel good about the situation. Sabrina could be dead by now.

Damn. Why didn't he see that coming?

Nerves unlike anything he'd felt in a long time rode up his back as he skulked along the side of the old stone farmhouse. A weathered patio covered the back part of the house, with a cobblestone pathway leading into the trees behind it.

As Kane was trying to figure out the best way to approach, a car engine rumbled to life around the front. He ran along the side, peered around the corner, and spotted one person inside the car. The motorcycle Sabrina rode sat in the drive, confirming what he already knew.

Considering the early hour, if Antonio was still playing the part of good guy, that could mean Sabrina was still sleeping. He didn't want to think about the possibility that he'd shown his hand and the fact she might very well be dead, either inside the house or within the confines of the car.

He tamped down the ominous thoughts. From everything he'd read about Antonio, he didn't like to get his hands dirty. He also knew her well enough to realize she wouldn't go down easily. Betting on the chance she was still inside the house, he opted for Plan B.

Getting inside was easier than he might have imagined; he slipped in an open window. He slid along the wall and felt his heart rate stumble and restart in his chest, all while hoping he'd made the right choice in betting on the fact she was still sleeping.

He crept along the perimeter close to the wall, allowing his eyes to adjust to the lack of light. The house was eerily quiet and he couldn't help but worry.

The knife came out of nowhere, nicking his bicep before he stopped its progress by grabbing the offending arm with a twist. When he turned and spotted a shaken-looking Sabrina in the dim light, the adrenaline subsided, relief in its wake.

Kane couldn't help but smile. "You're seriously starting to tick me off."

"How did you find..." She stopped and felt along the seams of her pants then shirt.

"No tracker this time." He put his arm around her shoulder because she looked as if she might drop to the floor any second. "I looked up your friend Antonio."

"How?" Her eyes went wide as she stared.

"It wasn't difficult, knowing the Petrovich connection." He gave her a hard look. "You do know that the guy is bad news."

She shrugged and avoided looking at him. "So am I. I don't see the problem."

"Antonio sells his services to the highest bidder. Rumor has it there's a reward out on both of us for Marco's murder. It's within the realm of possibility that he would sell you out for a couple hundred thousand euros."

"Maybe he and I are lovers." She steeled her gaze at him.

He worked his jaw for a few seconds before he spoke. "Naw, I don't see that either." Even though he dismissed her claim, the male part of him had a niggling doubt.

She huffed. "You're awfully cocky."

"I know guys like him. It's my job to bust guys like him."

"And me as well?"

"Geez, will you knock it off with the pity party." He shook his head. "Where did he go?"

She chewed her lip. "I'm not sure. He was going to meet with somebody this morning but thought it would be best if I stuck around here."

"How convenient."

She straightened her shoulders. "Antonio and I go way back with Petrovich."

"The same man who taught you and your brothers to be ruthless, except, despite what you think, you're not wired that way. Now there's a price on your head that would make Antonio not think twice about turning you in." Kane let loose a string of expletives. "And you didn't think it was suspicious that he conveniently had a meeting this morning. He's setting you up. We need to get the hell out of here."

"He said the guy—"

He could almost see as the truth tunneled deep into her brain.

"I thought it was a dream—" She stopped mid-thought as she turned and headed for the stairs.

He followed. She charged into a bedroom, gathered her things, and stuffed them into her backpack. Seconds later, they bounded down the stairs together.

"I'm right, aren't I? What happened?" Something in what he'd said scared her. It would be nice to know what.

"I'll tell you when we get to the car."

"This way. Through the back field. It's only about a quarter-mile."

When they got to the truck, she threw her bag in the back and jumped into the passenger seat. "Do you think he's on his way?"

"I know he is, and he brought some friends." He pointed to the trail of cars coming down the rural road in their direction.

CHAPTER ELEVEN

———

"Those aren't police cars. Which scares me even more." He glanced at Sabrina, his jaw set in a strong line. "Does Antonio know where you're going or who you're after?"

Mute, she shook her head. "No...I..." She couldn't seem to form the words, especially when her chest constricted. *No more mistakes. You're better than that. Stay sharp, Saby.*

The sting of Antonio's betrayal lay like a rock in her gut. She shouldn't be surprised, but she had been. Would she ever figure out that whole trust thing, or would it be only her brothers that offered her the security she needed?

Kane sucked in a breath and focused on the road. "Does he know about me?"

"I didn't get into specifics except to say I was hunting for a girl held captive by sex traffickers." She chewed her lip as she struggled to remember her exact words. "I mentioned Trinity but not you."

But he'd guessed about you. That made her wonder if he knew ahead of time she'd show up. She felt like Alice falling down the rabbit hole, without a bottom in sight.

He blew out a breath. "They'd have no reason to believe you have help with this, even though there's a reward out on both of us. They might assume we parted company, since you showed up alone. With a little luck, we still might be able to get out of this alive." He urged her to squish onto the floor of the truck. Then put on a hat with gray hair peeking out the back and plastered a phony beard and mustache on his face.

She had to admit, his cheesy disguise seemed to transform him enough to escape a superficial inspection. That, along with the old farm truck he drove, should get them past Antonio and whomever he'd contacted.

The idea of Antonio's disloyalty sank deep into her chest and squeezed. Confirmation of what she'd been feeling while she was at his home clanged around inside her gut. It was both unpleasant and unnerving.

Long ago she'd learned to trust no one but family, and now Kane wanted her to do the unthinkable. Trust him with her life.

She watched his fingers as he shifted the old truck into second, and hoped this worked, since this piece of crap couldn't outrun a donkey, let alone another car. Her own fingers held steady on the gun as determination steeled her spine. If it came down to it, she'd do what she had to do.

"*Caio*." Kane had managed to make his voice sound gruffer and older as he drove past what she could only assume was Antonio and his posse of bad guys.

Even though she wouldn't have suspected Kane had succumbed to nerves a few seconds ago, he blew out a breath once the car passed. "Four cars. Two guys in each car. I think I passed the smell test. They're still headed toward Antonio's house."

"Can I get up?" She was itching to see for herself. They needed cover, and this old pick-up wasn't going to do it indefinitely.

He glanced in the rearview mirror. "They pulled into Antonio's. We need to figure out a place to hide."

She eased up in the seat. "There's a small village about a mile down the road. Stash the truck there and we'll head off on foot. We probably can walk faster than this tank can move anyway."

He gave her a quick smile. "You're probably right. They might put two and two together and figure out that older farmer's truck doesn't belong around here."

"I want to be out of the line of fire when they do."

"Use the binoculars and try to see what's going on."

She stuck her head out the window and held them to her eyes. "They're still in the house as far, as I can tell."

"What exactly did you overhear this morning?"

Admitting she'd once again screwed up was difficult. Especially when betrayal licked at a sensitive spot inside her she'd learned long ago not to ignore. "Bits and pieces of a conversation." She blew out a breath. "I think he might have put something in my wine last night. I felt so exhausted and out of it I wasn't sure what was going on, but he was talking on the phone—" Her breath stutter-stepped as the men poured out of the farmhouse. "Uh oh, we're in trouble. They came running out and got into their cars."

"We've got to hope they wouldn't have suspected this old truck to be your getaway car."

"You were right. Eight guys including Antonio." Saying his name out loud brought a grinding sensation to her chest.

"Any ideas?"

"Give me your phone and I'll find the closest train station." He handed her his phone. No doubt they'd be suspecting that would be her first choice, especially if they thought she was acting alone, but if they could somehow evade them until the train came…

"Got it. Ten miles north." Sabrina glanced behind them and spotted a black car roaring down the road, gaining on them. "Trouble." She shook her head. "And we're not going to make it to the train."

He glanced in the rearview mirror. "Only one. They must have split up."

"That's the good news." The teaspoonful of adrenaline left in her body sprang to life. "I'll go back onto the floor. We shouldn't assume they're after us, but still…I'll take my gun and be ready."

"They're coming alongside." Kane maneuvered the gun into his left hand against the door as he slowed and moved to the right side of the road.

"Maybe they're only going to pass." Sabrina kept her finger on the trigger and sank further onto the floor while the itch crawled up her back. She had no doubt this was going to go bad. She didn't know when or where, but it was inevitable.

"Code word for they're not buying my line of BS is Uncle Salvatore." His jaw was clenched as he threw an old flannel over her squished form. "If you hear that, be ready."

She nodded and made herself as small as she could. The sounds of the engine rattled the frame on the old truck as she held her breath and tried not to move a centimeter. She could visualize the car getting closer until it had come side by side with the truck. Kane spoke to them in Italian. They returned the conversation in German asking if he'd seen a woman. He kept reciting "*Non capisco.*" But they kept hounding him with questions.

Her fingers trembled as she strummed the handle of the gun. Waiting was the difficult part. Not being in control was the *really* hard part. Sitting blind, letting her ears tell the tale was excruciating. How many times had she been in the same predicament with her brothers, and it had never felt good. Her heart tripped and started inside her chest more times than she could contemplate.

Every impulse inside wanted her to break out from beneath the blanket as Kane continued to act the part of feeble farmer, especially when they described her in detail to him. Being played by someone she'd called a friend wasn't something she relished. Then again, it proved her theory of never putting herself in a position of vulnerability, or relying on anyone but herself. Or her brothers.

They were survivors, pure and simple. Nothing could ever change their legacy.

Finally, she heard a car engine roar to life after one of the men called him a "*schwachen alten Mann,*" a "feeble old man" in German. She barely suppressed the chuckle as she emerged from beneath the cover.

"Oscar-worthy performance, Kane."

"It was, even if I do say so myself." He brushed his knuckles against his chest and helped her back into the seat. "I'm assuming you heard most of what they said?"

"Sure did."

"They showed me a picture of you as well. Definitely taken within the last couple of days, since your hair was short. They also had a photo of me. We're both wanted for Marco's murder, which only confirms what we already knew. So despite what you think about this crappy truck, it seemed to fool them."

She sat on the seat and tapped an anxious finger against the dashboard. "I'm worried about Antonio. He's going to know I had help getting away, since the motorcycle is still at his house. It wouldn't take a genius to figure out it was from you. We've got to get out of the area as quickly as possible."

The words were barely out of her mouth when a car barreled toward them. It was dark and sleek and looked suspiciously like the others they'd seen.

"This can't be good."

"Take the next turn. We'll head toward the town with the train station. Hopefully we'll beat them there and we can lose them on foot." She handed him back his phone. "The next train is in two hours."

"They'll be all over the train station. Sounds risky."

"Do I look like a gal who's afraid of risks?" She gave him a cheeky smile even while fear traveled down her back.

* * *

As far as plans went, hers pretty much sucked. But since Kane couldn't think of anything better, he hit the gas and hoped they'd make it into the town before the bad guys figured anything out.

"Grab the stuff and we'll try to blend in." He figured she was pretty much a sitting duck, and keeping to the periphery might be their best bet for now. It appeared to be a tourist town, based on the people milling about and the number of souvenir shops. The town included a bustling market and a terraced hillside, including what looked to be homes built a couple hundred years ago. Given the terrain and the number of people, they had half a chance of pulling this off.

"I guess we're lucky it's Saturday," she said. To his surprise, she grabbed his hand as they walked. The tremble in her fingers shot straight through his arm. She might talk tough and put up a great front, but it was all for show.

"Let's try to find a place where we can hunker down. The station is a little too obvious to be safe."

"We don't have too much time to kill." Despite her words, the wide-eyed expression told him more about the fear she felt than she'd ever admit.

Not that he blamed her. To his way of thinking, five minutes was too much time, knowing there were four cars with guys hunting them down. He raised his hand and pointed toward what appeared to be abandoned houses set into the hills. "I'll grab some stuff for us to eat and meet you back there. I can't guarantee they haven't put notices up about us all over town, so best for you to keep a low profile."

"I'll be fine." She patted her backpack and gave him a kiss on the cheek.

As he walked away, he felt the hint of trouble circling the air. All he kept thinking about was that they'd sent four cars.

The uptick in pressure had to mean that he and Sabrina were on to something, or at least somebody thought they were. Either way, it didn't matter. Both scenarios were bad news in terms of their current predicament as well as anything else going forward. They weren't safe now and wouldn't be until Trinity was behind bars.

As he strolled the small market, he couldn't help but think about the look on her face when she recognized the truth of Antonio's betrayal. In that half-second or so, she couldn't hide the evidence from her expression. He'd seen hurt quickly replaced by anger reflected in her eyes. She wasn't nearly as tough as she thought she was; then again, neither was he.

Kane sifted through the options for sustenance and selected some fruit and cheese as well as bread, and stuffed the bag inside his backpack. Despite the urge to return to her as quickly as possible, he plodded his way back toward Sabrina using his best old-man shuffle to avoid attracting undue attention. Suppressing the nerves running up and down his spine was the difficult part. It was only a matter of time before whoever was in those cars came looking for them.

As he turned the corner, he spotted a black car roll into town. Considering the later model, he had to assume it was part of the group they were trying to avoid. He tempered his pulse, which threatened to compromise his old-man hobble, and headed toward Sabrina.

Except when he got there, she was nowhere to be found.

* * *

Sabrina peered around the corner of the outbuilding and fought back the fear inching through her body. The prickle seemed to zero in on the base of her skull and project through every vein and artery in her head. They were not playing.

Two black cars cruised through the small town at a rate of speed that belied their intent. They were going so slowly that even people walking were moving faster.

She was seriously screwed. And so was Kane.

Coming here had been a mistake. Dragging him into her mess was another mistake. When would she learn? She pushed back the nagging thought of so many years ago and tried to blend into the scenery as much as possible.

Finally, she spotted Kane doing the fast version of the old-man shuffle. He must have gone to their agreed-upon spot and found her missing. But if she got too close to him, he'd be made as well. She needed to keep her distance until the men left.

She ducked into the shadow of a doorway and held her breath as the car rolled past. The rapid beat of her pulse began to pound in her ears as adrenaline, combined with increased blood flow, wound its way through her. When they rolled past Kane, she unzipped her bag and fingered the trigger on the gun.

Even though he feigned obliviousness, she knew him better than to be fooled by his casual stance. When he shifted the pack from his shoulder to his hand, she knew he was readying to shoot his way out of the mess if need be. Still, she couldn't help but admire his acting chops. If she didn't know better—

A plastic bag came over her head noiselessly while men surrounded her on both sides, grabbing her arms and wrapping them behind her back in what felt like industrial-strength bungee cords. Her feet were lethal, but not without leverage, and not without her ability to breathe. While she struggled to suck in air, a voice whispered in her ear as he pulled her along, "We've heard about you and aren't taking any chances." The sinister laugh that followed caused her mind to freefall.

Suck it up.

Wheeze. Instead of air, plastic hit her gaping mouth. Dizziness set in as spots vibrated before her eyes. It wouldn't be long before it was over.

The ping of a bullet sounded and the guy holding her on the left dropped away with a curse. She was too out of it to react until the tight grip on the bag loosened, freeing up some much-needed oxygen. A slip of air hit her nostrils, bringing with it a sense of awareness. She twisted her head, hoping to get the bag off her head. It wasn't working, but air was swirling underneath, giving her what she craved.

Another bullet sounded close enough for the guy on the right to bring her in front of him. Using him for leverage, and feeling a surge of strength, she stomped on his instep and dove left. Seconds later, another shot rang out.

Her shoulder hit the hard ground. Ouch.

"Sabrina, are you okay?" Kane didn't wait for an answer and yanked the plastic bag from her head, as he alternated between swearing and clucking like a little old lady. Somewhere along the way—she couldn't say when—he'd dropped the disguise. He made fast work of the things binding her arms and wrapped himself around her.

She worked her shoulder up and down and was glad she hadn't dislocated it. "How did you find me?"

"Dumb luck. I saw them park the car and get out and thought I should investigate."

A shiver wound through her. "When those guys don't respond, they'll send more."

"That's what I'm thinking too."

"The train's not due for another twenty minutes." She chewed her lip. Even while the craving for oxygen had subsided, her brain still flashed panic.

"Let's hide out until night when we can walk to the next station to throw them off." His voice was tight, his jaw clenched. He wrapped his arm around her shoulder and tucked her in close.

An inner wuss she didn't know existed didn't fight the contact. Memories from long ago tickled at the base of her brain but stubbornly refused to surface.

As they trudged silently up the century-old village steps, two men emerged around the corner of one of the buildings to point guns at them. With nowhere to duck and hide, they raised their arms in capitulation—at least for now. She knew Kane well enough to know he wouldn't go down easy, and neither would she.

"You're coming with us." The men spoke in German as they motioned with the tips of their guns to a point higher, where the likelihood of being spotted by a villager was even more remote. One guy was freakishly tall, with long, gangly arms. He moved behind Kane, forcing him forward. The other was about a foot shorter, with a mustache, and stepped in line behind her.

The men had every intention of killing them. She had no doubt about that. But first they needed to find out what she and Kane knew so they could report back to Trinity.

She knew Kane was thinking the same thing: they would use him to get to her and vice versa. In her estimation, that was a losing proposition. It would take a whole lot for either one of them to give in. They were alike in so many ways.

But she had no intention of getting to that point. And, she suspected, neither did Kane. Once they got to the torture thing, it was a vicious cycle that could easily spiral out of control. Stopping things before they got there was the best solution she could imagine.

The Uzi poked into her lower back as they went farther and farther into the ruins of the village and farther and farther away from the train that would be due in less than fifteen minutes. She glanced at Kane. He gave her a wink and mouthed counting back from three.

They struck in tandem, twisting and grabbing the guns, pointing them away until they fell from the men's hands. Leverage on the stairs was treacherous, but that worked to their advantage with the two out-of-shape men sent to capture them.

Kane and the tall guy were trading blows, while she knew better than to engage in a fistfight. She'd lose that battle for sure. Instead, she ducked and weaved among the crumbling architecture, hoping to find an opening. The uneven ground was making that nearly impossible. The mustached guy stalked her up the steps higher and higher. Kane and the tall one were still at it. Their abandoned guns had tumbled out of reach. But if she were quick, she might be able to secure one before Mustache

Man did. Just as she had the thought, the man lunged, grasping her foot and yanking. She lost her balance and fell.

A menacing smile broke out on his face as reached into his pocket and came after her with a knife. The shot rang out, clipping him in the shoulder and causing him to drop his knife. Sabrina expected to find Kane, but instead spotted Antonio holding a rifle. He motioned with his hands. "*Fretta, fretta,*" he shouted as bullets began to fly all around them.

Kane came up behind her and grabbed her hand. Together they tore down the steps toward the slowly approaching train.

Another shot sounded behind them. When she turned, she spotted Antonio with a giant red stain blooming on his chest.

CHAPTER TWELVE

———

They were both out of breath when they settled into their train seats. Sabrina couldn't speak for Kane, but it took more than a few minutes to calm her racing heart.

He clasped her hand in his. "Antonio made amends in the end."

"I guess he did." She nodded slowly, still trying to process the idea that Antonio was dead. Despite his double cross, shouldn't she at least have tears in her eyes? "At some level I understand him. If it weren't for my brothers, I might have turned into even more of a cold bitch than I am."

He chuckled. "That's only what you want people to believe."

"You're naïve, Kane. I never have been one of those touchy-feely kinds of people. I can't remember the last time I cried—probably not since I was a little girl and learned how cruel life can be." Why did he keep thinking she was capable of something that would never be? She'd made peace with it. Why couldn't he?

"That doesn't mean you're emotionless. It means you're guarded. I get that. No doubt it's a lingering effect of having a shitty childhood."

She shrugged, knowing he'd minimized her emotional desert. "It's who I am. I don't get all gaga over any man in my life; I don't sit around and talk about my problems or try to work them out; I never get overly attached. Most times I say screw it and move on." While nerves jumped around inside her, he looked the epitome of calm, cool, and collected.

"You told me a little too much about your past. That's your real fear, isn't it, Sabrina? Maybe people won't back away from you. Maybe they won't walk on eggshells to keep from pissing you off. Maybe they'll see you for the scared woman you are."

"What, are you my psychoanalyst now?"

"I'm more than that and we both know it." The firm set of his jaw irked her more than she could say.

She looked around the train, anxious for an out. "I don't need this." Her legs were shaky when she stood, brushing past him and moving to another seat.

Her plan all along was to go at this assignment alone. Just because he fell into her lap didn't mean she had to make use of his talents and the high-and-mighty power of the FBI. Besides, his talents weren't that great, and she had much more incentive to see this to its conclusion.

Seconds later, he settled next to her, spoiling the good vibe she was desperately working on. "Do I have to report you to the authorities?"

"Both you and I know that's not going to happen." His eyebrows rose up and down and he chucked her under the chin. "We don't have internet access; we have nearly a five-hour train ride before we hit the outskirts of Venice. We might as well hash things out between us."

She rolled her eyes. "How many times do I have to say there's nothing between us? I have connections with nobody. Take it or leave it. It's the way I am."

"That doesn't explain your commitment to Caitlyn, does it? It doesn't explain why you left me in the middle of the night, does it?"

"I told you I like to work alone." She knew he'd eventually go there. It was part of his makeup that wanted to see her exposed and vulnerable.

He nodded, but not in a way that felt understanding. Instead, his gaze narrowed as he took her in. "It's the whole sex thing, isn't it? It wigged you out." His comment came out of the blue.

She rolled her eyes. "I'd never get wigged out by something as trivial as sex."

He palm slapped his forehead. "That's right. It wasn't about the sex. It was about the intimacy. I'm betting you never told any other man about Petrovich before."

She wanted to protest, but the words seemed stuck to the roof of her mouth like a glob of peanut butter. When she glanced into his eyes, she knew she couldn't deny it even if the words themselves weren't trapped inside.

"Your non-answer speaks volumes." He nodded as if he knew what was going on inside her head. But he didn't. No one did. Not even her sometimes. "I get it now."

She wanted to spout off a pithy response to his observation but she couldn't think of a word to say. Did he actually understand what drove her to do what she did? Could that even be possible?

After keeping a metal case around her heart for as long as she could remember, that tightly wound spring keeping it closed loosened a notch.

* * *

Thankfully, their conversation on the train faded into oblivion when she faked sleep on the journey toward Venice. By the time they got to the small inn on the opposite side of the canal, Sabrina was more than anxious to tackle the information sent to Kane.

"Now that we're settled for the night, I need to see." She urged him to open the laptop and the program the FBI wizards had unearthed. When Sabrina inched closer, she saw the pictures: women, girls, hundreds of them. Sexual positions, naked, vulnerable. Bile rose up her throat in less than a heartbeat.

"Try to ignore the photos; it's the codes next to the girls we need to concentrate on." He placed his hand across the screen and looked into her eyes.

"Am I in those pictures?" She drew in a breath and tried to suppress the wash of vulnerability.

"We know the code next to the photo has to do with the airports where the women were abducted."

Sabrina couldn't speak. All she could do was stare at the screen, mesmerized by what she saw. Revulsion more potent than she could have imagined made a nauseous ball form in the pit of her stomach. It took every bit of willpower she possessed to not throw up all over the keyboard.

"Where's my photo? I know there's one of me in there somewhere." Judging by the women's drugged-out state, it had to be taken when she first arrived at Marco's.

She drew in a shaky breath and brought her hands together. The trembling started in her fingertips and worked through her hands to her arms to her shoulders, and on down until her whole body quivered.

He scrolled through the photos, finally stopping at a picture that looked like her, but didn't at the same time. Her eyes were closed as she was propped as if a naked rag doll against the wall of Marco's basement. "Who took that picture?" She wanted to look away, but at the same time couldn't. Seeing herself displayed in that way made everything more real.

"I'm not sure. I'm guessing maybe Petre or Arte." He grabbed her chin and forced her to look at him. "Sabrina, do not get sucked into this."

Although inside Sabrina felt close to tears, she knew they'd never fall. They never did. "How can I not?" Her voice sounded strained and raw, as it had to pass through the wash of emotions trying to keep it in place.

"Tell me what Caitlyn looks like."

Sabrina nodded. "Red hair, about five feet five, green eyes, freckles across the bridge of her nose." With a family that loved her more than life itself. She could picture their faces tinged with hope when she said she'd bring Caitlyn back to them. A shiver worked its way inside her chest and squeezed. Time was running out. Was she still alive? "This is perverted. What kind of man gets off on this stuff?"

"That's what we're trying to find out, isn't it?"

She opened her eyes again, steeling herself for the task at hand. This had to be done. And it might lead to Caitlyn. She could do this if she kept that thought in mind.

"How many pages are there?"

"Thirty or so. About four pictures per page."

Her fingers twitched on her lap as she fought the urge to press a button and remove it all from her memory. But she couldn't. "I need to find Caitlyn."

After the first few pages, she began to get immune. Maybe her perspective changed. Maybe she was able to focus on their faces, scrutinizing each for that silly lopsided grin, the huge, expressive eyes, the freckles across Caitlyn's nose and cheeks. That was now her focus.

Her heart felt it before her mind registered the picture. Then a moan erupted from her throat, starting somewhere deep down inside the pit of her belly.

Seeing it in blazing Technicolor heightened the madness. Made it all the more real. All the more frightening.

Tears hovered near the surface, but still refused to fall. Still her heart squeezed within her chest as emotion, raw and potent, set up inside and fought for control. As if he knew somehow, Kane stood her up and enveloped her in his arms and held her tight.

"We're going to find her, Sabrina."

"How?" Somehow the vulnerability slipped out more easily than she ever could have imagined.

"I'm not sure. But I know for damn sure we're smarter than whoever's behind this organization."

Desperate for a break in the crushing pressure lodged inside her chest, she bit off a chuckle. "Oh yeah, obviously you haven't seen my chemistry grade."

He smiled for the briefest of moments, as if he knew she couldn't focus right now. "I'll see if I can get one of the FBI specialists to take a look to see if there's a hint of a location somewhere in those numbers. There's got to be some kind of a clue that connects those numbers to people. It's the only thing that makes sense."

Bile revisited her throat. "You worked in the accounting end."

He opened his own laptop and pulled up a Excel sheet to show the transactions. "All the money was filtered through an account in Switzerland that can't be traced. Deposits were made under initials, but not necessarily representing their names."

"Is there someway to trace G through his phone?"

He shook his head. "Nope. He went the disposable route."

Trepidation lit up her spine. "We've got to figure out what that next code means. That's got to be about the locations or the names of the buyers." She tapped her fingers against the desk.

"Did the FBI run the two lists through their software to find anything to link them?"

Kane shook his head again. "As far as I know, they were concentrating on the hidden file, figuring the first file we found was a red herring."

"But what if it isn't? What if the two lists together somehow complete a picture?" When he didn't interrupt, she continued, "Bring up the original list on Marco's computer."

"The one that had all the random numbers?"

"Maybe the two are connected somehow."

He pulled up the list on Marco's computer and copy and pasted it into a Word file. "Give me Caitlyn's code number and see if we can match up a part of it somehow."

"2L1G(2)71AP4." She read off the code and held her breath. It was hidden there somewhere. She could feel it.

"No exact match. Let me search for combinations." He plunked at the keys some more and shook his head. "It's like finding a needle in a haystack."

"How many codes are listed on Marco's page?" She clicked and un-clicked the pen in her hand several times.

He went through the list. "A hundred and twenty."

She slammed her hand on the table. "And that's how many pictures you said were there, right? No way that's a coincidence. Start with the airport code. LGA."

He went through the list and five numbers popped up. "Got a couple of hits. What do you think?" After highlighting the numbers, he showed her the screen.

She pointed to the number that got her attention. "The same three letters are there. 44AP71GG11L. That's the one." She chewed her lip. "Now, what does it all mean?"

"The airport code is there but backwards." He eliminated LG and A from the sequence.

She high-fived him. "Good call. What else is there?" She studied the numbers until they started to blur together.

"How about the date? When was Caitlyn taken?"

At last he gave her something to focus on. "Around mid-February." She pointed at the number by the girl's photo. "2-1-7-1-4. Sounds like a date to me." The bubble of progress shimmied along her spine.

"What if the G(2) means GG?" He laid it all out. "Left in the first sequence is GP. Maybe initials? To keep with the backwards theme, we have GP but in reverse order."

There were still too many numbers left in the sequence to match up. "Maybe the whole date doesn't get transferred over. Maybe just the year. 1-4 in backwards order."

He ran his fingers through his short hair. "That leaves us with 4711. Could be an address, but that could mean anywhere."

She sucked in her bottom lip and chewed on it. "My guess it's in Europe." Despite the heightened circumstances, she chuckled. "That's really narrowing it down, isn't it?"

"We could have the tech people run that number through the database and see what they come up with."

"My gut says it's not an address. That would be too simple, considering what we've unwound over the last couple of hours." She glanced at the clock and recognized how much time they'd spent. But progress was a good thing, especially considering their lack of it over the last few days. "What else is recorded in numbers?"

"Latitude, longitude?" He plugged the numbers into the computer. "If I reverse the numbers it's in the middle of the Gulf of Eden."

"But what if you don't reverse the numbers. Keep it as is. Where do we end up?"

"In the mountains of Germany." He tapped on the keys. "Let me get a satellite of the location." A few moments later, he turned the computer toward her, a Cheshire grin on his face. "That house is massive."

"Can you find out who owns it?"

"Let me make some calls."

"That's got to be where she is." She grinned while the idea she might be close shimmied through.

* * *

A foreign part of her itched to cuddle deep within his embrace and stay there, sinking into the security of his arms. The more familiar side, the side she trusted to steer her away from trouble, the side she depended on time and time again, understood the folly of her thoughts.

Push. Pull. Push. Pull.

Overcome with sensations that warred deep inside, Sabrina longed to escape. Needing to dispel the uncomfortable rush of emotion setting low in her belly, she tossed back the covers and propelled out of bed, slipping on her clothes. Getting too complacent was never a good idea.

He patted the bed. "I had other ideas for starting the morning, but I guess you're ready to get started."

"We have a job to do. And when we're finished we can both go our separate ways. Don't make this sexual thing between us into anything more than it is."

The reassurance of her words brought a level of calm to her chaotic pulse. Although, for the life of her, she couldn't quite understand why that twinge of regret knocked around inside her.

His jaw clenched tight as he stood, yanking on his clothes. "What's going on, Sabrina?"

"Suddenly now you have a problem with me?" She arched her brow and gave him her best sneer. *You've gotten careless, Dragi. Don't let things get personal.*

He shrugged. "If you're happy with it being a roll in the hay, then so am I."

"Good." She nodded as a twinge of disappointment ebbed through. Being with this man made her feel strange, sick, wonderful, and edgy, all at the same time.

Sabrina didn't want to think about anything more than the here and now. Right now, at this stage of the game, she had no time for warm, fuzzy feelings. Who was she kidding—she didn't have a warm, fuzzy bone in her body. She'd proved that over and over again.

She chewed her lip as she contemplated the risk she might be taking. "On second thought, I think I should go this alone." Sabrina packed up the backpack in the early morning hours and strapped it to her back. That might be the key to getting her head on straight.

Kane shook his head. "Are we back to that again?"

"It's not fair to involve you in this. Your job is up in the air, no matter what you say, or they would have given you more support on this."

"Their lack of support is more about official channels than anything else. They need to make a case against Trinity. That's why I was on the inside."

She raised an eyebrow at him. "And you don't need to make a case?"

He sighed. "There's more than one way to make a charge stick. Trust me—I will not let this guy slip away."

"But you could get killed and it would be all my fault." That was the rub. She didn't want to see anything happen to Kane, which alarmed her. She'd somehow crossed an invisible boundary she swore she never would, and couldn't figure out how to jump back to the safety of numbness.

He laughed, the sound breaking a little of the tension floating between them. "I'm not going to die." He paused. "And we are getting Caitlyn back home."

* * *

"What are we doing here?"

When Kane pulled into the small, nondescript airfield, Sabrina had to force down the shiver. For all her bluster and bravado, small airplanes made her go all squirrelly. As far as she was concerned, they were only marginally safer than flying with a lawn chair attached to helium balloons.

"Easiest and fastest way in. Ron arranged it. Don't want any trouble at the border with the price on our heads."

"I don't know about this, Kane…" There wasn't a 747 in sight.

He shook his head as he dragged her past the hangar and between the two airplanes on the left. "We'll parachute in close enough to give us an edge, but not close enough to be seen. We don't know what we're getting into. And given the remote location, this is the best option."

Suddenly, she felt a little dizzy. "I agree with you one hundred percent, except for the whole parachuting thing."

"How did you think we'd get in there?"

She rolled her eyes and tried to stop the flutter of fear at bay. "Drive like normal people."

"It's so remote—they'll see us coming a mile away. There's a clearing in the forest a couple miles from the house. The pilot will get us in close enough, the parachutes are in back, and I'll give you a short lesson."

"How are we going to get back out with Caitlyn?" She could hear the irritation in her own voice. "Walk? Yeah, sure, that sounds like a wonderful plan."

"I spotted a helicopter pad on top of the garage. Once we're successful securing the place, the FBI has agreed to airlift us out." He gave her a cheesy grin.

"But...I don't...know how to jump..." She gulped down the wad of fear clogging her throat. "...from an airplane."

"Nothing to it. It's like jumping off a giant step."

"I don't think so."

"Sure it is. Just larger scale. Besides, we'll do a tandem, so I'll handle the parachute part. I've parachuted at least a hundred times. You just need to know how to land without breaking something."

When he went through his explanations, she couldn't focus. Her mind was a blur as fear overtook her thought processes.

Jumping out of an airplane? She'd rather be thrown into a cage match with Attila the Hun, and have people chanting "two men enter, one man leaves" than fly through the air. Boundary-less. And totally and completely out of control. She didn't do out of control. He should know that by now.

Heights petrified her. Ever since Max nearly died, it had been her worst nightmare.

Kane brought his hand behind her back, ushering her toward one of the planes. Her mind faded in and out as a bout of panic overwhelmed her. Before she knew it, the pilot started the engine, and Kane strapped on their parachute. Seconds later, they'd lifted off the ground and all options had disappeared.

Sabrina glanced at Kane then out the window of the small plane once again. She gulped, feeling the anxiety forced down her throat and into her gut.

"Couldn't we fly the plane in close and land like normal folks, not some crazy daredevils?"

His lips inched up in a slight smirk before he let loose a chuckle.

"You think this is funny? I'm going to be covered in a cast from my neck to my toes and you're laughing."

He laughed again and she barely resisted the urge to pop him one. "After all the dangerous stuff you do, you're scared about jumping out of a plane?"

She folded her arms across her chest, refusing to give in to his tease. "I don't see the point. I'm sure there's a better way to handle this."

"We're parachuting in because there's no landing strip nearby. The place is in the middle of a forest with only dirt road access. Besides, we don't want to get too close and give ourselves away."

The plane banked to the right then leveled out. Sabrina had a death grip on the seat cushion, while the prospect of breaking every bone in her body seemed inevitable.

"Would it be so bad to hike in? Maybe drive close, then continue on foot."

"Are you crazy? Look out the window. Do you honestly think we have the time to climb up and down those mountains? They know we're getting close."

"Really, I think—" He moved in behind her. The clink sounded seconds before she opened her mouth and let out a bloodcurdling scream.

CHAPTER THIRTEEN

———

Every curse word in every language Sabrina knew flew out her mouth as she dropped the twenty thousand feet—that felt as if a million—in slow motion.

She kept her eyes closed for as long as she could, then dared to open her left eye for a fraction of a second. The ground closed in beneath her with amazing speed. Trees surrounded the miniscule patch of green that Kane had decided they could easily land upon.

If she got out of this alive, she was going to strangle him. With her bare hands. When she touched ground, he was one dead FBI agent.

"Come on, Sabrina. Relax." Kane's voice was close, but still he had to shout in order for her to hear him.

If she could open her eyes she could get her bearings. But the sensation of hurtling toward the ground at breakneck speed was more than enough visual for her.

Suddenly, her whole body was yanked up when he pulled on the cord, and she flew back up into the air. Her stomach lurched into her throat as she opened her eyes.

Death was definitely too good for Kane.

Sucking in a deep breath, she watched as he guided them through the trees to the clearing. His toes touched down first. Her head knocked into his chest. As he unclipped the binding between them, she slipped off her harness, more thankful than ever to be on solid ground.

He was still taking off his harness when she tackled him to the ground. She scrambled off, only to glower at him from a dominant position.

"Ouch."

"If I really wanted to hurt you, believe me, you'd know it." She drew in a breath and forced her hands onto her hips to keep from hitting him again. "You pushed me out of that plane."

"It didn't look as if you were going to do it on your own." He folded his arms across his chest and rocked back on his heels. "And the timing was right."

"I told you I had another plan." Adrenaline spurted through, making her jumpy and nervous.

"What? Waiting around until the damn plane ran out of gas and crashed into the side of the mountain?"

"I—"

"You were scared. I can respect that. You needed a push. I supplied it. Simple as that." A smile brought up his lips. "But you screamed like a girl."

"Excuse me?" Of all the things she expected him to say, that was not one of them.

"I've seen you take a punch like a heavyweight boxer and not mumble a sound. But toss you out of a plane at twenty thousand feet and you're a screaming Mimi." He chuckled. "Yep, you screamed like a girl."

"Maybe that's because I am a girl." Okay, so she didn't feel so mad anymore. He really was kind of funny—even though the joke was at her expense.

And she supposed part of what he said was a compliment. Of sorts.

"I kind of noticed. I had my doubts when I saw you street fight, but as I can now verify, you have all the right equipment."

She chose to ignore his comment. Besides, she didn't have a snappy comeback.

"Let me see that tracker." Sabrina held out her hand. Desperate for a change in the tenor of conversation, to work on a plan of action seemed to be a good strategy.

He pulled the device from his pocket. Sitting down on the grass, he encouraged her to do the same.

"We're about five miles from the compound." He pointed to a red circle. "It shouldn't take us long to cover that ground."

Sabrina patted the piece strapped to her side. "What are we waiting for?"

* * *

They got close and took turns resting until darkness fell, then continued their hike through the forest, utilizing the trees as a natural cover to mask their movement. The snap of a twig. The sudden flight of a flock of birds—all heightened her senses. All forced Sabrina to look around, observe, and remember in vivid detail the scene that night seven years earlier. Everything had gone horribly wrong.

Max. Bleeding profusely.

Jake, for the first time in his life, panicked. Which only made her panic more. Alone. The three of them. Double-crossed by the man they'd sworn allegiance to. He'd never responded to their distress call. They were on their own. Just like before.

"There it is." Kane's voice brought her out of her memories straight to the present.

The imposing structure before them was enormous. More castle than house, it stood alone, surrounded by nothing but forest, with a helicopter pad on the garage roof.

"The iron fence and guards patrolling the grounds with Uzis makes me believe they're guarding something or someone real important," he whispered in her ear.

This. Was. It.

She wasn't sure of the origins of that telltale sixth sense. Petrovich? Or some genetic component passed down through the Shaw legacy? Either way, she couldn't be sure. But the itch was kicking up a storm at the base of her neck.

She nodded, taking in the scene as she calculated odds. "How do you want to play this?"

Caitlyn was here somewhere. It was almost as if the girl's voice whispered to Sabrina among the soaring treetops. She needed to stay focused and not allow her emotions to overtake her abilities. There was no doubt she was good at what she did, but focusing on the task at hand took every ounce of concentration within her. Some things came naturally; others took the very life out of her.

A massive iron gate guarded the front. Despite its location in the middle of a forest, the house was surrounded by manicured vegetation and well-tended gardens. The serenity of the exterior reminded her of Marco's place—a stark contrast to the horrors inside.

"Let's walk around the perimeter and see what we're dealing with." His whispered words brought her back into focus.

They crept in a wide arc around the compound, getting the lay of the land and a sense of guard assignments. One guard was stationed at the front gate; two were lazing around the porch, seemingly shooting the breeze.

But it was an outbuilding way in the back that caught her attention. Apparently Kane noticed it as well, as he stopped and pointed. While it looked to be nothing more than an old structure in need of repair, the two guards stationed outside said otherwise.

Kane inclined his head and mimed climbing the fence. When she nodded, he gave her the thumbs-up sign. They waited until the guard passed by, then scaled the fence in tandem.

They hunkered down near a large bush to catch their breath, and waited for the guard to pass by before they approached the smaller building. Both guards were stretched back in their chairs, as if sleeping, but with guns strapped across their chests they could still be trouble.

She nodded toward Kane, and together they sprinted toward the outbuilding. She peered inside the window, at first seeing nothing much of interest but a threadbare home with a makeshift kitchen. But a sweater tossed across the back of a chair made her heart clench inside her chest. It meant somebody lived there.

When she peered inside the next window, her breath caught in her throat. Between the blur of dirt on the windows and the bars denying entry or exit…she couldn't tell their age, but two girls slept on cots inside the first room. While they could be servants, her gut said otherwise. The second window revealed another two girls. She motioned for Kane to come look. After all this time, she needed to know she wasn't hallucinating. When he joined her, nodded in agreement, and tilted his head toward the guards in front, she followed him along the perimeter.

She rustled the brushes along the side of the house, hoping to draw some attention. One of the guard's snoring stopped as the chair creaked.

"Did you hear that?" He spoke in Italian.

The other man yawned and muttered, "Probably an animal."

"I'd better check it out."

It didn't take more than a second for Kane to take care of him. The other man had already returned to snoring, so it didn't take much to overpower him as well. She and Kane left the men tied and gagged on the porch with their hats tipped over their faces, appearing to anyone passing by as if they were asleep. Judging by what she'd seen so far, the other guards didn't venture this way, but just in case, it would be best to make things appear normal.

Her fingers trembled when she eased open the door. With both a penlight and the Uzi tight in her grasp, Sabrina tiptoed inside. Kane was on her heels. She pushed through the chaos and fear running roughshod down her spine and cautiously searched the first room. A well-worn couch, a rudimentary table, and a straight-backed chair were the only furniture she spotted.

As she slipped into the first bedroom, her heart pounded so frantically it felt as if any minute it might pop out of her chest. Worry, fear, and a host of other emotions bubbled to life inside her.

A sliver of light filtered through the window, allowing her to see without her penlight. Two girls slept in their beds. The first one was blonde; the second dark-haired.

Neither was Caitlyn.

Sabrina fought against disappointment as she made her way to the second room. The threadbare covering didn't do much to dissuade the chill from the midnight air, and each of the girls shivered in their sleep.

As quietly as possible, Sabrina went from one bed to the next. Neither one of those girls was Caitlyn either. A third cot lay in the corner, unoccupied, but the sheets and bedclothes appeared rumpled. She shook her head in response to Kane's raised eyebrows, even while she wondered about the whereabouts of the third girl.

She knew nothing about these young women. They could be house servants for all she knew. But that didn't explain why there would be two armed guards stationed outside the door. Could she have jumped to the wrong conclusion?

Despair gnawed at her temples. But still she couldn't leave. Was it about stubbornness, or should she pay attention to the itch running down her spine?

Somehow she knew. Caitlyn was here. Every bone in her body shook in awareness. But she'd been wrong before.

Kane looked at her and shrugged. Clearly these girls were being held against their will, even if Caitlyn wasn't among them. The smart thing to do would be to leave, but she couldn't.

She went back to the first bedroom and turned on her small light. This time she didn't care if she woke the inhabitants. Even if she was wrong, and Caitlyn wasn't there, maybe they would know where she could be found.

First she illuminated the perimeter. Then she brought the light up to travel the length of the empty bed, her hand trembling more now than before.

"*Esca della mia casa.*" *Get out of my house*. The low growl came from somewhere behind her, followed by a curse.

"*Siamo qui per aiutarti*," Kane's muffled voice protested. *We're here to help*. When she turned, she spotted two girls hitting him with wooden objects—they looked to be spoons, or maybe pieces of a bowl. It was hard to tell.

Kane fended off the blows with his forearms as he tried to secure their makeshift weapons. One of the girls cursed at him, mumbling in German, but they continued the assault.

Sabrina tried to intervene, but it was nearly impossible, especially when the girls from the other room joined in.

Kane kept muttering, "We're here to help," in German, then Spanish, then French, but it seemed to fall on deaf ears. The girls were relentless. Sabrina grabbed one and tried to secure her arms, but the girl fought her off as if she were in a death match and spouted off a litany of curses in what sounded like Russian.

"Ouch. Damn it. Any bright ideas?" Kane called in her direction.

"None that I can think of at the moment." Sabrina had her hands full, as two of the girls had taken to hitting her as well.

She didn't want to hurt them, and corralling their punches and kicks without doing damage was difficult.

"We're looking for someone," Kane said to the girls surrounding them.

One of them muttered an oath in response. Given the lack of light, it was difficult to distinguish one girl from the next. But based on the way the others looked to her for direction, she was clearly something of a leader.

Now desperate to take advantage of the temporary lull, Sabrina said. "You don't understand."

"No, you don't understand. We're not going to do this anymore. You either set us free or you'll have to kill us," one of the others said. Her accent made Sabrina believe she might have been French.

Kane glanced at Sabrina. "We're not going to hurt you."

"Ha, we've heard that before. Now we fight back. It's the only way," another of the girls said, a makeshift knife in her hands. "You have guns. We know what that means."

"Watch, we'll put down our guns. We mean you no harm. We're here to help," Kane said before he slid his Uzi to the floor.

While Sabrina followed suit, she struggled to regain her composure.

Think.

"I'm going to turn on the light so you can see our faces. We're not going to hurt any of you. I promise."

Before she could, the ringleader tackled her to the ground. The others went after Kane once again, this time grabbing the weapons that had been surrendered.

CHAPTER FOURTEEN

———

Sabrina hit the ground, the wind knocked out of her lungs. The girl's wiry legs landed on either side of her chest. Sabrina grasped tightly on to the girl's arms to stop the blows coming her way. She needed to make her understand. "I promise I won't hurt you. I'm looking for Caitlyn Collins. Maybe you know her."

The girl emitted a wail. Sabrina couldn't tell if it was pain or some sort of acknowledgment. Cautiously, she let her fingers slip from around the girl's biceps.

While the girl's posture slumped from its formerly rigid position, Sabrina turned to the girls harassing Kane. "*Arresto*," she shouted in Italian. When that didn't work, she tried German. "*Anhalten*." No luck. Spanish? "*Detener*." Either she hadn't hit the right language or nothing was going to stop them short of force.

The girl moved to a sitting position before she turned her attention to Sabrina. "Who are you?" The words came out almost as a curse.

Sabrina's heart kick-started in her chest as she sat. With trembling fingers, she touched the wisp of hair surrounding the girl's face. The girl jerked back in response, bringing her hand up to protect herself.

Sabrina breathed in deeply as a knowing sensation barreled through her. "Caitlyn," she whispered. "My name is Sabrina Shaw and I've been working with your parents to find you. Your birthday is November 13th. Your favorite color is red. Your room is white with a red, striped comforter and a four-poster white bed. Your dog is named Riley. "

Caitlyn let out a sob then clutched at Sabrina's shirt, pulling her into an awkward embrace. "I've been…" She drew in a ragged breath. "...waiting...so...long." Sabrina felt tremors run the course of the girl's body as it pressed against her. The words came out in a mixture of Italian and English, mixed with bone-deep sobs. "I...want...t...to go home."

Caitlyn pulled back, examining Sabrina more closely, as if not quite believing help had arrived. She shook her head, scared, delirious, or a combination of both while tears streamed down her cheeks and great big sobs retched from her chest to her throat.

"Sabrina Shaw, you're my hero," Caitlyn uttered.

Sabrina enveloped her in an embrace, while the girl held on as if trying to convince herself being rescued wasn't a mirage. Her body felt emaciated, far different from the robust photos taken of the girl. But right now, it didn't matter.

Kane rubbed at her shoulder, breaking into the moment. "We gotta go. The sun will be up soon."

"What about the others?" Caitlyn turned toward the girls, a hint of strength in her words.

Kane peeked out the window, then back toward the group. "What kind of vehicles do they have in the garage?"

"That pig has a Hummer." One of the girls spewed the information in a combination of Italian and German.

"What's the name of the man who has you?"

"Guillermo Ponci. He has this place here and an island off Venice somewhere," Caitlyn supplied. "He left a couple of days ago in a hurry. That's why there are only a few guards."

Kane and Sabrina exchanged looks. No doubt he was thinking the same thing as her. The initials were in the code: GP.

"I'm going to break into the garage. You get the girls ready," Kane announced as he made a move toward the door.

Despite the fact they'd been ready to kill him moments ago, they now stood in front of him. "*Lassen Sie*," the girls pleaded. *Please stay.*

"I'll be right back," he whispered, even as the girls shook their heads and latched on to his arms. He glanced at Sabrina for support.

Her brothers had started on their missions for Petrovich several years before her. She hadn't known what it was they did, but she could see a sense of fear mixed with determination in their eyes. Each time they'd left, she'd begged them to stay. Each time she had been petrified they wouldn't come back, and she'd be alone.

She understood well the sense of desperation. Now that these girls saw a sense of hope, they couldn't let it slip away.

"We'll go with you." She nodded to Kane's questioning glance. "I'll bring up the rear." She forced a smile. "Besides, you know I'm much better at hotwiring a car than you are."

Kane blew out a breath and shook his head. "Really bad idea," he muttered. Despite his words, he pulled out his cell and called the FBI, relayed the name Guillermo Ponci, and let them know what his coordinates were and the fact they were headed back with five victims.

Sabrina translated the plan to the girls in as many languages as she could muster. Based on their nods, she was pretty sure they understood. She gave them a few minutes to change out of their nightclothes.

Caitlyn whimpered, her body trembling. She turned her head into Sabrina's chest. "I'm not strong enough. Besides, I'm going to die soon. I'll slow everybody down."

Max's similar words flew around her brain from that night seven years ago. She had to force herself to focus.

"That is not the girl who attacked me ten minutes ago." Sabrina grabbed Caitlyn by the shoulders and steadied her. "Don't worry, I'll help you." Sabrina grasped Caitlyn's hand.

One of the girls pulled on Sabrina's sleeve and whispered, "She hasn't had anything to eat in a week."

Sabrina wanted to ask why, but now was not the time. "I won't let anybody hurt you again, Caitlyn."

Kane ushered them out, the barrel of his Uzi leading the way. They walked past the guards on the front porch, who had started to come around. Kane made short work of putting them back out. That left only three guards to worry about.

The expansive lawn seemed as long as the eighteenth hole on a golf course when Caitlyn faltered at nearly every step, trying to keep up as they tiptoed single file to the garage. Sabrina couldn't be sure if it was lack of food, drugs in her system, or something else that caused the girl's weakened condition. But it seemed now that the adrenaline rush was over, Caitlyn was hard-pressed to walk a straight line, let alone move quickly. Caitlyn's teeth chattered, and her body shook once exposed to the cool evening air. She emitted a drone-like buzz to mirror her unsure demeanor. Every step seemed to take minutes rather than seconds.

"Come on, Caitlyn. We have to hurry," Sabrina whispered.

Caitlyn started to trot, but then her knees gave out and she stumbled to the ground. Sabrina grasped on to one bicep while Kane grasped the other. Together they brought her to an upright position. With her feet barely touching the ground, they moved her closer toward the side door on the garage.

Kane got through the lock with minimum effort. Sabrina felt she could relax once all the girls were safely inside the car. Caitlyn teetered a hair's breadth away from an emotional breakdown.

"Care to try out your magic fingers?" Kane asked as he locked and barricaded the door from the garage to the house, as well as the side door.

Sabrina ushered the girls inside the car then slid behind the driver's seat and went to work. The new technology didn't make it easy.

A sense of *déjà vu* rode down her back, but she pushed it away. Shouts coming from outside made her believe something was up. Seconds later, someone pounded on the side door. The girls screamed in unison, and a flurry of gunfire pinged against the metal garage door.

"Come on, come on." The anti-theft device kicked in, preventing her from putting the car into gear. "I need the key. Check the garage somewhere." Panic rose within her throat, threatening to prevent her from swallowing.

Kane swore as he rummaged through the garage. Bullets came from the front of the garage. This was going from bad to worse.

The girls kept screaming, which only inched up her fear. Failure. If they were caught, they'd all die. And everything she'd done would be for nothing.

Caitlyn's eyes glazed over as she whimpered, "The mat. Check under the mat."

Sabrina bent down and ripped up the car's floor covering but found nothing. Kane rushed to the passenger door. "No key."

"Caitlyn said to check under the mat."

He looked at her quizzically, but he pulled back the floor mat. With a big smile on his face, he handed over the key. "Get down, ladies."

She pushed the steering column back together and turned over the engine. When the garage door opened, she didn't waste any time before barreling through. The men were waiting for them, Uzis firing a steady stream.

Bullets pinged off the frame as if a hammer pounded on it. The girls were hysterical by now. Everything seemed surreal as she mowed through the grass, small trees, bushes, and branches in her path to get them out of there.

The only road leading in or out was nothing more than a dirt track made through the forest. It was impossible not to be jostled about the cabin, especially when pursued by a Jeep filed with bad guys shooting.

Kane popped through the sunroof and shot off a couple of rounds. He came back down seconds later. "I couldn't hit a side of a barn in this terrain."

Even driving the Hummer, she had them at an advantage; the slow progress of the unwieldy vehicle seemed to erase any potential gain. She glanced in the rearview mirror and they'd disappeared. "Where did they go?"

"Damn it. There must be another trail."

"Look for them." Tension seeped down her shoulders and into her arms as she fought to keep the vehicle on the narrow road and avoid the trees that seemed inches away from the sides.

The girls had gone from screaming to whimpering. Sabrina couldn't decide which was worse. Caitlyn seemed to have passed out and remained slumped in the seat. If not for the soft whisper of the girl's breath, she'd be worried.

Day or night, this road had "treacherous" written all over it. Due to an abundance of trees, even on a bright, sunny day, Sabrina doubted much light would penetrate through.

The Jeep appeared in front of them blocking the road. They were either suicidal, or they were close to the mountain road that would get out into the open.

"I'll try to pick them off." Kane shifted in his seat and readied to poke out through the sunroof again.

Sabrina shook her head and pressed the gas pedal to the floor. "I'm going to plow right through them." She briefly glanced in back. "Hang on, ladies."

Once the men in the Jeep spotted her intent, they jumped off the vehicle. She didn't think about stopping as she rammed through, not stopping until she'd pushed the Jeep to the road. The mangled car spun until it finally came to a stop, resting on its side. The Hummer went airborne as she landed on a real road.

But they were free. That was the important part.

* * *

As far as partners went, Kane figured Sabrina was the best he'd ever had, even if she fought the word with a ferocity he still couldn't quite comprehend. They stopped to get some water and food for the girls.

"Caitlyn, do you want to call your parents?" Kane offered his cell phone. She hadn't said a word for the longest time, preferring, it seemed, to slump between him and Sabrina.

He helped her take some sips of water while Sabrina drove. A sense of fear permeated the interior of the Hummer, even though it had been at least fifteen minutes since they'd seen anyone on the road.

Caitlyn seemed unable to muster the energy to press in her phone number. Instead, she rattled off the number as he punched them in and handed her the phone.

She seemed to perk up a bit, and tears rolled down her cheeks as she spoke. "Mom. Dad. It's me. Sabrina found me." Between the emotion and her weakened state, she couldn't continue, and handed the phone to Sabrina.

Kane could guess the gist of the conversation based on Sabrina's one-word answers. "Germany." Then seconds later: "Probably Zurich. Sounds good. I'll let you know once we check into a hotel." She handed the phone back to Kane and continued to drive for a few moments. "Where is the Bureau meeting us?"

"Switzerland border. The girls will be released to their care, visit the hospital to make sure they're okay, and they can be returned home."

"No. No. No," Caitlyn screamed as she sucked in giant gobs of air. She tried to climb over Kane to the door, but he held her back. She started to hyperventilate and Kane couldn't help but wish he had a paper bag handy. Sabrina reached over and rubbed the poor girl's arm. Caitlyn's head shook back and forth as a prelude to her words. "No hospital. Ponci will find me and bring me back." Her voice so strong, so forceful, he blinked at the intensity.

She scratched her arms, leaving giant marks in her flesh. He corralled her to keep her from doing serious damage. Her limbs started to shake, even as Kane tried to soothe her. She kept whispering, "I'll die if I go back there." Over and over again.

Kane and Sabrina exchanged looks.

"Okay, no hospital. We'll check into a hotel. Kane has a gun. I have a gun. Ponci won't get you." Sabrina's voice was soft as she stroked the girl's arm and shoulder.

It didn't take a doctor to know Caitlyn's hold on reality was tenuous. One wrong word would send her over the edge.

She needed help. Psychological help for sure. Probably medical help as well. But more than anything, she needed to get back to the United States and with her parents.

Through the miracle of exhaustion, Caitlyn fell asleep against his shoulder as they made their way toward Zurich.

Except for Caitlyn's meltdown, all in all, he'd say it was a great day. But capturing Trinity still was his number one objective. Tracking down the clients on Marco's list would be one thing. But how many other Marcos were out there doing the exact same thing—brokering deals for the man who made it happen. All with a connection back to Trinity. He couldn't rest until he tracked the man down. Dead or alive didn't really matter much to him.

CHAPTER FIFTEEN

———

Sabrina sat on the bed in the hotel suite and wrapped multiple blankets around Caitlyn. She pulled her into a hug to further stave off the cold that didn't seem to want to leave. The FBI had made a stink about Caitlyn not going to the hospital, and compromised with a doctor coming to the hotel. He'd checked her out, diagnosed her with dehydration, and had given her an IV of saline. She seemed to perk up a bit after that, but hadn't said much. Judging by the photos Sabrina had seen, she would guess the poor girl had lost fifteen to twenty pounds in the last couple of weeks.

This case was messing with Sabrina's head, bringing her to times she hadn't thought about in years. As she watched Caitlyn give in to the vulnerability and fear, she couldn't help but wonder why she hadn't been wired that way. Or if she had, what happened to her to allow her to cut herself off so completely?

As she watched Caitlyn exhaust herself by crying, part of Sabrina wished she could allow herself the same type of release. But she didn't think she remembered how. She remembered crying after the loss of her parents, and being on the verge of crying when Max had nearly died, but everything in between and since had been an emotionless void. It was as if sadness or fear for someone else had been extinguished from her internal makeup. Most times she didn't miss the whole emotional connection thing, but right now she felt its absence more acutely than she'd dared to admit. Part of her would give anything to let loose the clog of fear stuck inside her, but the other part, the one who felt vulnerable and alone, stripped naked and bare when exposed in that way, thought better of it.

Why couldn't she feel? Would she ever feel? Prior to these last few days, the numbness of her existence felt comfortable, like a nice, warm sweater on a cold day. Now it seemed as if that sweater was suffocating her.

More anxious than she cared to admit, Sabrina scooted away from Caitlyn's vise-grip to scour the place for food. Caitlyn whimpered, then brought her arms around herself and rocked back and forth.

Sabrina held out a bottle of water. "I'll order room service. What would you like to eat?"

Caitlyn stared off into space as if still caught up in a nightmare. But then she reached for the water. Seconds later, she shrugged. "I'm not very hungry."

Kane gave Sabrina a this-is-scaring-the-crap-out-of-me look before taking control. "I'll order a bunch of different food, and we'll see what strikes your fancy when it gets here."

Caitlyn had a far-off look in her eye as she stared back at him. Sabrina couldn't help but think it was only the beginning of her trauma settling in.

Memories from her first night at Petrovich's rose to the surface.

She had never been so scared in her life. After months of not letting their guard down, the home he brought them to was warm and inviting, a giant fireplace heating up the place.

She sat on Max's lap, close to the fire, a blanket wrapped around her. Still she shivered as he fed her soup from a large cup. She remembered crying and begging for Max to find Mommy and Daddy. The vivid memory of the expression on his face—somewhere in between terror and despair—had burned itself into her brain. She recalled everything as if it had happened yesterday. Thinking about that night and what it meant to Max still made her heart break.

When they had first arrived at Petrovich's, Max was on edge, but he had been since their parents died. Being the oldest, he'd always been bossy, but being the self-appointed father to her when he was barely twelve only made him more vigilant. He never left her alone in the room with Petrovich and ensured she slept in the same room as him and Jake every night. He'd monitored her every move and was a general pain in the ass as she got older.

Some people might believe she'd had a tough childhood. But it was all she knew. When she considered what Kane told her of his own, she wasn't sure. A vagueness about her parents shrouded her memories. They were happy. They were in love. And then they were gone.

When she was younger she had daydreamed about running around, playing hide and seek with her brothers, but as the years went by, those thoughts disappeared. Her mother's ruby necklace that she had always worn had never been passed down to Sabrina. Somehow that had gone missing, and nothing had been asked or said about it that she could remember. Each night while her mother braided her hair, she had let Sabrina try on her ruby necklace before she went to sleep at night. Even now, she could feel the weight of its imprint on her neck. The smooth feel of the stone; the gold chain woven through it; the initials on the back—M&M—Marina and Max. Thinking about it now, and that hole in her heart that remained due to their absence, didn't even bring a tear to her eyes.

She loved her brothers more than anything else, but the man who was part father, part mentor, part drill sergeant who was impossible to read, especially the day he sent them to what he thought was their death, was something else. Remembering each and every lesson he'd taught until they were instinct didn't dull the pain; it only made it more contradictory.

Kane interrupted her thoughts when he touched her arm and mouthed, "Are you all right?"

That was the million-dollar question, wasn't it? Would she ever be all right? Would she ever be normal? At this point in her life she highly doubted she could be anything but what she was trained to be. An unemotional killer.

* * *

Caitlyn had finally eaten a grilled cheese sandwich and an apple out of the plethora of food Kane had ordered. Sabrina figured at least it was something.

"Kane stole some sweet FBI sweats if you want to take a shower and change. Maybe then you'll be able to take a nap."

The girl's eyes went wide. "I don't want to be alone."

Sabrina patted her hand. "You don't need to worry about that. I'll help you." She shook her head. "Maybe, on second thought, you should take a bath instead. I could help wash your hair and we could put on some American music and relax."

The girl still seemed as weak as a baby when Sabrina helped her undress. She helped her take off her threadbare clothes and uncovered what looked like healing wounds along her back. Sabrina sucked in a breath and immediately regretted it when Caitlyn started to sob.

"I'm going to send Kane out for some ointment."

Caitlyn hiccupped through a sob. "There are still the guys at the door, right?"

Sabrina nodded. "Yep, two big, burly FBI dudes carrying guns. Nobody is going to get past them." She wasn't about to admit her own fear about their safety. And wouldn't discount another attack from Trinity or his minions.

After she helped Caitlyn into the deep tub, Sabrina put on the radio and found a station playing American music. Then she opened the door and whispered her request to Kane. To his credit, he didn't ask any questions.

Sabrina knelt next to the tub, leaning her back against the wall, and tried not to focus on Caitlyn's emaciated body. Worse than that were the bruises on her wrists, her legs, and numerous other spots, along with the welts and burn marks.

Sabrina trounced down the roar of anger. She had to keep her focus. Caitlyn needed to be safe and secure before Sabrina could move on to step two.

She sucked in a breath and thought about stopping Trinity from ever causing harm to another girl. Memories of being at Petrovich's mercy paled in comparison to what these girls had endured. It wasn't fair that this man was getting away with sexual slavery at a hefty profit.

Kane knocked on the door and handed her the antibiotic cream, bringing her out of her thoughts. A few moments later, Caitlyn exited the tub with a little more color to her cheeks than when she went in. Sabrina dried her hair and braided it, mimicking the movements of her mother so long ago. Once she'd finished, Caitlyn sucked Sabrina into a hug and started to sob again. "It was horrible."

Sabrina felt a tug in the middle of her chest as she patted the girl on the back. "You don't need to tell me anything you don't want to."

"Did Kane…find that…" Tears rolled down her cheeks as she struggled through emotion. "…creep, Ponci?"

"They're getting very close." She didn't want to lie, but to distress the fragile girl with the information that they hadn't yet tracked him down would only make her more anxious. Besides, between her and Kane there wasn't a chance anyone would get through to Caitlyn.

Sabrina administered the cream to her back, wincing every time Caitlyn whimpered. Ponci had better pray the FBI got hold of him before she did. They had to abide by rules. She didn't.

"Why don't you lie down? Remember, Kane and I will be right outside the door." She helped the girl to the bed, tucked her under the covers, and closed the blinds. Within moments Caitlyn was sound asleep.

Sabrina tiptoed out of the room, closing the door behind her. "She's finally asleep." She sat down on the sofa and stretched her legs. The swirl of emotions and memories wouldn't stop coming, and she needed some respite from her thoughts.

Kane had been nonstop texting since they'd walked into the room several hours ago. And was still at it.

"Did they arrest Ponci?"

"They're trying to track him down, along with the other names on the list. The girls' parents have all been contacted and they're in the process of heading home. Ron said they're still sorting everything out. They haven't located Ponci yet. He's not on his private island. But they found a few young girls there." Kane shook his head. "What a sick bastard."

Sabrina tapped her fingers along the table. "We need to make sure Caitlyn stays safe. As long as Ponci and Trinity are roaming free, she's in danger."

He hesitated for a minute and looked at her. "Did she say anything about what happened?"

Sabrina shook her head, undecided if that was a good thing or bad thing. "Based on the burn marks and welts on her back, I can only imagine what they did to her while she was there."

"Probably should have taken some pictures for evidence." He grasped her hand, but she didn't look him in the eye.

"I couldn't bring myself to do it. Besides, some dickwad prosecutor would probably say I screwed them up." Sabrina closed her eyes and shuddered. "Once she's home with her parents, the doctors can take care of her there."

Sabrina could only imagine how long it would take for Caitlyn to recover mentally. Nothing she'd ever experienced had come close to what Caitlyn had. "What's the theory about Ponci? Where do they think he's hiding out?"

"Don't even think about it," Kane cautioned. "Let the FBI handle it now. Caitlyn's safe. That's all you signed on for."

"What about all the other Caitlyns we don't know about? Who's going to make sure they're saved?" Letting this go wasn't an option as far as she was concerned. Once she'd seen Caitlyn and all the other girls held in Ponci's home, she'd known she was in this with Kane until the end.

He cradled her chin. "Don't go there. Why don't you take the plane back with the Collins?"

He was worried about what she might do, and she couldn't blame him for that. "You know I can't do that."

"We have to prove the case in court against Trinity. No doubt his attorneys will run circles around the court process. Do not go vigilante on me. It will compromise everything. The FBI will make sure whoever's involved gets what they deserve as they build their case."

"Will they?" She locked her jaw. "I'm not so sure. If you hadn't gone off map on this one, they'd still be sitting around with their computers and their statistics and probabilities while young women were suffering." And she wasn't planning on allowing either man to evade what they deserved.

"You can't kill Ponci. We have to find out what he knows."

"I won't kill him. At least not right away." She folded her arms across her chest and leaned back on the couch.

"The girls are talking. They've been kept in the dark for the most part, but they've mentioned some names that we've tracked down, and we have those guys in custody for questioning."

Her heart squeezed as the breath caught in her throat. She closed her eyes and tried to focus.

"What's taking them so long? Shouldn't they have Trinity behind bars by now? We did everything but tie him up in a neat little bow." Frustration trailed along her spine. She wanted Trinity. She wanted the man behind all the heartache for Caitlyn and every other girl who'd fallen victim to his scheme. She wouldn't rest until that happened.

"The guys who bought these girls from his network aren't saying, even with the promise of immunity. Besides, most of their contact was through Marco. It seems no one knows Trinity's identity."

"They don't know or aren't sharing?"

"I'm not sure. But let's face it, if this guy operated as long as he did, he had to keep his identity well under wraps."

"I want Trinity." Those three little words pounded through her system like a shot of conviction. Knowing no other young woman would fall prey to his scheme was the single thought tunneling through her brain.

"You need to be patient, Sabrina."

After all they'd been through, she didn't need his patronizing tone. She wanted the man who did this to Caitlyn held accountable.

"I'm not letting this rest until he's found."

"I promise you that will happen."

If not for Caitlyn walking in at that second, a smile lighting up her face, Sabrina was fairly certain she and Kane would have had words. For some reason, she was spoiling for a fight, and with him towing the FBI line of bull, he was a good target.

"Hey, you two. I'm hungry," Caitlyn announced, the innocence of her words slicing through the air and releasing the tension. At least for the moment.

"You could definitely use a little meat on your bones."

Sabrina wasn't naïve enough to believe all Caitlyn's problems had disappeared over the short time she'd slept. She knew, without a doubt, it would take time and patience to regain what she'd had. But compared to how Caitlyn looked when they'd found her, this recovery was nothing short of a miracle.

"To think all those times I dieted. Now I'm looking to put on weight. The irony of it all." Caitlyn laughed, the sound as close to normal as Sabrina could expect given the circumstances.

"The stuff from earlier has gotten cold. What would you like?"

"Breakfast." She giggled. "Although I think it's closer to dinner. I have a taste for"—she shrugged, a smile lining her face—"anything and everything."

"I can do that," Kane responded, picking up the phone.

It didn't take long for room service to arrive and the food and coffee to be brought in. Croissants, jellies, eggs, breads, fruit, and pasta piled high on the plates.

They sat down at the table, and ate in silence for a few minutes before Caitlyn spoke. "What's with you two? Are you boyfriend and girlfriend or something?"

Kane glanced over at Sabrina, one eyebrow raised, his dimpled smile firmly in place. He was definitely enjoying the sense of discomfort the question provoked in her.

A shot of nerves skittered through. It was weird after all she'd been through that such a simple question brought about that type of response.

"Kane helped me find you. Of course, I did most of the work," she teased, trying to lessen the knot of tension in her stomach. "But he did come in handy a time or two."

"Come in handy? Is that all the thanks I get? You need somebody to rein in that impulsive streak of yours."

Caitlyn giggled. "You two look good together. You should definitely be a couple."

Sabrina felt heat flame her face. How could she kill a man without a hint of nerves, but one relationship question and she was about ready to crawl out of her skin?

"I'm never in one spot long enough to be a couple." Finally, the words spurted out of her mouth.

Caitlyn didn't seem to be listening as she paled and stopped eating, putting down the fork she was holding. Tears sprang up on the corners of her eyes. "It's the little things I missed. My dad always burns the bacon and my mom…well…she burns everything. But Dad eats it anyway."

Sabrina nodded. Although she didn't have the same experience as Caitlyn growing up, she could remember tidbits of her life before her parents' death. She could remember having some great times with her brothers. Times that weren't consumed with fear. Even Petrovich had his kinder side at times.

"Families might get on your nerves, but that doesn't mean you don't love them," Kane said.

Sabrina felt a little queasy as the need to flee overtook her in a rush. Something about what Caitlyn said, the words she spoke, unnerved her. Long-held beliefs tumbled inside her head as she fought to make sense of it all.

"I'll be back in a few. I need to borrow your phone."

Kane gave her a stare-down before handing her the phone. She knew he was curious. But also knew he wouldn't ask. She turned and headed out the door without another word.

Her heart pounded in her chest as if she'd run a couple of miles uphill. Need and desire and pain and hurt tousled inside like a giant tornado.

Sabrina fought with the urge to succumb to memories. She'd done some horrible things in her life. But had she done them for the right reasons? Would she ever know? Rescuing Caitlyn she could feel good about. But lingering doubt seemed to dog her every step of the way. Remnants of striving for perfection to gain Goren's approval tumbled through her head. He wasn't abusive to her or her brothers, but none of them ever wanted to disappoint him. Was that about fear that he'd cast them out, leaving them once again vulnerable to the whims of others? Or more about that sinister side to him he showed once in a while that kept them in check? And why, in the end, did he set the three of them up to be killed?

She rushed through the lobby and into the cool evening air, and the soft breeze sifted through her hair. She walked the streets of Zurich for about twenty minutes. Discharging all the feelings swirling around her brain was a welcome relief.

At thirty, she was much too old for make-believe. She was way too old to think the past could be erased. And she was way too smart to think Caitlyn and Kane Travis could change her cold heart.

Her brothers would help her find Ponci. Then they'd help her track down Trinity. She didn't waste a minute before she made the call and filled them in on everything she'd been up to, including Caitlyn, Trinity, Ponci, and Kane.

"What do you need?" Max asked.

"Money and a phone, and most of all I need both of you to help get this done."

"Give me the info on your hotel, and I'll have a phone in your lobby within an hour. And we'll take the next plane out," Jake said.

A sense of relief hit her as she hung up. Together they could do this. After Ponci, they'd hunt down Trinity. Maybe then she'd be able to sleep and put to rest her past transgressions.

After walking around town to waste some more time, she picked up the phone Jake had sent. She sent her brothers a text so they'd have her new number. Only then did she make her way back to the room. Stepping off the elevator, she heard music. Then a giggle. And a warm, tingly feeling rushed through her before she opened the door and spotted Caitlyn and Kane laughing. And dancing?

The normalcy of the scene made her believe Kane was right about Caitlyn. Maybe she was a lot stronger than Sabrina believed.

Caitlyn shouted as soon as Sabrina walked inside, "Look, Sabrina. I'm teaching Kane how to dance. I thought he'd be much too old to learn." Caitlyn laughed again as Kane mimicked the girl's movements while music blared from the TV.

"Pretty smooth, don't you think?" He winked, sending a wash of an unidentifiable emotion slithering through her.

How could he do that? She had rectified all this weirdness in her head about him and then he did something so darn…well…adorable, even if he'd loathe her use of the word.

"Come on, Sabrina, join us," Caitlyn said, motioning toward Sabrina.

"Naw, I don't think so. I'll let Kane make a fool of himself while I watch along the sidelines."

He tugged at her arm. "Oh no, girlie. I don't think so." He pulled her alongside him.

Caitlyn and Kane continued their dance, her with the concentration and skill, him…hot damn…he looked downright sexy. Although she'd rather die than reveal that bit of information to him. It cost her enough admitting it to herself.

"Come on, Sabrina," Caitlyn urged.

"I don't think she knows how. She's led a rather sheltered life, filled with boring stuff that made her a rather dull little lady." A wicked sneer pulled up the left corner of his mouth, and the dimple popped to the surface.

She elbowed him in the stomach. "All right. That's it. You've left me no option but to show you both up."

The pull was irresistible. The normalcy of it all blended together with hope as she jumped in the middle of the step. Never prone to flights of fancy, letting the music guide her body felt more freeing than she'd dared believe. Was this some kind of weird metamorphosis taking place in her? One that she wasn't very receptive to even while simultaneously drawn to it.

For the first time in a very long while, Sabrina felt at peace. The sheer joy of the moment overcame her, as something she couldn't even fathom, let alone remember, oozed along her spine.

When the song finished, and the next began, Caitlyn stopped. "You two dance together. I need to sit down for a minute."

Fear sat low in Sabrina's belly while Kane shimmied up next to her, his arms outstretched. When she shook her head, he motioned over to Caitlyn, who then replaced her smile with a pout.

Push. Pull. Push. Pull.

Reluctantly, Sabrina moved toward Kane as if marching off to her execution. Touching him, or letting him touch her, brought out the worst in her. When he did that, she felt out of control. Definitely not a feel-good.

Something about him made her insides go all mushy, for lack of a better word. And she didn't appreciate that feeling. She was not a mushy kind of gal. Besides, it made her feel raw and vulnerable. And that was not something she could welcome with open arms.

But there she was, between the proverbial rock and the hard place as she glanced over at Caitlyn, who seemed to be relishing in her newfound matchmaking skills. Without an option, she slipped into Kane's embrace, fighting against the pull.

Not having the energy to resist, every muscle in her body relaxed. With his left arm positioned at her back, his right hand wound within hers and rested on his shoulder. Letting her head relax against his chest resembled coming home.

He whispered provocatively into her ear. Memories of his touch on her body tumbled through her brain. Had it not been for Caitlyn's presence, Sabrina wouldn't have an ounce of will to resist the chemistry that sparked between them. But she didn't believe in this. In fact, everything about who she was demanded she resist this kind of lunacy.

But she couldn't. At least not right now. Her brothers would be here soon, and she'd come to her senses and morph back into her old self. For right now, she could enjoy the moment or two of mindless sensation.

With precisely that thought in mind, she gave in. Let his hands touch her, sparking her nerve endings to a jolt. The fresh scent of soap and Kane enveloped her as a shroud bringing with it memories long since denied.

Part of her wanted to give in. Part of her knew there was never any happily ever after. That was only in the movies.

And the part she didn't want to think about hoped she was wrong.

When the song ended, he didn't let her go. Rather he stood there, one hand on her back, the other still wound within hers. He chucked under her chin, forcing her head up to look into his eyes. "What nefarious purpose did you want my phone for?" he whispered.

Even though she expected the question, it still caught her by surprise. She clenched her jaw tight. "Checking in with the family."

He slowly nodded and glanced at the readout on his phone. "I wonder what that conversation was about."

"Have you become my keeper?" She'd predicted he'd go there, but she still couldn't help the swell of resentment for no other reason than he had the upper hand.

"I know this might shock you, but I worry about your impulsivity."

"That's my problem, isn't it?" She needed to push him away, and this seemed a good time to do exactly that.

He lifted his fingers to her hair and stared into her eyes. "I don't want you to spend the rest of your life in prison."

"Don't worry. I'll be fine."

"Hey, what are you two talking about so secretively?"

"Nothing much. She dared me not to dip her." He winked. "But I love a good dare." Swooping in with all the style and grandeur of an old-fashioned movie, he bent Sabrina over his arm, until her head nearly touched the floor.

Before she could struggle back to a standing position, the hotel phone rang. He pulled her to an upright position and grabbed it.

"Kane Travis," he spoke into the receiver, then nodded. "You have the right number. Let me get your daughter."

He handed the phone to Caitlyn. "Mommy, are you on your way?" Tears dribbled down Caitlyn's face as she spoke. "I'm…all right…thanks to Sabrina…and Kane." She hiccupped as emotion ebbed through her body in a violent torrent, ripping the words from her throat. "Sabrina's boyfriend." Rather than say anything else coherent, she only nodded and grunted. "Uh huh," Caitlyn managed to say before handing the phone to Sabrina.

Caitlyn flung herself at Kane. He enveloped her within his arms, allowing her to release all the emotion until she was spent. With one hand, he patted her back, while he whispered that everything would be okay.

Sabrina longed to have someone give her that sense of security even though she knew she would never be willing to give over that amount of control. "I'll make sure the FBI meets your plane in Zurich in the morning," she told Martha Collins. Sabrina jotted down their flight information. "I'll pass that on."

"Will it be safe for Caitlyn?" Martha asked, her voice filled with fear. "Will you be coming back with us? I'd feel much better if you were with us on the plane." Sabrina wasn't surprised by the irrational fear. They'd been through a lot in the last six weeks or so.

"That won't be possible right now." She eyed Kane. "But the FBI will be ensuring everyone's safety. And I have total faith in them."

Kane didn't even bother to hide his laughter.

CHAPTER SIXTEEN

———

Sabrina glanced at the clock. She'd slept for nearly twelve hours. While Sabrina and Caitlyn shared the bed, Kane took over the pullout couch in the sitting area for the night.

With sounds of CNN in the background, she heard Kane moving about outside the door. She threw off the covers and tiptoed out of the room, closing the door behind her.

He had already ordered coffee and a slew of pastries from room service. "Good morning." He smiled and poured her a cup of coffee. "Snag a pastry and let's talk out on the terrace. I don't want Caitlyn to overhear." He grabbed his laptop on the way out.

She sat down at the bistro table, as did he. "What's going on?"

"Ponci's dead. It looks to be a professional hit." He stopped and let her digest that information before he continued. "They're closing in on Trinity. One of the men who was taken in for questioning on human trafficking charges decided to exchange information for immunity. He's given us an address in Paris for a man by the name Pierre Lennard, who is alleged by this man to be Trinity. As we speak, the FBI is doing due diligence. They're looking into the guy's financial situation, his website activity, and searching for a connection to Marco."

She sucked in a breath. "Did they make a positive ID on Ponci?" She grabbed his arm. "I mean a hundred percent."

"He has a couple of scars that match up positively."

"What do you know about this Pierre Lennard guy?"

"He's a wealthy businessman who has several homes throughout Europe. Also owns a condo in New York."

"What kind of business is he in?" Maybe she was suspicious by nature, but something seemed a little too convenient. Then again, maybe she was ready for the challenge and having this all over with so easily and being left out of the action annoyed her.

One step at a time. That meant that her journey with her brothers would get easier. Finding the man and getting the charges to stick were entirely different things.

"Here's a picture. Does he look at all familiar?" Kane pointed to a picture he pulled up on his computer.

She examined the face for signs of familiarity, but the middle-aged man with blond hair and blue eyes didn't ring any bells. "Don't know him. When will you hear something definite?" She let the question hang in the air. Something about this seemed a little too pat.

He eased out a smile as he examined his watch. "Not sure when I'll hear something. But since Caitlyn's parents will be here in a couple of hours, would you mind if I went to Paris to see this settled?"

Maybe she was a control freak and wanted to be there when it happened. Maybe she felt worried they'd let the slimy bastard slip through their fingers. Maybe something about the scenario didn't click into place for her.

"No problem." She sucked in a breath, "But are you sure this is for real this time? It all seems a little too convenient."

"Anybody's fair game when it means a few less years in prison."

Sabrina bit at the nail of her index finger. "But it doesn't make sense. From everything we found, nobody knew who Trinity was. Even Marco. Why would this guy know?"

How did it go from nobody knowing the real identity of Trinity to suddenly some guy turning over on him? Smelled of a decoy to her.

"We'll know soon enough if he's the right guy." Kane fidgeted a bit before he spoke again. "And if he is…this is over."

"Let's hope."

"And we both go back to the States. Alone?"

Sabrina paused, trying to read Kane's blank expression. "What are you trying to say?"

"I'm trying to say we didn't make a half-bad team."

Sabrina snorted, trying to cover an unwelcome tide of emotion pooling in her stomach. "We made a terrible team. We fought the whole time."

Kane took a step toward her, his fingers lightly grazing her cheek. "Not the *whole* time," he said, infusing the words with a meaning that made Sabrina's face heat. "But you and I need to talk."

Sabrina bit at the corner of her lip, feeling a different sort of sensation ride along her spine. She trounced it down, narrowing her eyes as she stared back at him. "I don't do relationships."

Kane shrugged. "Right. Neither do I." But he took another step forward, so close that Sabrina could feel his breath on her cheek. Was it her imagination or was it coming faster? Stronger. As if emotion was backing up in his chest as well.

She forced herself to take a step back, feigning indifference that was completely at odds with the feelings tingling up and down her spine. "There's nothing between us. It's the emotional intensity we've been under. Come on, you know how the scenario works. It's Stockholm syndrome or something."

"That's about captors and their victims."

"Whatever. You know what I mean. It was adrenaline. Intensity. Sex. That's it."

"That's it?" Was she crazy or did she detect a note of disappointment in his voice?

She shrugged, allowing the unease building inside her to ooze out. "Look, you're off the hook, okay? I'm not the romantic type. I'm not the type of gal a guy brings flowers. I'm more the type they buy a beer, talk about their bitchy girlfriend, wife, lover, or whatever, and hope to get laid."

Kane's eyes narrowed, but before he could respond, Caitlyn poked her head out of the door. "This is where you guys are hiding. Come on inside. It's too small out on that patio, and I'm starved." Taking a bite of a croissant, she ushered them inside and plopped down on the couch. "Hey, what's going on? You two seem weird."

If Sabrina didn't have this visual popping through her head of reaching across to shake some sense into Kane, maybe she could have thought of something clever to say at the moment. Something that would make this awful feeling inside her go away. But nothing came to her.

Push. Pull. Push. Pull.

"Are you two fighting?" While Caitlyn's voice held optimism, panic rode along Sabrina's spine. The word *conspiracy* hinted at the edges of her awareness as Caitlyn and Kane exchanged looks.

"No, Caitlyn. It's not that—" Sabrina looked at Kane. When he nodded, she continued, "Ponci is dead."

Tears twittered at the edges of her Caitlyn's lashes. For a moment, Sabrina was envious of the emotions lying below the girl's surface. It made her who she was—a capable, loving young woman. "Are you sure?"

"Positive," Kane responded. "He can't hurt you anymore."

"That's good." She sucked in a deep breath. "Do the other girls know?"

"I'm not sure, but I'll make sure they're contacted if they haven't been already."

"Then you two should be happy. Why do you look all stressed out and scared?"

"It's complicated," Kane offered.

"I thought you two were…you know…together." Caitlyn looked first at Kane then Sabrina, as if trying to figure out what was going on.

"We're not," Kane quickly said.

Too quickly. Something about the words hit Sabrina harder than they should. She should be relieved, right? So what was the sinking feeling in the pit of her stomach at the finality in them?

"What else?" Caitlyn asked, clearly unwilling to let the subject drop.

"I've got to leave for Paris in a few minutes, but don't worry. The men outside will see you and your parents safely to the airport. I guess this is goodbye, Caitlyn." He wrapped the girl in a hug. "When I'm in the States, I'd love to check on you and see how you're doing."

"I'd like that." She kissed him on the cheek.

Sabrina grasped Kane's hand in a handshake. He brushed off her touch and wrapped her in an unexpected hug, bringing with it security, safety, and a solidarity that caught her off guard. Despite her inability to feel, she found herself hugging him back. Fiercely. She drew in a breath, but she had to work at it as his embrace crushed her chest, robbing her of breath. Or maybe that was the elusive emotion clawing at her.

He hugged her and whispered, "I'll find you, Sabrina."

Right then she couldn't say if it was the words that startled her or the feeling of his peppermint-tinged breath wafting around her nose. But the accompanying shiver was born of something foreign.

He winked at Caitlyn and left through the door. For the first time in her life, Sabrina felt the terror of being alone, even though that had been her preference for as long as she could remember.

"Kane seems mad. What's going on?"

Sabrina shrugged, trying to lighten the mood. "You know how men get some times. And they say they don't get PMS. Ha."

Caitlyn laughed, as Sabrina knew she would. But then she stopped abruptly as something on the TV riveted her. The only station broadcasting in English was CNN, which Kane had left on for background noise.

Caitlyn started pointing to the set, her voice mute, as tears rolled down her cheek. "It's him. Trinity."

Sabrina stopped the broadcast and hit rewind. The broadcast continued. "Ambassador Quarto is in Venice during Carnivale, sponsoring a benefit for the Children's Hospital. He's very active in helping children get free cancer treatment in many of the clinics he's established throughout Europe. He utilizes his own private jet to ensure they get sent to the best hospitals throughout the world."

She turned toward Caitlyn. Her one hand trembled as she pointed, while the other covered her mouth. "He's close by."

"Are you saying Ambassador Quarto is Trinity?" Sabrina asked while a different kind of fear set up low in her belly. That was not the same man Kane had showed her a picture of. That meant the FBI was on the wrong track, and the man she was after was more powerful than she could have imagined. An ambassador, with the power and privilege that went along with that.

"That's him." Caitlyn's voice shook, and tears started to flow down her face.

Sabrina blinked, unable to comprehend what Caitlyn was saying. It all seemed too unbelievable.

"How do you know?"

Caitlyn nodded. "There's proof." Two little words that made all the difference in the world. "I heard Ponci mention something about having insurance in a safe deposit box, but I'm not sure where it is."

Nothing ever happened this easily. But apparently Sabrina's luck was about to change. She knew this for certain when Caitlyn spoke again.

"Don't let him get me again, Sabrina." She shook so hard, her body a mass of jumbling nerves, that Sabrina ushered her over to the bed, urging her to sit on the mattress.

Of course. It was the only thing that made sense.

A diplomat. A big shot who used the guise of helping sick children to continue his sick plan. How he was able to get the girls out of the US unnoticed always bothered her. But now it all fit together. He drugged them and claimed he was sending them to Europe, where he'd set up his own charity for children needing cancer treatment, for medical services. The slime ball. Now Sabrina knew she wouldn't have to go too far to find him. He was virtually in her backyard.

Game changer. Should she call Kane and let him know? But how could she do that when she couldn't be sure herself?

She brushed Caitlyn's hair as she pulled her in close. "Do me a favor? Don't mention any of this to anybody. Nobody can know."

Caitlyn whimpered. "He'll find me."

"He's a sewer rat. He'll want to keep his reputation in tact. With all the buzz around his benefit and the Carnivale over the next couple of days, there'll be reporters dogging his every move."

Caitlyn tugged at her arm. "You've got to come with us. He's dangerous, Sabrina."

"I need to stick around and make sure he pays."

Caitlyn drew her into a hug. "He came one time…I pretended to be asleep. He and that creep, Guillermo Ponci, went to some fancy school together. They were tight. Anyway, Guillermo complained I was difficult." She giggled, more out of hysteria than mirth, as evidenced by the tear sitting on the corner of her eye.

"You don't have to talk about this, Caitlyn." Sabrina felt torn between wanting to know and not wanting to know.

Caitlyn brushed at the tear. "I'm a lot stronger than you think." She huffed out a breath. "Besides, it helps to talk, doesn't it?"

Sabrina didn't have an answer for that one.

But on the other hand, she couldn't deny her the opportunity. The pain etched on Caitlyn's face was so palpable, a line of worry creased above her brow.

"By the time Trinity arrived, I'd picked up a little Italian. Ponci wanted his money back. I guess I wasn't quite what he bargained for. I caused a lot of trouble." A weak smile pulled up the corners of her mouth.

Sabrina nodded. Maybe Kane was right after all. Caitlyn did seem to be a lot stronger than she'd thought.

"Trinity assured him I could be managed with the right drugs." A visible shiver wormed through her. "I wouldn't cooperate with those pictures they wanted me to make. I ran away a couple of times. At one point, I attacked one of Ponci's guards with a poker from the fireplace." She squeezed Sabrina's hand tighter. "Instead they decided they could isolate me, barely feed me, and I would cooperate and do what they wanted." Her voice was low, barely above a whisper, but laced with a strength Sabrina never envisioned. "But I told them I'd rather die. And that was what was happening when you came to rescue me. I would have starved to death for sure."

"How did you—"

"I couldn't let them win." She sucked in a deep breath. "At first it wasn't too bad. I mean, I was scared and all, but it was okay. Then things got progressively worse. I learned Ponci and Trinity, maybe some others, were big on making porno flicks.

Everything in the place where we stayed was wired with cameras."

Caitlyn wiped at an errant tear, and Sabrina once again wondered why she herself couldn't cry. Why her emotions remained trapped inside like a safe with no tumbler lock to open it.

"I didn't know how much longer I was going to be able to make it. I kept waiting to be rescued, but every day seemed as if a year."

Sabrina grasped her hand. At that moment, the relief oozed through her body like a shot of Valium directly into her bloodstream.

Anxious to break the focus, Sabrina once again pointed to the picture frozen on the TV screen. "You're absolutely sure about this, Caitlyn?" It wasn't out of the realm of possibility with the drugs she'd been given and the trauma that she'd misconstrued or imagined what happened.

Caitlyn shook her head. "I'm positive." Her bones seemed to rattle beneath her skin. "Usually they drugged me to keep me subdued and out of it. But one time, the guard forgot to give me the heavier dose. I heard Ponci on the phone talking about a meeting later in the day with Ambassador Quarto. After he hung up, he said something like, 'Goddamn asshole Trinity thinks he can tell me what to do and when to do it.' Later that same day, that man came to visit. "

It could be this guy was only another grunt like Ponci rather than the lynchpin of the organization. Could she trust the word of a girl who'd been scared and drugged out of her mind?

In terms of witnesses, she couldn't be sure this girl could hold up to any sort of interrogation or probing. No doubt she'd dissolve under the hint of cross-examination. And the guy was an ambassador who was known for doing charitable works. Proving he was behind all this might be a lesson in frustration.

Could Sabrina trust this girl's word and follow through without some sort of evidence? She knew darn well the FBI couldn't. That left her and her brothers to take the man down and hope they weren't being led astray.

Going with her gut, she sent off a text to her brothers telling them about the change in locations. She was headed to Venice.

CHAPTER SEVENTEEN

———

Kane wasn't sure if it was Sabrina's doubts running through his head, but he had a bad feeling about this whole operation. Then again, maybe it was the way things ended between them. Unsettled.

And he still had to wonder what she was up to. He confirmed that she'd called her brothers. He had airline manifests checked and, as he expected, they were flying into Zurich later in the day. Her brother had arranged for a cell phone to be delivered to the hotel for her. It would be a simple process to track and get her new number. He had no doubt they were going after Trinity. Would they show up in Paris, or were they headed off in another direction?

The strategy meeting for Lennard was in about an hour, so he'd arranged to meet Ron prior to that. He'd been sitting in the bar at the hotel for about fifteen minutes waiting.

"Still in one piece, I see." Ron grasped his shoulder and sat on the stool next to him. "Where's Sabrina? I expected her to tag along."

Kane shrugged. "Yeah, me too. But…well…she's complicated." Although that word hardly came close to describing her.

"That's not too surprising, given the Petrovich connection you told me about. She give you any insight into the guy's psyche?"

He shook his head. "Not much. He took her and her siblings in when her parents were killed. There are a lot of gaps in her memory that I wonder about. Maybe the investigator in me can't seem to accept anything at face value."

"And?" Ron did a *come on* motion with his hand.

"She's up to something with her brothers. I think they're planning to take down Trinity. And by that, I mean kill him."

"You think they're in Paris?"

"I'm not sure. They could be."

"Are you going to bring this up in our strategy session in"—Ron turned his wrist to look at his watch—"thirty minutes?"

"Hell no." Kane would never betray her. But he still had to figure out a way to keep her from doing something stupid. He'd seen the look of raw determination in her eye when he'd left, and he knew all too well what that meant.

* * *

John and Martha Collins burst into the room, encompassing Caitlyn in a hug that lasted a good five minutes. Sabrina couldn't help but reflect on the love swirling between the threesome.

Family. The concept seemed to flitter outside her reach. For as long as she could remember it had only been her and her brothers. Outside of the three of them, she hadn't felt an emotional connection to anyone else. Even Kane, as much dysfunction as was present in his family, seemed more evolved on the emotional scale than her.

What was it in her family's past that had scarred them so completely that none of them could commit to anyone for longer than a couple of weeks? They each carried undeniable baggage. Why couldn't any of them move beyond it?

"Mom. Dad. This is Sabrina." Caitlyn giggled. "Then again, I suppose you guys already met. Kane's not here. And he's great too. But can we go now? I never want to visit Europe again. In fact, I'm never leaving New York. Maybe never leaving home."

"I'm forever indebted to you," John said, unashamed of the tears that littered his cheeks.

"You should have seen Sabrina, Dad. She kicked butt like Angelina Jolie in *Tomb Raider*."

They laughed, breaking the hint of awkwardness that had risen. No one wanted to discuss the details of what had happened to Caitlyn. Which was fine with Sabrina. She didn't want Caitlyn to divulge any more than she needed to right now.

"What time does the flight leave?" Sabrina asked, more anxious than ever to see this matter to its conclusion.

John twisted his wrist, checking the time. "We'd better get going back to the airport. The plane leaves in about two hours."

Sabrina nodded, not quite sure what else to say. It had been a long journey. One she couldn't help but think wasn't yet over for any of them. "I'll look you up when I get back to the States and see how you're doing." Would she do as promised, or would it be another one of those unfulfilled commitments she couldn't get herself to complete?

Caitlyn's eyes misted over as she wrapped her arms around Sabrina. "Thank you for everything." She pulled back and smiled. "And you and Kane need to figure that whole thing between you two out."

"This gal doesn't need a man by her side to finish the deal." She winked at Caitlyn. Somehow now the words didn't ring a hundred percent true.

* * *

Kane set up in the apartment across from Pierre Lennard's house. Using his binoculars, he tried to keep watch, but considering the place had every drape closed tight, he didn't have a hope of seeing inside. The other agents were wandering around, waiting until the final orders to apprehend came through.

Nellis was still punishing him for going against orders, and he'd relegated him to watchdog duty. Which, in the end, was fine. This way, he could keep an eye out for Sabrina or her brothers. Every second, he half expected they'd pop up on the street.

He trained his binoculars on the old woman waiting at the bus stop. Her build was similar to Sabrina's, so he zoomed in closer and blew out a breath. Short of getting a makeup artist from Hollywood to give her the lines and wrinkles of a woman in her eighties, that wasn't Sabrina.

If she wasn't hanging around here, where could she be? She'd sent that text to her brothers yesterday. He had no doubt they'd landed by now. There wasn't a doubt in his mind they were gunning for Trinity.

Before he could make himself crazy with worry and speculation, the powers that be must have given approval to bring Pierre Lennard in for questioning, because six agents entered the downstairs door. All he could do now was wait. Ten minutes later they exited, escorting what appeared to be a recalcitrant and handcuffed Lennard.

That was when guns started popping and all hell broke loose.

* * *

Sabrina got off the train in Venice and glanced around. For the first time she could remember, it felt awkward being alone. He'd been so much a part of her life over the last week, she expected Kane to pop up every time she turned around. But he didn't. And she'd made peace with that. At least she thought so.

Why was she struggling with guilt about not passing along the information Caitlyn had given her? It wasn't as if Kane weren't holding out on her as well. She pondered that for a moment, letting the idea sift through her brain. He'd filled her in on details he probably shouldn't have. But that didn't mean she needed to do the same. She liked to work alone. Except for assistance from her brothers at times, she preferred it that way.

Besides, Caitlyn was headed back home, and that was the important part of this journey. Her brothers were the only men she could or would ever truly count on to finish off this task.

The voice inside her head couldn't stop at Caitlyn. She needed to figure out if Ambassador Quarto was Trinity. Still, it could very well be that Kane's lead proved right, and she and her brothers were on some wild goose chase. The idea was possible given the fragile nature of Caitlyn's psyche. But Sabrina needed to know for sure.

Sabrina had barely come down from that emotional rollercoaster when she felt fingers dig into her biceps. Fear snaked along her spine as she primed her elbow to strike, right before her brother laughed.

"Taking down a child trafficker is a little too hard to resist."

She hugged her brothers one at a time and felt an ease in that tightness in her chest. Just like old times. As quickly as the thought came up, she pushed it back. Old times were not necessarily good times.

Working as a threesome had been Petrovich's idea from the start. She didn't want to focus on that black period of her life and the reverberations it caused.

Instead she focused on how happy she was to see them, and squeezed them again for good measure. Max, Jake, and Sabrina. Max looking like he'd just stepped off the pages of *GQ*, and Jake looking like he'd been on the cover of *Rolling Stone*. She almost laughed at the absurdity of their differences but sameness at the same time.

"Okay, all this hugging is making me nervous," Jake said even while he snaked an arm about her waist.

"This has got to be some kind of suicide mission for you to be so happy to see us," Max added as he joined ranks on the other side.

"It's just that I'm not real sure about the girl who gave me the info. That's the problem." She felt confident about what Caitlyn had revealed but couldn't help but question her state of mental health. She fought the urge to call Kane to find out how the raid had played out.

"Okay, why don't you call your FBI guy and find out what he knows?"

"Yeah, about that. He's got a lead he's following, but Caitlyn confirmed they were going after the wrong guy. It shouldn't be too hard to see who's right."

* * *

Kane catapulted down the steps and pushed through the door. By the time he hit the street, the bullets had stopped, and an eerie silence had descended. Lennard lay on his back with a bullet wound in the center of his forehead, while sounds of the ambulance making its way to the location broke through the awkward silence. Twenty feds stood around, trying to make sense of what had happened. A couple had been injured during the process, but it didn't look like anything too serious. It was more than clear the target had been Lennard.

Sabrina.

The possibility circled his brain, making his head ache and his stomach clench. He scanned the surrounding buildings and zoned in on where the shots might have come from. Old-school agents were doing their due diligence by looking upwards and doing the same thing.

No doubt all sorts of fancy trajectory workups were already being formulated on somebody's laptop about now. As for him, he scrambled to the most likely building and roof location and prayed he'd find no evidence it had been her.

His heart kept up the frenetic pace before he burst onto the rooftop. He ran from one corner to the next, searching for evidence. To one of his fellow FBI agents, he gave the appearance he was doing his job. And he was.

As much as he believed in justice, he hoped he wouldn't find anything to implicate Sabrina. But he had to know for sure. He fingered the piece of paper with the number of the phone her brother had bought for her in Zurich.

He dialed the number and hoped she'd answer. If she did, there was a fairly decent chance he could track where she was even if she wasn't forthcoming about the information.

* * *

"Not that I don't love you, Saby, and you know I love Venice, especially at Carnivale, but are you sure what this girl told you is accurate? I mean, she'd been held captive for several weeks. She could be hallucinating about facts and faces at this point," Jake commented.

Sabrina chewed her lip. "We're good either way. If Kane's bust turns into a red herring, we've got a lead they don't know about."

"That reminds me, why didn't you tell him about what Caitlyn revealed to you?" Max asked.

"He'd already left by the time she gave me the lead." Sabrina rubbed her temples as something that felt suspiciously like guilt rose to the surface. "Besides, you know those feds. They were on a mission. And there was nothing that was going to stop them. I swear if Kane hadn't gone off map with me they wouldn't be where they are right now."

She shook her head, more than a little thankful for the diversion of her brothers. The idea she was a tiny bit worried about Kane didn't settle well in her gut. The nagging thought of his parting words about finding her trailed through her brain.

When her phone rang seconds later, she glanced at the readout. How had he…? Those annoying fed connections, that was how.

"I should have figured you'd track me down." She tried to keep a bite of anger in her tone but worried it wasn't working too well, since a part of her was oddly happy to talk to him.

"Lennard is dead. So my question is, where are you and your brothers?"

The words reverberated through her body. He thought they were somehow involved. Once an assassin, always an assassin, no doubt. Not that she hadn't thought of it herself, but still…

"We're not anywhere near Paris, if that's your question. So no, we didn't orchestrate the hit." Her snarky tone this time would be impossible to miss. "Now if you don't mind—"

"I didn't think so. But I want to know what you know," he interrupted.

So this wasn't a call to get her to confess. This whole thing with Kane had her confused.

"Why do you think I know something?" Her brothers were staring at her as if she'd suddenly developed two heads. Max started giving her the *come on* sign, indicating his thoughts as to the matter. She wasn't about to cave that easily. They could accomplish what they needed to do on their own.

"Because I think it's a little too convenient both Ponci and now Lennard were killed execution style. Since you didn't have anything to do with the hit on Ponci, I'm guessing the same person is responsible for Lennard as well. Putting two and two together, I'm thinking they are the two people who knew Trinity's identity. Because of that, they're dead. As the saying goes, dead people tell no lies."

"Good hypothesizing, FBI dude." She felt the rush of comfort set in. That wasn't exactly a feel-good. She didn't want to get comfortable with Kane. Getting comfortable meant she'd lost her edge. Losing her edge meant she was a hair's breadth away from disaster.

"I have my moments. So you gonna tell me where you're at, or am I going to have to track you or your brothers through your cell phones?" He bit off a laugh. "You do know I have some mad skills."

She couldn't help but laugh. How did he do that? Laughing was another one of those expressions that seemed to elude her. Except around him, it seemed.

"I'm sure you do. But we've got this whole thing under control. Besides, I wouldn't want you to violate any of those precious FBI rules." Without another word, she hung up, even while she couldn't help but think she'd made a monumental mistake.

CHAPTER EIGHTEEN

———

"What was that all about?" Jake asked.

"He wanted to horn in on our fun." She drew in a breath and tried to ignore the little voice in her head. "Let's get to our hotel suite and strategize."

"I hope you appreciate the room I scored. It overlooks St. Mark's Square, and should give us a bird's-eye view of most of the festivities." Max shook his head as they walked the streets of Venice. "You don't even want to know what I'm going to have to do to satisfy one sexually repressed hotel manager by the name of Francesca." He smiled as he sighed. "Yes, it's a tough job, but somebody's got to do it."

"Seriously? Cry me a river," Jake said. "I've got a line on somebody who's privy to the costumes and masks, not only for us, but for what the dignitaries are wearing." He brushed his knuckles against his chest. "Can you say score?"

"Good start. Let's check in so we can come up with a plan," Sabrina said.

The walked together to the hotel that held grandeur by size as well as proximity to the landmark square. Even though she'd spent the better part of her life in Europe, she couldn't help but marvel at the ancient architecture with a reverent eye.

They entered their suite and dropped their meager belongings on the couch. "Impressive, Max. Dibs on the bedroom," Jake said as he opened his computer. "I need to see if my contact has some costumes for us and has learned what Ambassador Quarto is wearing."

"Since we don't have any real evidence, except the shaky eyewitness, how do we play this?" She hated the thought she might not be victorious. In many ways this journey had been years in the making. "Caitlyn says that Ponci had evidence hidden in a safe deposit box, but didn't know where or which bank. Which pretty much leaves all of Europe as a possibility."

"As much as I like the idea of going all Jason Bourne with this and getting into a safe deposit box, we don't have time. This guy has gotten away with it for a very long time without anyone knowing who he is. We've gotta hope we can somehow trick him into confessing," Max said.

"I say we fake it till we make it." Jake rolled his eyes. "The guy doesn't have to know we don't have the goods on him. We've pulled this scam before."

"I'm not sure it will work this time." She was second-guessing freezing Kane out. With his connections, he could run a list of registered safe deposit boxes. Maybe she should have used him to bring this to a close. Then again, with all the bureaucratic red tape, their opportunity might evaporate.

"It might be our only option," Max said.

She shook her head even as the possibility had been in her thoughts for the last several hours. "Maybe I can propose a new venture opportunity for him in the Far East. I'll tell him that I've already recruited some girls but need his connections in order to make it happen."

"Let's face it, the guy wants to corner the market, as sick as that sounds. I think your plan might work," Max said.

"All right. If we're all onboard, when?" Jake asked.

"He's having a benefit at the Carnivale for all the children he helps—yeah, I think I'm going to puke." Being in masks would keep their identity hidden, and the festivities would obscure anything they needed to do. And if they had to take matters into their own hands, they always planned for an exit strategy.

"I hate to talk about the elephant in the room," Max said, his eyebrows signaling to her she was in for a lecture. "But since you're buddy-buddy with an FBI guy, why not utilize those resources?"

"If I leave it to the FBI, they'll go after the wrong man, won't they?" Okay, she sounded a tad defensive, but she didn't care.

"They're following protocol. Something we don't have to do. I get that." Jake shrugged. "But, despite what you think, it makes sense for him to be in on this. At least as a fallback if the ambassador doesn't go for your ploy."

"What's with you two? All of a sudden you're afraid of a little challenge?" If they wanted to push, she'd push back. While they knew her Achilles' heel, she knew theirs as well.

She needed to stay as far away from Kane Travis as humanly possible right now.

* * *

Kane trudged up the stairs, along with four other men, to take apart Pierre Lennard's home. They were looking for evidence that confirmed the intel they'd received that the guy was Trinity. To him, it was looking more and more like the FBI had been led in the wrong direction.

The opulent residence was in Paris' 3rd District on the Right Bank. Known for its art galleries, small stores, and cafes, along with Renaissance architecture, it was trendy and expensive. The guy definitely had money. How much and where he got it remained to be discovered.

The other agents had given Kane high-fives for taking down the largest trafficking ring in decades. He wasn't so sure. And he couldn't help but wonder what Sabrina knew but wasn't telling.

"Start with his computer and see what you find." Kane drew in a breath. "We need something to back up what our informant told us."

"You don't think he's Trinity, do you?" one of the agents asked.

"I think either he was set up or somebody didn't want him to talk. Maybe he's got some notes somewhere to confirm his part in this, or leads us to the real identity of Trinity. Either way, keep digging until we find something."

"Will do, sir," the young agent said, making Kane feel every bit of his age.

His phone rang seconds later. "Travis."

"We managed to triangulate that cell phone to Venice."

"What's going on in Venice right now?"

"Carnivale."

"Thanks." He hung up and contemplated the significance of the Shaw family trip. He knew it had nothing to do with enjoying the festivities. They were there for a reason. As soon as he could, he'd hop on a plane and find out what.

His phone rang seconds later. When he glanced at the readout, his heartbeat sped up. Something was going down. "Travis."

"This is Jake Shaw. Max and I talked about it...and well...I think we might need your help."

* * *

Where were they? Sabrina paced the room, waiting for her brothers, who swore they'd be back two hours ago. When they had left that morning around ten, they'd mentioned something about meeting up with some old friends, which was Shaw-brother-speak for getting laid. Sometimes, her brothers were so predictable.

She strapped a knife to the pouch around her thigh and slipped into the floor-length silver dress that Jake's friend had provided. Covered in rhinestones and sequins, it shimmered as she walked on strappy heels onto the balcony overlooking St. Mark's Square.

Noise filtered from the crowd below as she scanned, both for her brothers and Trinity. Jake had been informed that Ambassador Quarto would be wearing a gold mask with a large black-and-white beaked nose, a black hat, and a black-and-white harlequin checkered suit. She hoped his costume would be unique enough that he would stand out, but given the numbers of people, she wasn't too sure.

For more than a few pensive minutes she thought about her decision to leave Kane out in the cold. Was it a foolhardy choice or all about self-preservation? With the phone clutched in her hand, one simple call would enlist his help. Even though she hadn't heard from him since yesterday, she had to assume he was in Europe, trying to nail down more information about Pierre Lennard. Her fingers paused over the keypad as she contemplated what it might mean to solicit his help.

By tomorrow this would all be over, and Kane Travis would be out of her life. Everything she knew about herself had not changed, and she would once again return to her solitary existence and the job she did best. But still…

Before she could make a decision one way or the other, her brothers charged through the door. "Sorry we're late. We…got detained," Jake said.

"Redhead? Blonde? Or was it a raven-haired beauty that snared your interest?" She shook her head and made a waving motion with her hands. "You guys have to hurry and get ready."

"Did I tell you how beautiful you look, Sabrina?" Max winked as he tore off his shirt and made his way to one bathroom, while Jake headed to the other.

She sat at the vanity table, applying white face makeup and slicking back her hair with gel. Next, she did her eyes and lips with dark liner. After filling in her lips in a deep red shade, she put on a silver mask adorned with black and red plumes of feathers along the top and sides.

Nerves, for the first time, trickled inside. She fought against the sensations of doubt that accompanied it. Now was not the time to question her abilities.

Three hours from now this would all be over. As that realization hit, a swell of memories rushed up to squeeze at her chest. Why was she thinking of all this now?

She walked back onto the balcony to soak in a breath of air as the nerves threatened to get the better of her. The crowd had grown in the last hour, and the square was nearly wall-to-wall people as it neared seven in the evening. For the first time she contemplated the futility of the mission.

They were working against so many obstacles. What were the chances she'd be able to find Ambassador Quarto in this sea of humanity? Granted, the ball they were attending had been sponsored by him, but that didn't mean he'd be easy to find.

She took one last look over the crowd and hesitated.

Kane.

Standing outside the hotel…waiting…oh no, they didn't. She marched inside, catching her brothers as they walked out of the bathrooms showered, shaved, and ready to go.

Was it her? Had the air in the room suddenly become so tense, she could have cut it with a knife? Or was that the betrayal swimming through her veins?

"Is there something you two want to tell me?"

Jake and Max glanced at each other than back to her. Finally Max spoke. "Kane's here."

"I spotted him." She closed her eyes and drew in a breath as a combination of anger and relief rolled through. "Why?"

"You weren't thinking clearly. Somebody had to be the voice of reason," Jake said.

"You think it's okay to go behind my back?"

"We thought of it more as making an executive decision, since you weren't thinking straight."

* * *

Kane had a plan, thanks to Jake and Max and their phone call earlier today. The FBI had located a safe deposit box under the name of Guillermo Ponci in Zurich. Right now, the powers that be were getting the proper authorization to open the contents and find out if Caitlyn had been right about it containing some sort of proof of Trinity's identity, even while they were trying to find an excuse to keep going with their original scapegoat, Pierre Lennard. Kane needed to buy a little time in the interim, since without proof, nobody at headquarters was willing to believe that Quarto was anything but a respectable philanthropist and pillar of society.

Now he had to make sure he could build his case. He tried not to dwell on the fact that Sabrina had pushed him away so easily. But it was hard to ignore her rebuff.

He knew if the opportunity presented itself, she'd take Trinity down in a heartbeat. There was no way she'd leave this place without Trinity's head on a platter, in the figurative sense if not the literal sense. That was definitely the part that worried him.

Unlike most of the other people milling about in elaborate costumes, he didn't want any of that to interfere with his job. Instead, dressed in a tux to hide his Glock, he waited in front for Sabrina and her brothers to appear. He wasn't sure what, if anything, her brothers had told her.

Ten seconds later, he had his answer when she charged out the door and seemed ready to take a chunk out of him.

CHAPTER NINETEEN

———

Sabrina let all that tension steam through her as she shoved Kane in the chest. "What is this, some kind of boys' club?" All the frustration she'd been feeling coalesced into anger. Anger toward her brothers. Anger toward Kane. Anger toward a man who got rich by selling the bodies of young girls.

Even though the crowd seemed to be growing by the second, she spotted her brothers moving alongside her. To their credit, they didn't interfere. She figured she'd have a whole plane ride home to chastise them for their betrayal.

"We've located a safe deposit box in Zurich that belongs to Ponci and are waiting on approval to go in there." He had the good grace not to touch her, but she could tell by the way his hands clenched that he was fighting the urge. "It would help to have solid proof rather than put the onus on Caitlyn's recollection."

"What about Lennard? Are they still thinking he's Trinity?" The crowd seemed to be getting rowdier as the seconds ticked by, and she found it increasingly difficult to have a conversation.

"They've found some porn on the hard drive on his computer that connects with sheltered accounts, but nothing solid yet. They're not keen on digging too far into Ambassador Quarto, but they were willing to pursue the safe deposit box for now."

Her teeth seemed to rattle when she clenched her jaw. "I suppose you're coming with us to Ambassador Quarto's ball?"

While she let the question hang in the air, a swell of people moved her along the crowd. A man in a jester's costume grabbed her arm and tried to dance with her. She smiled but refused, and allowed the crowd to move her along toward her destination. All four of them were headed in the same direction. They'd meet up there.

The classic Renaissance-style building, with ornate columns and arched windows and doorways, was on the right. She struggled to make her way through the crowd toward it, knowing her brothers and Kane couldn't be far behind.

Sabrina smiled at the jester, despite the circumstances. Or maybe *because* of the circumstances. This was her day. Her day of reckoning. She would bring Trinity and his whole organization down. Maybe it was the similarity of him to Petrovich that set her teeth on edge. Maybe she was finally going to be able to feel free of the bonds of the past that haunted her.

She would expose him. The heady sense of victory brought about a smidgen of calm to her otherwise erratic pulse. Everyone would know the man for the scum he was. He no longer could hide behind the veil of nobility and fool everyone, as Petrovich had done.

Her pulse rate doubled, then tripled as she surveyed the crowd, looking for signs of her brothers. As for Kane, even though she'd be loath to admit it, she had to fight to ward off the warm feelings simmering beneath the surface he brought about.

Her inner cynic rationalized that with him here, at least she'd know what he was up to. The relief she'd felt seeing him and knowing he was okay must have been her imagination. He was a big boy. No doubt he could take care of himself. If she was unattached, as she'd professed to be, why did the idea that he could have been hurt in Paris make her chest constrict? Now was not the time.

She drew in a breath and forced herself to focus on the task at hand. With Lennard and Ponci both dead, that meant Trinity had no reason to worry about being discovered. No doubt he didn't know about the evidence Ponci had stored in a safe deposit box. She could only hope that part of the information was correct as well.

She brushed back the futility of worrying and soldiered on. Sabrina attempted to relax as she tried to break through the swell of people toward the building. The familiar feel of the strap of leather against the skin of her thigh brought a measure of comfort, even if she could never get to it, considering the crush of people surrounding her.

Unable to find the ambassador in his costume amongst the crowd, she bit back at the hint of anxiety. Probably nothing. More than likely, he was already in the building getting things ready for his gala event.

As she struggled to make her way through the crowd to the steps, the man in the jester's costume came alongside her once again. He smiled with his painted lips and offered his hand, as if he somehow knew where she was headed.

When his gaze slid from her hand to her eyes, a slight twitch in his right eye forced her heart to beat faster. "Are you going to the ambassador's ball?" he whispered.

She nodded as thoughts swirled around her head, too confusing to separate truth from paranoia. "I can't seem to break through the crowd."

"Grab my hand. We'll try to go along the side."

She glanced into his eyes, partially hidden by the mask he wore. The same red and black checked pattern surrounded them, giving the illusion of something she couldn't yet identify. "That's okay. I'm meeting some people. I'll try to make it alone."

He smiled. "Good luck." When he waved her off and forced his way through the crowd toward the side, she felt a sense of relief.

Nerves were playing havoc with her common sense. Focus was the key to making this job a success. But worrying about where her brothers and Kane were set her teeth on edge. They had anticipated the craziness surrounding the Carnivale but had underestimated the impact it might have on their plan.

Max and Jake came up next to her, on either side, each grabbing an arm. It was more than enough to send her nerves into a tailspin.

"Easy, there, Saby. It's us." Jake laughed as he spoke into her ear. "For a minute there I thought you were going to yank out your knife."

She attempted a tight smile, but when Kane appeared in her peripheral vision waiting on the steps, nerves took over for some odd reason. It always had been the three of them, and now Kane slid effortlessly into their group. The idea unsettled her.

"Everybody have their invitation?"

Her brothers nodded and linked arms with her as they fought their way through toward the palace. "Let's do this thing," Jake said.

They met up with Kane at the entryway and handed off their invitation to the guards at the door. Compared to outside, the interior was comfortably crowded. Still, she couldn't help but look around, anxious to spot the ambassador in his harlequin costume. If nothing else, her goal was to keep him in her sight.

They each took a glass and helped themselves to champagne. "Any sign yet?" Max asked.

Kane spoke up. "Nothing. It's his party, and I understand he arrives late in order to make a grand entrance. It's part of his shtick."

Something foreign and uncomfortable oozed between her and Kane. She couldn't quite decipher what it was, but she knew it went much deeper than irritation at him showing up at the behest of her brothers.

Her brothers must have felt the discomfort, as they begged off seconds later with the excuse of doing reconnaissance. That worked for her. She had a thing or two to say to Kane, and now was as good a time as any.

He touched her elbow. "You're pissed."

She rolled her eyes. "Gee, ya think?" Frustration rolled through her, gaining momentum. "I didn't invite you here."

She spotted a hint of disappointment in his downward glance. "Nope, but your brothers did."

Traitors. "They had no right."

"Why? Because they had the foresight to think that it might be best to work at this from two angles versus one?"

"So now you're saying I'm incompetent, is that it?"

"You're letting your fears get in the way of thinking straight. What are you so afraid of, Sabrina? Do you think you might actually let your guard down and begin to care?"

A shiver whipped around inside her. "You are so wrong. I'm all about myself and nothing about anybody else. I risk nothing for nobody. As far as I'm concerned, you take your chances hooking up with me. I'm a son of a bitch. If things get dicey, and it's a choice between me getting out of here alive or rescuing you, I'll save my own skin. That's how I roll."

She saw the hurt in his eyes but somehow couldn't back down. He needed to understand how it was with her. From all accounts, she would have figured he'd know this by now. Clearly, he didn't. She'd have to spell it out.

"That's how it's going to be?" He forced her to look at him by tilting up her chin.

The look on his face told her he didn't believe anything she said. That was a good old bout of self-preservation on his part. But why was that hint of doubt taking up residence in her spine, saying she might not be right this time?

"Believe me, to save my skin, I'd leave you in a heartbeat and not lose any sleep over it. I left you with a sprained ankle to fend for yourself, didn't I?" She brushed back the unwanted bout of emotion brought about by her words. She was telling the truth, wasn't she? She was, and always would be, a solitary kind of person. Meeting Kane Travis and spending time with him would never change that.

He brought his hand up to his chest to the area by his heart. "Wow, you don't pull any punches."

"That's the way it is with me, Kane. Take it or leave it."

He forced her eyes to meet his. "You try to play this hardass role, Sabrina, but I'm not buying it."

"Then you're the fool, Kane," she responded, fighting down the urge to do anything else. The parameters of their relationship needed to be clear. And if she had to be the bad guy in that scenario, so be it.

Sabrina felt a wash of unidentifiable emotion. The whole time she'd told him she wanted to go at this alone. Now when the prospect hit her in the face, why did she feel so lonely and disappointed? How did Kane get her to feel that way?

Never in her life had she been dependent on another person. The last thing she needed right now was to have that ugly dependency thing rear its ugly head.

Being a loner had been advantageous for her. She made her own luck. She enjoyed the solitude. She didn't need others to make her feel worthwhile or important. She certainly didn't need the extraneous and mundane conversation.

So why, at this moment, did everything feel so strange? Why, never having experienced loneliness in her life, did a bout of it come at her and grab her by the throat?

Why then did she suddenly feel so alone and vulnerable? More so than she'd ever felt in her life. The urge to flee overtook her in a rush. "I'm going to use the ladies' room." Without another word, she walked away, uncertain where she was headed. But getting away from Kane right now seemed to be the best option.

She pushed through the door of the ladies' room and leaned against the sink as she willed the constriction in her chest to ease. Her eyes closed as she fought through the demons that continually nipped at her heels.

"So we meet again." A strong hand surrounded her bicep from behind. Goose bumps broke along her arms, and the hair stood up at the back of her neck as a gun poked her in the spine. The man in the jester costume reappeared at her side. This time she wasn't fooled. No mistaking the sixth sense. It was Trinity.

"Not a word. I have my men trained on your brothers. One word, and they're dead. Now go where I tell you," the hoarse voice whispered into her ear.

She gulped down the wad of fear lodged in her throat. A heavy-duty case of nerves made her legs quiver, and the itch crawl up her back.

She sucked in a breath. *Caution. Don't overreact.* Think, above all else, even if impulsive seemed to be her middle name at times.

His touch was tight, circling her arm in a vise-like grip. Breath tinged with champagne and cigarettes oozed like slime across her cheek as he muscled her through the partiers.

"I know all about you," he whispered softly, as if saying the words was enough to convey his message.

Sabrina fought with impulses, deeply embedded within her, to react. She struggled for control and a twinge of reality. This was a public place. Regardless of what he knew or thought he knew, he couldn't do anything to her right here. Right now.

She forced out a "Hmmm?" and hoped to God her voice didn't shake too much. Where were her brothers? Kane? They couldn't be far away. Unless what he'd said was true.

"You've done something…with your hair…but you're Sabrina Shaw. You and I share a mentor. In fact, I was one of his earliest students. Along with your parents."

The words bounced around her head until they finally settled. How dare he tell lies about her parents.

She wouldn't let his mention of Petrovich, her parents, or anything else register on her face. Any telltale sign of fear, shock…any kind of emotion would allow him to go for the kill. "Congratulations. You're able to do a good internet search." She gulped back the bile sticking to her throat and ignored his earlier claim.

"I remember you and your brothers when you were children. In fact, I sat in on some of your training. I'm shocked you don't remember me. Then again, I was pretty young myself."

Her skin started to itch, but she fought off the sensation. Part of her wanted to look him in the eye; the other part couldn't stand the idea of confronting her past. "Why doesn't that surprise me that you and Petrovich are connected?"

"Don't want to think about your parents being assassins as well, I see." He chuckled before continuing. "I was barely out of my teens at the time, but I still knew Petrovich was missing an idea for expansion. Using you only for trained assassins seemed rather shortsighted when he could have expanded his repertoire to all sorts of other enterprises, like I did. Foolish man in the end." He tsked. "Unlike Petrovich, I'll never allow a lightweight like your brother Max to get the goods on me."

"I wouldn't be too sure about that." Information bombarded her from all sides. Her brother, her parents…what was he saying?

She couldn't think of that now. Concentration was the key to not only getting out of this alive but being successful as well.

She hadn't been prepared for any of his revelations. Maybe that would come to bite her in the end. Still, the security of the knife strapped to her thigh made her believe there was hope. "The FBI is tracking down proof of your identity hidden in a safe deposit box as we speak." She enjoyed the hint of surprise that briefly passed across his face.

"You're lying. Those imbeciles still believe Trinity is Pierre Lennard. There's enough evidence planted at that guy's place to put him away for over a hundred years." He let loose a chuckle, as if she'd told him an amusing story for anyone looking in their direction. "Too bad he was the target of an assassination. Hmmm...where were you and your brothers yesterday afternoon?" He laughed again, and this time any touch of merriment was replaced by pure evil.

Past mistakes threatened to overtake her future as everything she'd done rose to the surface. Things she'd done out of fear, commitment, and misguided loyalty mishmashed within her head, making it impossible to think. She needed to fight through it. Right now, he had the upper hand. Someway she needed to flip that.

"Cat got your tongue, Ms. Shaw?" He sneered at her beneath the mask he wore. "Truth is, I've always admired your family's chosen occupation. It's a shame you and Jake decided to get all righteous." He lowered his voice and whispered against her ear, "That evilness never leaves you, does it?"

Even though she knew he was playing mind games with her, she couldn't seem to avoid getting sucked down the rabbit hole anyway. It took every ounce of energy to fight through his words and recognize her strength. She wanted to glance around and see if her brothers had spotted her but didn't dare. No doubt he would take that as a sign of weakness.

Responding to his bait would only give him leverage. If she denied his claim about her parents, her brothers, herself, she'd come off as defensive, only leading him to believe he was right.

She sucked in a breath, steadied her spine, and cleared her mind. *Eye on the prize, Saby.*

Chess.

Channeling conversations during her heated chess matches with Petrovich helped clear her thoughts. For once she didn't detest the game.

"This is a game of chess we're playing. The problem is you think you're a positional player, which gives you a false sense of security. You mistakenly believe you can keep taking all of my good moves away from me." She faked a sad face. "But in the end, it won't work out for you."

He forced a cheesy smile for someone passing by, pretending they weren't discussing life and death, good and evil. "Very astute observation." He touched her hand, and the flesh crawled up her arm. Instinctively, she yanked it away. "If I'm a positional player that makes you a tactical player. And, as we both know, that type of player depends on forcing me into making an error. I'm afraid that will never happen."

"You know the old saying that tactical players do it to you. Positional players make you do it to yourself—or at least try, in your case." She refused to drop her stare. "You are at a stalemate with me."

He laughed, the sound sharp and nerve-rattling. Realization that she was in the presence of the devil in human form became a palpable fear gripping at her chest. She and her brothers were so different from this monster that Petrovich had created, they weren't even of the same species.

"You sound as if you don't believe me, Ms. Shaw." With a sudden move, he brought her in close. She felt the pressure of a gun barrel to her ribs. "This is what is called check and mate."

CHAPTER TWENTY

———

Kane didn't bother to knock before barging into the ladies' room. But as he'd guessed, it was empty. Panic began to rise as he spotted a door left ajar. Maybe she went out the back way to avoid him? But Sabrina wasn't the type to avoid confrontation. Something had happened. He phoned Max and Jake.

He went through the first hallway, opening every room along the way before they caught up with him. Kane glanced around the ballroom filled with people and knew he'd been outsmarted. "Any sign of Trinity?"

Jake shook his head. "Unless he deviated from the costume we were told he'd chosen." Jake worked his jaw as he glanced around the room. "Sabrina knows better than to go it alone. She wouldn't have left without a fight. Let's not panic yet."

Kane wanted to believe in the mundane excuses, but after the fiasco in Paris, he knew they were dealing with somebody who was one step ahead of them. Somehow the guy seemed to be able to read their movements before they happened. He hated to think of the guy as a genius, but that was the only explanation he had. Unless someone had been tipping him off?

His heart squeezed inside his chest. Trinity was playing a cat-and-mouse game, and all three of them knew it. They'd all underestimated the man's reach and power.

"You take the first five rooms on the left. I'll take the first five on the right. Kane, you focus on the ones further down the hall. We'll join you when we're finished," Max said.

Kane ran toward the end of the hallway and saw it split off into yet another hallway with a set of stairs. He spotted a small sequin lying on the marble floor. He rushed up the stairs, only to be confronted with yet another cavern of spaces. He updated Jake and Max via text and continued the search.

She could be anywhere.

* * *

Trinity urged Sabrina into a roped-off hallway, up a flight of stairs, and pushed her inside one of the rooms. Being isolated was not a great scenario, but she remained confident she could figure a way out.

"It doesn't matter what you do to me. The FBI probably have the evidence as we speak." *Fake it until you make it.* Her brother's motto had just become hers.

He stopped, a nervous twitch bobbing his head. "You're bluffing." He regained his swagger. "And even if they manage to come up with something, I'll make it disappear, as I do every other threat that comes my way."

"Believe what your big ego wants you to." Her brothers and Kane would be looking for her by now. If she could only stall him another minute or two, they'd figure out what had happened to her. Unless they'd been overpowered by his men, like he'd threatened. She refused to think of that scenario.

He yanked her outside to a veranda and locked the French doors behind him. It came down to the two of them as the music and crowd noise faded into the background.

"You have nowhere to escape. There's only the canal." Sabrina glanced over the edge, hearing the lap of the water several floors below.

"But this is the perfect place to make you disappear as if you were never here to begin with." He spat on the concrete at her feet. "You can't let anything go, can you?" His rhetorical question seemed to fade into the night. "Really, what's a few young girls here or there? They're unhappy with their life situation anyway."

Grabbing her shoulders, he shook her. Knowing she had to pick the right moment was a lesson in patience. He knew her skills, as no doubt they were identical to his, assuming he wasn't lying about the Petrovich connection.

"And being sold to disgusting old men for sex is the solution to their unhappiness? Is that how you justify your vile enterprise?" She tried to keep the emotion out of her voice, but that was nearly impossible.

Feeling the lessening of his grip, she brought her elbow back into his gut, while she twisted around. Even though he lost the gun, he was able to counter her move and put a chokehold on her. She broke his hold. They went at it as if warriors, trading and blocking strikes. At this point it wasn't about who was bigger or stronger. It was about who could anticipate the other's move to take advantage.

If she only had a second, she could get to the knife strapped to her thigh, but his practiced moves didn't allow for respite. He anticipated every blow, as she did with him. The impasse lasted for what felt like an hour, but was probably more like minutes. She kicked between his legs, but the tight fit of her dress inhibited the movement until the seam ripped. By then it was too late. He had the upper hand as he brought her arm behind her back, inching her hand toward her shoulder. The pop and strain of the muscles and tendons brought a wave of pain. She spiked her heel into his foot and spun around. But he was waiting for it.

The punch sent her sprawling along the cool stone floor. She scrambled away while reaching for her knife. He pounced, pinning her to the floor. His hands around her neck made her gasp for air.

She tried to break his hold, but he knew that move. Instead, she ripped at his hands as spots appeared before her eyes. His thumbs dug into her windpipe, increasing the pressure. She tried to wedge her knee between them to release some of the force, but her strength was waning.

She. Needed. A. Breath.

To her shock, he let go. She sucked in a breath, even while she started to cough. It felt so good.

"On second thought, killing you is too good for you. With the right drugs, you'll command a hefty profit." He fumbled in his pocket, but her mind was still fuzzy, unable to focus on the needle in his grasp. She tried to gather the strength to fight back, because it was that or sure death—one way or another.

The sound of a crash registered somewhere in her mind as she twisted her neck to avoid the prick of the needle. Trinity looked up for a half-second, which allowed her time to grasp the knife. Before he registered her intent, she swung. She struck his chest and arm with a wide sweep, before the knife skittered to the ground. His recoil allowed her enough room to wiggle from beneath him.

She heard someone call her name. When she glanced toward the sound of the voice, Kane stood on the adjacent balcony, ready to jump to hers. There were several feet separating the two. He'd never make it.

"Kane, don't." The words stuttered out of her mouth.

He made the leap as a gun sounded. His body seemed to stall in midair as if hitting a pause button on a TV. He let go a litany of curses when he missed the edge, his hands slipping down the railing.

Her heart squeezed in her chest as he grappled for purchase. Bits of stone crumbled into chunks, plunking into the water below. Her breath stalled as she turned to see Trinity charging toward Kane, his gun aimed at the flailing man.

"Nooooooo." The word tore through her throat as she ran, grasping the knife she'd lost earlier.

She didn't have much time. A shot pulsed through the air. She launched the knife, striking Trinity in the neck. Blood spurted out, but he didn't collapse. Instead he stumbled a few steps, the gun still raised, ready to finish Kane off.

Something foreign wet her cheeks as she tackled Trinity from behind, sending him sprawling headfirst into a stone bench. His body pulsed as blood soaked the back of his jacket and dripped onto the floor.

"Kane." She rushed over to him, offering her hand to pull him to safety. Blood spread along his shirt, and the wetness she now recognized as tears rolled down her cheeks. He smiled when he saw her, but his face was deathly pale. She could almost see his strength slipping away with every beat of his heart. "Do not give up."

His skin was slick from blood, making it difficult to get a strong grip. If he fell, he'd be lost in the murky waters below and would surely die.

She kicked off her shoes and propped her feet against the pillars. The increase in leverage compensated for his waning strength. It seemed to take forever as she watched the blood spread down the sleeve of his shirt, but she finally managed to get him to the railing where she could shift him over.

Bracing his fall as much as she could, she placed her fingers to his neck to find a pulse and sucked in a much-needed breath. Her brothers burst onto the balcony seconds later.

"Get some help. Kane's been shot."

Jake left while Max crouched down beside her, removing his jacket and pressing it to Kane's arm. "He's got a vest on. Looks like he got shot in the arm."

"Vest?" She padded Kane's chest, feeling the reassurance of Kevlar beneath her fingertips. Thank God. She brought her lips to his cheek, relishing the warmth in his body. A sense of relief bounced around inside her while the tears continued to fall. Her fingers trembled as she stroked the stiff fabric of his shirt. Thoughts and fears of what-ifs tumbled in her head.

His eyes popped open. Then he sucked in a rush of air— the sight itself bringing with it an unexpected chill to her spine. He blinked twice, as if trying to remember where he was. Then, as recognition hit, a smile eased up the corners of his mouth.

"Are those tears?" He brushed at her cheek with his hand. She grabbed it, holding it to her face, relishing in the touch of his skin to hers. Unable to talk, she nodded. She was being such a wuss, but she couldn't seem to make it stop. Besides, the wetness against her cheeks felt good.

He struggled to sit. Both she and Max urged him back to the floor.

"Trinity?" The word eked out of his lips in an almost-whisper.

For the first time, she glanced in that direction and spotted the now lifeless body. "Dead."

"You did good." He smiled at her, although he still seemed weaker than a new puppy.

Jake arrived seconds later, bringing a doctor along with him. The doctor pushed her and Max away as he attended to Kane. She chewed her lip and tried not to worry.

Max grabbed her hand. "Are you okay?"

"I'm fine. Trinity..." She struggled to get the words out. "He worked with Petrovich. He said..." No, she couldn't utter the vile words of a madman right now.

"What did he say?" Jake asked.

Before she could even contemplate her response, the doctor called her over. He had propped Kane against one of the pillars into a sitting position.

"I told him he should be transported to the hospital, but he's refusing. He said you and your brothers will get him there. He bumped his head, but the wound on his arm nicked an artery, which is where all the blood came from." The doctor smiled and grasped her hand. "No need for tears. He'll be perfectly fine." Without another word, he walked away.

Sabrina still couldn't speak. Every time she attempted to open her mouth a bubble of emotion in the form of tears resurfaced, and she once again was blubbering like an idiot. She chewed on the inside of her cheeks, but that didn't stop the flow either.

Kane wrapped his hand in hers. "Come closer." He forced her lips to his. "I don't think I've ever seen you this quiet," Kane remarked as Max and Jake helped him to a standing position.

Tears pricked at her eyes, dotting the corners momentarily until a full-on stream ran down her cheeks once again. His thumb brushed along her face, feathering the wetness with his touch.

"See what you've done." She sniffled, drawing in a shaky breath. "You've turned me into some sniveling, crying female." She shook her head.

"I knew you were crazy about me," he teased, revealing his dimpled grin.

"Crazy? We've established that a long time ago." Anything resembling the L-word she couldn't say for sure. But this feeling bursting inside her for Kane was close. Closer than she'd ever been before. And with a start like that, who knew where it might lead?

ABOUT THE AUTHOR

Wendy has a Masters in Social Work and worked in the child welfare field for twelve years before she decided to pursue her dream of writing. Her first two books, *Fractured* and *Mama Said* were published in 2011 and 2012. *Mama Said* was a finalist in the Gayle Wilson Award of Excellence Contest. She self-published *The Christmas Curse* in 2012.

Between teaching college classes, trying to get her morbidly obese cat to slim down, and tempering the will of her five-year-old granddaughter, who's determined to become a witch when she turns six so she can fly on her broom to see the Eiffel Tower and put hexes on people—not necessarily in that order—somehow Wendy still manages to fit in writing. She spends the remainder of her days inflicting mayhem on her hero and heroine until they beg for mercy.

To learn more about Wendy Byrne, visit her online at
www.wendybyrne.net

Enjoyed this book? Check out these other reads available in print
now from
Gemma Halliday Publishing:

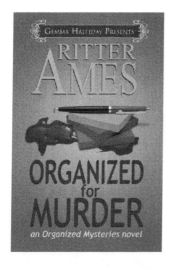

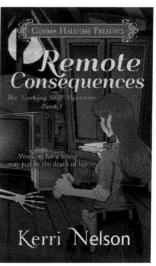

www.GemmaHallidayPublishing.com

Made in the USA
Charleston, SC
26 November 2014